Praise for the Boo.

"A thoroughly entertaining series debut, with enjoyable yet realistic characters and enough plot twists—and dead ends—to appeal from beginning to end."

—*Booklist*, starred review, on *Booked 4 Murder*

"Filled with clues that make you go 'Huh?' and a list of potential subjects that range from the charming to the witty to the intense. Readers root for Phee as she goes up against a killer who may not stop until Phee is taken out well before her time. Enjoy this laugh-out-loud funny mystery that will make you scream for the authors to get busy on the next one."

—*Suspense Magazine* on *Molded 4 Murder*

"Engaging characters and a stirring mystery kept me captivated from the first page to the last."

—Dollycas, Amazon Vine Voice, on *Divide and Concord*

"Well-crafted sleuth, enjoyable supporting characters. This is a series not to be missed."

—*Cozy Cat Reviews* on *Death, Dismay and Rosé*

"A sparkling addition to the Wine Trail Mystery series. A toast to protagonist Norrie and Two Witches Winery, where the characters shine and the mystery flows. This novel is a perfect blend of suspense and fun!"

—Carlene O'Neil, author of the Cypress Cove Mysteries,
on *Chardonnayed to Rest*

Books by J. C. Eaton

The Wine Trail Mysteries

A Riesling to Die
Chardonnayed to Rest
Pinot Red or Dead?
Sauvigone for Good
Divide and Concord
Death, Dismay and Rosé
From Port to Rigor Morte
Mischief, Murder and Merlot
Caught in the Traminette

The Sophie Kimball Mysteries

Booked 4 Murder
Ditched 4 Murder
Staged 4 Murder
Botched 4 Murder
Molded 4 Murder
Dressed Up 4 Murder
Broadcast 4 Murder
Saddled Up 4 Murder
Grilled 4 Murder
Strike Out 4 Murder
Revved Up 4 Murder
Pinned 4 Murder

The Marcie Rayner Mysteries

Murder in the Crooked Eye Brewery
Murder at the Mystery Castle
Murder at Classy Kitchens

The Charcuterie Shop Mysteries

Laid Out to Rest
Sliced, Diced and Dead

Pinned
4
Murder

J. C. Eaton

BEYOND THE PAGE
PUBLISHING

Pinned 4 Murder
J. C. Eaton
Copyright © 2024 J. C. Eaton
Cover design and illustration by Dar Albert, Wicked Smart Designs

Beyond the Page Books
are published by
Beyond the Page Publishing
www.beyondthepagepub.com

ISBN: 978-1-960511-77-5

For Mona Williams, the classiest bowler at Johnson Lanes in Sun City West. Keep turning heads and knocking down those pins! You're incredible!

CAST OF CHARACTERS

Protagonist:

Sophie (Phee) Kimball, forty-something bookkeeper/accountant from Mankato, Minnesota, turned amateur sleuth

The Sun City West, Arizona, Book Club Ladies:

Harriet Plunkett, seventy-something, Phee's mother and book club organizer; owner of a neurotic chiweenie named Streetman and a cat named Essie

Shirley Johnson, seventy-something, retired milliner and teddy bear maker

Cecilia Flanagan, seventy-something, devout churchgoer and more modest than most nuns; sneaks off holy water when needed

Lucinda Espinoza, seventy-something, attends Cecilia's church and translates Telemundo soap operas for the club

Myrna Mittleson, former seventy-something New Yorker and aspiring bocce player with a penchant for self-defense weapons

Louise Munson, seventy-something avid bird lover and owner of precocious African gray parrot

Ina Melinsky, Harriet's sister and Phee's aunt, married to saxophone player and gambler *Louis Melinsky*; more eccentric than Lady Gaga and Andy Warhol combined; seventy-something but don't tell her that

The Sun City West, Arizona, Pinochle Crew:

Herb Garrett, Harriet's neighbor and pinochle crew organizer, seventy-something

Bill Sanders, seventy-something bocce player

Wayne, seventy-something carpenter, jack-of-all-trades

Cast of Characters

Kevin, seventy-something

Kenny, seventy something, married

Williams Investigations in Glendale, Arizona

Nate Williams, sixties, owner, retired detective from the Mankato, Minnesota, Police Department

Marshall Gregory, forties, partner and retired detective from the Mankato, Minnesota, Police Department, Phee's husband

Augusta Hatch, secretary and Wisconsin transplant from a tool and die company, sixty-something; as quick with a canasta hand as she is with her Smith & Wesson

Rolo Barnes, cyber-sleuth extraordinaire, puts the CIA, FBI and Homeland Security to shame

Maricopa County Sheriff's Office

Deputy Bowman, fiftyish, grizzly in looks and personality

Deputy Ranston, fiftyish, somewhat toadish in looks and personality

Sun City West Residents

Cindy Dolton, sixty- or seventy-something, local community gossip and dog park aficionado

Gloria Wong, sixties or seventies, Harriet's former neighbor and unofficial book club member

Paul Schmidt, seventies, avid fisherman and radio show host

Lyndy Ellsworth, forties, widowed, Phee's neighbor and best friend; works for a medical billing company

CHAPTER 1

"**P**rince Charming is fine," I announced to my mother when I brought Streetman into her house. She was waving a red laser light on the floor and watching the cat chase it. "I got your precious chiweenie out of the dog park before the park monitor showed up. You should have told me someone registered a complaint. By now the rec center probably has a dossier on him."

"He's just rambunctious. And inquisitive. Like Essie."

"Are those euphemisms for overly amorous and neurotic? And I'm referring to your dog, not the cat."

"He's making progress."

Must be he's on the ten-year plan.

"Okay, fine. Listen, it's after seven. I've got to get to work. Sorry about your ankle. Just keep it iced and stay off it."

"Don't worry, I'll take it easy. I can't believe I twisted it on my way into Sher's for their clothing sale yesterday. They only have those full weekend sales a few times a year."

"You're just lucky someone didn't trample you. Catch you later!"

"Oh, before I forget, the book club ladies and I will be going out for Buffalo Wild Wings tonight. You said Marshall was out of town on a case, so why don't you join us? The last two times you came up with excuses."

If only I could remember what they were so I don't repeat one of them.

"Um, uh . . ."

"Six-ish at the restaurant on Bell Road, not the new one on Waddell."

"I, um . . ."

"Think about it. I'll save you a seat. It's just the women this time. No grumpy, grumbling pinochle-playing men." Then she paused. "Except for maybe Herb."

"In other words, *all* of them."

My mother shrugged and I raced out of there before I was forced to kiss the cat and give Streetman a smooch as well.

I'm Sophie Kimball Gregory, better known as Phee, and I can't believe it's been over four years since I relocated to Arizona as a result of temporary insanity. The surname Kimball was my takeaway from my first, albeit short-lived, marriage, and it sounded a whole lot better than Plunkett, my maiden name.

1

Gregory is my married name, and had it not been for a weak moment when I agreed to help my friend Detective Nate Williams as the bookkeeper/accountant for his investigative agency in Glendale, Arizona, I'd still be shoveling snow in Mankato and signing my name as Kimball. Call it kismet, but when Marshall Gregory joined Nate's agency, an old spark we had back when we worked for the police department in Mankato turned into much more. Sometimes the best results come out of the craziest situations.

• • •

"Come on, Phee," our secretary, Augusta, said when I got into the office. "Humor your mother. Maybe she'll let you off the hook next time."

"Fat chance. But chicken wings do sound better than day-old salad."

"Especially the Parmesan-encrusted garlic ones."

"Fine. I'll think about it."

"Any word from Mr. Gregory?"

"Yep. He's still in St. Johns tracking down that missing sibling."

"Beats poor Mr. Williams. He'll be in late. Stayed out till all hours on that infidelity case from Goodyear. And tonight won't be any different. He texted me to reschedule his nine o'clock appointment for tomorrow since he anticipates another long night."

"Guess he'll be sleepy today, huh?"

"Oh yeah." Augusta fluffed her bouffant hairdo and adjusted her tortoiseshell glasses. "Glad I'm not one of those night owls. Nope. Not after years of working on a dairy farm. Up early, go to bed early. That's why us Hatches have longevity on our side. And don't let anyone tell you it has to do with food. It's red meat and real butter, eggs, and milk that make for a long life. Not to mention sugar. It's that substitute stuff that'll kill you."

"If you say so." I laughed and opened the door to my office.

With relatively little on my agenda, I finally acquiesced by midafternoon and let my mother know I'd join them. At a quarter past five, Augusta and I locked up and I headed off to Buffalo Wild Wings. Nate was out more than in, making it a relatively quiet day. It was the bliss of spreadsheets and invoices, where tallying up numbers was a whole lot easier to deal with than stressed-out or cranky clients. But then again, it was to be expected when people needed the services of an investigative agency.

The good news was that Williams Investigations acquired a stellar reputation in its few years since opening. Not to mention getting a contract with the Maricopa County Sheriff's Office for joint consultation as needed.

Consultation being a loose word for solving most of the cases.

Judging from the full parking lot in front of Buffalo Wild Wings, I knew it was going to be one of those evenings when the book club ladies competed vocally with TV sets blaring, children shouting or crying, and the usual patrons conversing at the top of their lungs.

As I stepped inside, I looked at the long lineup in front of me and regretted not saying no to my mother. Thankfully, as luck would have it, Myrna rushed in behind me and announced, "We're with the Plunkett party of thirteen." Then she looked at me and pointed to the rear of the room. "Your mother made reservations for all of us." She thundered toward the table as I struggled to keep up. It was like following a lumberjack in a skill competition.

"There are thirteen of us?"

Myrna shrugged. "You never know who'll walk in."

I was inches behind her as we reached a long table with a cushioned bench against the wall. Shirley, Lucinda, and Cecilia were already seated on the cushion side along with Herb, Bill and Wayne, but that didn't stop Myrna from pushing her way in next to Cecilia.

"Phee," Cecilia said, "it's so good seeing you." She looked around and then unbuttoned the top button of her black cardigan, revealing the collar of her starched white blouse.

"Good to see you as well."

Herb waved my way, sat upright and leaned toward my mother. "Kevin just came in. That cinches it. I'm not waiting for your sister to get here. Let's order as soon as the waiter shows up. Hate to mess around with my blood sugar."

"You don't have a blood sugar problem," my mother said, "but you can relax. That's Ina in the red and pink fedora. Good grief. It looks hideous with those long braids of hers. Shh! Don't say a word."

Then Myrna announced, "Here come Louise and Kenny. I didn't know Kenny was joining us. How did he ever get away from his wife?"

"Bridge club," everyone answered at once.

It took a bit of scrambling but finally, the entire crew was seated. Or at least I thought it was the entire crew.

"We can't order yet," Shirley said. "Gloria Wong's joining us too. I really wish she liked reading cozies instead of those romances of hers. She'd be such a welcome addition to our group."

Gloria was my mother's former neighbor and unofficial book club lady. And while she didn't read mysteries, she was no stranger to gossip. She sold her house a few years ago to move into a larger one in Sun City West that she and her twenty-something daughter could share, along with their Great Dane, Thor.

My mother scanned the room before focusing back on the table. "Maybe we could find a romance-mystery she would like."

"Or a waiter!" Herb suddenly spotted a waiter and waved him over like a traffic cop. The poor man all but collided with Kenny, who rushed to grab the cushioned seat next to Myrna, totally oblivious to the fact that he had narrowly missed knocking over the waiter, who could have passed for a high school junior.

"Am I late? Did you order already?" Kenny asked. "Parking is a bear."

"Are you folks ready to order drinks?" the waiter asked.

Then, it began.

"Do you have diet drinks?"

"Do you have decaffeinated soda?"

"Do you have alcohol-free beer?"

There weren't enough mental eye rolls in my brain to deal with the unending barrage of questions. And finally, when the drink orders were taken, Gloria walked in. She was petite with short dark hair and looked closer to fifty than seventy.

"Sorry I'm late, everyone, but I got wrapped up with an email and didn't realize the time."

"I know how that goes," Lucinda said. She tried to put her shoulder-length grayish blond hair behind her ears but it only resulted in sending it everywhere except there. "I've been dodging emails and calls from a horrid man who gave a presentation at my church a week ago. It was called 'The Circle of Life,' but it was really about life-care communities in the West Valley. He extolled the joys of independent living, assisted living, nursing care, palliative care, and, well, care beyond the grave. He represented one of those 'circle around until death' communities and wanted us to sell our homes and sign up for that. Can you imagine?"

"I most certainly can," my mother said. "Well, I've got news for them. The only way I'm leaving my house is when they drag me out feet-first."

"Can we talk about something else, Mom?"

"Fine. We probably should order now that Gloria's here."

If the drink orders were such a monumental task, the wing orders were worse. With a zillion sauces to choose from, it was a veritable nightmare. And, after all of that, the whole crew only selected two different varieties— Buffalo sauce and Parmesan garlic. I could have crossed the Atlantic in the time it took them to agree on the orders.

Finally, when the food came and everyone was satiated, Kenny plopped his elbows on the table, looked around and announced, "Folks, we've got a problem."

"What kind of a problem?" my aunt asked. "Don't tell me some food I just bought has been recalled. Louis pitched a fit over the Pacific salmon last week. And the pickled herring before that."

Kenny shook his head. "Not food. Bowling."

With that, Gloria sat straight up. "What kind of a problem? I didn't hear about any problem." Then she turned to Kenny. "What problem?" Then back to us, "Kenny and I are on the same team, the Lane Chasers."

Kenny glanced at Gloria. "Better check your spam folder. Half my email winds up there. Our captain just informed us that the board voted to allow residents who are nineteen years old and older to be on the teams. Might as well start a babysitting service for them."

Gloria recoiled and didn't say a word. Then Shirley spoke. "Nineteen? Can they live in Sun City West? This is a retirement community." She reached for a napkin and I saw that she had redone her gorgeous nails to a lovely bronze tone that accented her ebony skin.

"As long as you are nineteen or over, and living with someone who is fifty-five or older, it's okay," Herb said. "A lot of people say it's for caregivers, but if you want my opinion, it's either for ne'er-do-well grandkids who can't make it on their own, or gold diggers looking to cash in early."

I all but fell over in my seat. "Um, that's quite the generalization."

"Generalization or not, it's the new norm around here."

"Yeah," Kenny said. "And here's the problem. I don't want to compete with a teenager or youngster. I'm in my seventies. I moved to a retirement community to be with people my age. Next thing you know, the rec center will say we're too old to be on the teams."

"Can they do that?" Gloria looked stricken.

I shook my head. "I doubt that. Read the bylaws."

"Bylaws, schmylaws!" My aunt tossed her braids off her chest and onto her back. "It's the same in the Grand, where Louis and I live. The entire community is being overrun by the new generation. We were perfectly happy when it was Sun City Grand, until someone on the board decided we needed to rebrand ourselves to attract younger people. What's wrong with our generation?"

Oh no! This could take all night.

And then, as if things couldn't go down the rabbit hole fast enough, Kenny said, "That's not the worst of it, they want to hire Harris and Blake Wainwright from New Media Entertainment to redo the bowling alleys."

"Redo?" everyone asked at once.

Kenny nodded. "Remember the Metro Mall in Phoenix? They tried to redo that, too, and look where it got them. It wound up being demolished."

"No one is going to demolish our bowling alley," Myrna said. "Not on my watch. Last thing Bill and I need are for all those people to crowd us out of bocce." Then she looked at Gloria. "No offense, Gloria."

5

"None taken. By the way, why does the name Wainwright sound so familiar?"

"Don't you remember?" Lucinda asked. She whisked some hair off her forehead and clasped her hands. "They were on trial for attempted murder in Idaho a few years back but got off due to lack of evidence. Then, they sued the state for duress and walked away with enough money to start their media entertainment venture."

"As long as they don't make an attempt on someone's life here, I suppose we'll be all right," my mother said. Then she looked directly at me. "You work for an investigative agency, Phee. Find out everything you can on those two. Last thing we need is for someone to get murdered in our bowling alley."

"'Murdered in our bowling alley'? Who said anything about anyone getting killed in our bowling alley? We were talking about redoing it!"

"You can never be too sure."

A lump formed in my stomach and I knew it wasn't from the wings. What I didn't know was how close to the truth my mother's words would be.

CHAPTER 2

"How was your evening?" Augusta asked when I got into work the next day.

"Upsetting, unnerving, and unbelievable."

"Don't tell me your mother brought the dog with her?"

"Worse. She brought Kenny and he opened a Pandora's box that we'll never be able to close. Anyway, I'll be glad when Marshall gets back this afternoon. I can't wait to tell him about it. Care to listen?"

For the next two or three minutes, I walked Augusta through the events of the prior evening. When I finished, all she could say was, "At least the Parmesan-encrusted garlic wings sounded good."

"I honestly don't know what that crew will come up with next. So far it's just the usual grumbling but I can never be too sure."

I headed to my office, booted up the computer and began my usual process for reconciling the monthly accounts. An hour into it, Augusta called out, "Phee, you've got someone on the line and it's not your mother."

"Thanks, Augusta." I picked up the phone and before I could speak, I heard a voice that sounded vaguely familiar.

"Hi. This is Lydia Wong and I hope I'm speaking with Phee Kimball."

Lydia Wong! My immediate reaction was that something awful had happened to my mother and for some reason, Gloria Wong's daughter called to let me know.

"Yes, it is." Positive the tone of my voice expressed fear, I waited for her to say something.

"I'm sorry to bother you at work but I didn't know where else to turn and I need your help. This is all my fault and I think I've put my mother in danger."

"Danger?"

"Not life and death, but it could be. Um, I can't really talk right now. I'm on a break at the hospital. Is there any way you could meet me after work? My shift ends at five. I want to be discreet about this and Sun City West is the last place we should talk. I can meet you somewhere in Peoria or Glendale near your office. I also don't want to be seen going into your investigative office because you never know who could be watching."

The more Lydia spoke, the more cloak-and-dagger everything sounded. I knew Marshall would understand so I told her I'd meet her at the Starbucks on Lake Pleasant Parkway at five forty-five. It was out of the Sun Cities gossip range as far as clientele went and it was close enough for both of us.

"Lydia," I said, "you *do* realize I'm a bookkeeper/accountant, not an investigator, right?"

"I know. But I also know you're smart and clever and able to untangle the worst messes. And believe me, I sure have one."

"Thanks for the vote of confidence. I'll try to help. See you later."

When I got off the phone, I told Augusta about the conversation.

"What do you suppose is going on?" She took out a small cloth from her top drawer and proceeded to clean the lenses on her glasses.

"Whatever it is, it has Lydia rattled. Knowing those book club ladies, my mind's conjured up all sorts of things, but if it was really, really bad, I'm sure my mother would have heard something. Those women can't keep anything to themselves. Besides, I just saw Gloria last night and she seemed perfectly fine to me."

"Maybe something happened this morning."

"Could be. Guess I'll find out tonight."

Nate arrived at a little before noon with dark circles under his eyes. I had made myself a new cup of coffee when he walked in.

"Good morning, all! I've been playing night owl and early bird. It finally paid off. Caught the scoundrel in the act and got the proof for my client. Now I'll be able to sink into that temperature-controlled mattress of mine tonight and get a decent sleep. Anything new?"

I shook my head at the same time Augusta answered, "Phee has a new case of her own."

"Huh?" Nate gave me a funny smile.

"It's not a case. Per se. It's Gloria Wong's daughter and she thinks something's going on with her mother. Wanted me to meet with her after work, that's all."

"Oh, for a minute you had me worried." I literally could see the relief on Nate's face. "Something's always going on with that book club. Who gave who the evil eye, who stole someone's family recipe, who cheated at bingo . . . I'm surprised Bowman and Ranston aren't grouchier given the reports they wind up taking."

"Those two detectives are ornery enough," Augusta said. "I was hoping they'd retire and some good-looking forty- or fifty-year-olds would take their place in the sheriff's office."

"Don't count on that happening any time soon," Nate said and laughed. "I think they're both married to the Maricopa County Sheriff's Office."

Just then my cell phone rang and I saw it was Marshall. "I've got to take this," I said. "It's Marshall." Then I walked into my office and closed the door.

"Hey, hon! Just wanted to let you know I'm still on the chase. Even though I thought I'd have it wrapped up today, it looks like I'll be headed south to Eagar. Got a really good lead and I don't want to waste time. Will keep you posted. How are you doing? Everything okay?"

"Everything's fine. Nate straggled in from his case and he caught the philanderer. Now he needs to catch some sleep."

"Yeah, I know how that goes. I'm not burning the midnight oil but I don't sleep well when I'm away from you."

I could feel the heat rising in my cheeks. "Me either. Stay safe. Text when you can."

"Speaking of which, I just texted Nate to let him know what's going on. If I'm right, I should be able to locate that sibling in the next twenty-four hours."

"Just don't take any risks."

"It's a long-lost sibling case, not a fugitive from justice. No worries."

We spent the next few minutes saying sweet cozy things to each other before we ended the call. Then, I returned to my accounts and blissfully immersed myself in documents and figures. With the exception of tearing into a late lunch pizza with Nate and Augusta, I spent my time at my desk, glued to my work.

At a little before five, I got up to stretch and grab a donut. That's when I overheard Augusta on the phone.

"I understand it's a delicate matter, Mrs. Lanne, but our investigators are extremely discreet. And, I might add, everything is strictly confidential. It would help us greatly if you could give me an idea of what your situation is so that I could let our investigator know in advance."

Then silence on Augusta's end. Finally, this: "All right, then. You're scheduled to meet with Mr. Williams at eight thirty a.m. on Thursday. We look forward to seeing you."

"The day after tomorrow, huh? That was pretty quick for scheduling." I bit the donut and let the chocolate linger in my mouth.

"Mr. Williams had an early slot available and our new client was anxious. Anxious and quite circumspect. Hmm, maybe the two of us should place a bet about what they're hiding."

"Shame on you, Augusta. That's not very professional." Then I broke up laughing. "Okay, here's a dollar. My money says your case is a cheating spouse and mine is, well . . . some tidbit of gossip that spread around and now poor Gloria has to fess up."

"Didn't the daughter mention danger?"

"She didn't say life or death. And in Sun City West, danger could mean anything from getting unfriended, ghosted, or not invited to whatever hoo-hah someone had planned."

"Okay. My money's on blackmail for Mrs. Lanne and trouble with the HOA for Gloria. How's that for starters?"

"Better than extortion, embezzlement or murder."

"Let's face it"—Augusta grinned—"our imaginations are far worse than anything that's going to land on our plate."

If only Augusta had been right, it would have made for an easier month. But March Madness in this case, which was a month away, had nothing to do with college basketball.

CHAPTER 3

There was a handful of people at Starbucks when I walked inside, but only a few were chatting. The rest were on their cell phones or laptops and oblivious to anything except their screens.

No doubt we had picked a good place to meet. As I approached the counter, I heard Lydia's voice behind me.

"Thanks so much for meeting with me. There's an empty table in the far corner. Let's grab it once we order our drinks."

A few seconds later, we sat face-to-face and I held my breath for what was to come.

"This is all my fault, you know," Lydia said, her voice low and soft. "I can't believe I'm responsible for getting my mother into this situation. And the worst thing is, she doesn't realize it. Or believe it."

"Okay, can you backtrack a bit so I can understand what's going on?"

Lydia nodded. "My mother's had a hard time adjusting to the twenty-first century up until now. By that, I mean she shied away from any kind of technology—smart phones, computers, you name it. Heck, she was even scared of the microwave when my father bought it for her in 1986. According to him, she used it as a bread box for months."

"That's kind of normal in a way. It took my mother a while to get used to the new technology. But now she likes it because it gives her something more to complain about."

Lydia laughed. "If only I had left her alone. But no, I insisted she get a computer and taught her how to use it for email. Then, I got the bright idea to introduce her to Facebook. I told her she'd see photos of her grandkids in California and would be able to chat with friends."

"Uh-oh. I think I see where this may be going."

"My mother's a very trusting person. I wouldn't quite say *gullible*, but close enough. Recently, she friended someone who's been sending her lots of messages and now they chat over Messenger all the time."

"What about texting? Does this friend text her?"

"Nope." Lydia shook her head. "You need a cell phone to text and hers isn't equipped for that. Thank goodness. They chat strictly over the computer."

"I take it it's a male friend."

"Uh-huh. All my mother would tell me is that she met a very nice engineer who works on an oil rig off of Louisiana and plans to retire in a year. According to her, he's a widower whose son passed away a few years ago from cancer."

"That's either a sad scenario or very convenient."

"So you're thinking what I am?"

"That he's scamming her?"

Just as Lydia was about to answer, the barista called out our names for the lattes.

"I'll get them," I said.

When I returned to the table, Lydia had wiped her cheek with a napkin.

"Sorry," she said, "but I don't know where else to turn. I'm convinced this guy is a fraud, or worse yet, is emailing her from some cyber-café in Nigeria or Libya. He's stringing her along for sure. Sending her poetry, telling her how wonderful she is. You name it."

"How did she friend him in the first place?"

"He saw her profile and sent her a message. That's my fault, too. I was the one who helped her write it. Anyway, this man told her she sounded like a very sweet person and wanted to get to know her. That was all it took for my mother to push the Friend button."

I took a sip of my latte and sighed. "I hate to say it, but it's like waiting for the other shoe to drop. The next step in these so-called romance scams is that the guy will tell her he wants to meet her and will fly to Phoenix. Then, something will go wrong and he'll need money. Then someone will fall ill. These scammers have a zillion plausible scenarios and they can be very convincing."

"I know. But she refuses to believe it's the case with him."

"I'm surprised she hasn't shared it with the book club ladies. Those women can't keep anything to themselves."

"My mother's very old-fashioned and somewhat superstitious when it comes to things like this. She probably doesn't want to jinx it. I keep telling her it's a ruse, but she refuses to believe me."

"At least she confided in you."

"Not exactly. I noticed her spending an inordinate amount of time on the computer, so one night when she took Thor out, I went into her room and looked. She was in the middle of a conversation with him."

"And you told her what you did?"

"I'm not crazy. But I was sneaky. I suggested she consider dating some of the men who've paid attention to her at bowling and that's when she informed me that she had a gentleman friend whose 'friendship was blossoming.' I kept prying and that's how I learned how deep into this my mother was."

I sipped my latte and listened as Lydia continued.

"It may get worse. That is, if my sister finds out. At least she and her husband are in Chandler and only venture into the West Valley once in a while."

"I think I remember my mother saying something about an older sister who worked for FedEx."

"Yeah, she's in corporate. And her husband is a bank manager in Phoenix. I call them the power couple. No kids. Just workaholics. Phee, if this situation with my mother escalates, my sister will blame me for not leaving well enough alone. Worse yet, she'll call my brother in Fresno and he'll insist she leave Sun City West and go live with him and his family."

"Isn't that an overreaction?"

"Not if you knew my brother."

I looked at Lydia and handed her a napkin. "Tell me how I can help. And keep in mind, I'm not an investigator but you may wind up needing one."

"I understand. First of all, I'd like to know who's really on the other end of these conversations but I have no idea how to go about it."

"I know someone who can find that out but he doesn't come cheap. Well, I shouldn't really say that. His remuneration falls into the category of 'other.'"

"I'm not sure I understand." Lydia bit her lower lip and widened her eyes.

Heck, I'm not sure either when it comes to Rolo Barnes.

"We had an incredible cyber-sleuth in IT when I worked for the police department in Mankato, Minnesota. His name's Rolo Barnes and the FBI, CIA, and Homeland Security can't hold a candle to him. He's that good."

"I won't be able to afford him."

"Hold on. Here's the weird part—Rolo likes to be paid in kitchen gadgetry. The more complicated the case, the more expensive the products. I truly believe IKEA's stock oscillates due to Rolo."

"It's worth a try. I'll do anything to prevent my mother from getting mixed up in something like this."

"Okay, here's the caveat. Rolo will most likely take your case but he'll initially communicate with me, as in Williams Investigations. Probably best that way. I'll contact him and let you know. Meanwhile, get the IP address from your mother's computer and text it to me."

"I can do that. Is there anything else you need?"

"That's it for starters. Just so you know, many people caught up in these things refuse to believe it's true, even when shown the evidence."

Lydia welled up. "I was afraid that would be the case, but I guess I'll cross that bridge when I get to it."

"Good idea. We'll take things one step at a time."

"Um, is there any charge for your consultation?"

"Heavens no! Our mothers are friends. And I'm no detective. Rolo will come at his own cost. Better peruse Amazon for the latest kitchen gadgets." I laughed and for the first time, Lydia smiled.

• • •

I told Marshall about my meeting with Lydia when he phoned later that evening. He'd made the drive to Eagar and was able to contact a few reliable sources. Positive that he'd have the missing sibling located by the end of the day, he gave me a tentative, "I'll be home tomorrow."

"I'm counting on it," I told him. "In fact, I'll be so elated that we should eat out at Twisted Italian or Chef Fabio's."

"You've got a deal."

Oddly enough, I had a blissful night's sleep, but I when I woke the following morning, I had an uneasy feeling something was wrong. I'm not prone to that sort of thing and tried to write it off to missing Marshall, but when I turned on the news, I began to wonder if I didn't have a sixth sense after all.

"That's right," Bonnie Williams announced on channel 10 news, "students from Willow Canyon High School in Surprise discovered a dead body on their way to school this morning. The unidentified man was found behind some bushes and was noticed only when one of the students snuck behind those bushes for a smoke."

"I bet his parents won't be too pleased," her co-anchor said and chuckled.

"And I'll bet that'll be the last time that kid goes behind some bushes for a smoke. We'll have more news on this grim discovery once the police department gets their investigation underway."

Then the comment that rattled me for sure. "Something else to ponder before we move on for a traffic update. The students found a bowling roster from Sun City West next to the body. It may have blown in from anywhere, or it could be connected. We'll have more when we get it."

"Blown in, my foot!"

I kept my fingers crossed that whoever the unfortunate victim was, he lived in a community other than my mother's. However, given that track record, I was prepared for the worst. Including a phone call from my mother.

14

CHAPTER 4

Sure enough, within minutes my mother's voice blared through the landline. "Did you turn on the morning news, Phee? They found a man's body in Surprise. With the Sun City West bowling roster on it. I'm calling Gloria as soon as I get off the phone with you."

"Whoa. Slow down. I watched channel 10. The bowling roster was found *near* the body, not *on* it! Until the victim is identified, we have no idea if he was a resident in your community. Don't go scaring Gloria. Or anyone else. For all we know, he could have been a walker who suffered a heart attack." *Not likely considering the location under the bushes but she doesn't need more coal for her fire of rumors.*

My mother continued speaking as if she hadn't heard me. "If it turns out to be Sun City West, then the Surprise Police Department will be working with Bowman and Ranston."

I cringed at the mention of their names. "Let's hope it doesn't come to that or our guys will inevitably be dragged along. Meanwhile, put it on hold. Okay?"

"Fine. Those bowlers have enough to worry about, I suppose."

When I got off the phone, my confidence level in my mother's ability to keep this to herself was nil. Even Augusta agreed with me when I arrived at work a short while later.

"Mr. Williams was already informed about that situation," she said. "He's on his way to chat with Bowman. The police found a wallet with a Sun City West rec card in it. Looks like the guy was a resident after all."

"Suspicious death?"

Augusta shrugged. "Most likely. Not usual for someone to strangle themselves."

"How do you know?"

"Mr. Williams was informed there were ligature marks on the victim. Doubt they were caused by those bushes."

I was positive my face had turned ashen. "I'll need another cup of coffee."

While I fumbled with the Keurig, Augusta pulled up the weekly schedule and said, "I suppose it's as good a week as any for a murder. We've only got small domestic cases on our docket."

"Wonderful. Just what those book club ladies need to hear."

"Maybe some other nefarious situation will waft their way."

"It'll have to be a doozy for them to drop this one."

We both laughed, but little did I know that Augusta's offhand remark

15

would take center stage and hang around for a good long time before its final bow.

I retreated to my office and remained there until my body cried out for coffee at my midmorning break. At that time, I checked my text messages and saw that Rolo returned the one I sent at the crack of dawn. It was his usual "impossible to interpret" emoji, followed by two words—*burner phone*.

"Here you go," Augusta said as she reached into the bottom of the file cabinet near her desk and handed me the phone. "Honestly, that man makes security at the Pentagon look like amateurs."

"What else is new? Next thing you know, we'll need a secret password and a decoder ring."

"You're dating yourself," she said with a laugh.

"Nah. I'm just a good historian."

Rolo answered on the first ring and informed me he was back to intermittent fasting. I crossed my fingers it didn't involve some sort of break-the-fast appliance that specialized in cooking gut-recovery recipes. After a quick hello, I explained the situation.

"Do you think you can track down whoever's baiting Gloria Wong?" I asked.

"No problem. Send me the IP address and her email. I'll ferret around. Shouldn't take me that long."

"Any idea of the cost? I imagine the daughter is on a limited budget."

"Depends on what I find and how long I need to dig. Will let you know."

"Rolo, if Gloria refuses to block the guy, can you do it?"

"Yeah, but she'll only friend him again. The trouble with those romance scams is that the recipients get totally brainwashed by these con artists. And it's not one person. They work as a team. It's their business."

"Can't the authorities intervene?"

"Most of the scammers are in the Middle East. Good luck with that. Not happening. I'll let you know what I find."

"Thanks. And good luck with the fasting."

"My next step may be a colon cleanse. Not sure yet."

I tried to block that image from my mind and ended the call.

Fortified with a cup of McCafé, I returned to my desk and the pile of invoices that awaited me. At a little before noon, Augusta leaned into the doorway and announced that Nate would be tied up most of the afternoon with the deputies.

"I'm sure they've identified the victim but haven't shared it with the press. Did Nate tell you who it was?"

"Nope. Only thing he said was to get him a giant meatball sub and put it in the fridge. I'm calling Firehouse Subs and ordering one for myself. They deliver. What about you?"

"Might as well make it three orders."

By midafternoon, I'd completed the invoices and started on the billing. That's when Marshall called to let me know he located the sibling and was in contact with the family. Mission accomplished. He'd be back home by evening.

"Have you spoken with Nate?" I asked.

"And then some. We're on that murder case. They identified the body but there's one problem."

"Other than the fact he's dead? Sorry, I shouldn't be making light of this."

"Hey, I've joked at worse. Hold on for this one—He had a rec card that said Sun City West, an Arizona license and an expired one from Idaho. He could be a recent transplant. Or a snowbird. Listen, I really don't want to talk about this on the phone so we'll pick up later. Miss you."

"Me too."

When I told Augusta, she furrowed her brow, removed her glasses, and bit the tip of the temple. "Hmm, sounds like a snowbird to me. Most transplants can't wait to get licensed in Arizona. It's the vanity plates that do it. Then again, they wind up touting their former states. We've got NJGIRL and ALOHAAL parked out front if you take a look."

"I'll take your word for it."

"How long do you think this will sit quiet until your mother's book club goes off the rails?"

"A nanosecond if I'm lucky. All I know is that if something doesn't grab the attention of those book club ladies, this murder will. There won't be enough Screamers on the market. Myrna ordered a new kind, complete with a strobe light to temporarily paralyze any attacker."

"Looking down the nose of my Smith & Wesson is paralyzing enough, I'd say."

"I hope the sheriff's office can wrap up this case quickly, before it catches like wildfire."

"You mean the more those book club ladies turn it into the crime of the century."

"Yeah, *that*."

And while it wasn't quite the crime of the century, or even the decade, it was still a homicide and no amount of sweet-talking would change that. However, Kenny made sure something would rival it in the eyes of the book club ladies. It was the "nefarious situation" I hoped would surface. Unfortunately, it turned out to be worse and there was no way to toss it back.

"Your mother's on the line, Phee," Augusta shouted a little before five.

Now what? I expected the rumor mill to be in full force, but instead, it was a bona fide announcement from the rec center that prompted her call.

"Phee! The worst has happened! Remember last night when Kenny said the board was considering hiring Harris and Blake Wainwright from New Media Entertainment to redo the bowling alley? Well, it sounds like it's a done deal! It's on the cover of today's *Independent*."

"Didn't it have to go through a vote or something?"

"It did! *Their* vote. Then they'll just shove it down our throats when we vote on the budget for next year. Half of the residents won't even realize they voted for the plan. Listen to this! The article says, 'New Media Entertainment plans to convert the antiquated bowling alley of the seventies into a modern structure complete with laser-lit lanes, holographic images, and even a virtual reality bowling area. In addition, there will be a sports bar, an arcade, a sports theater and even a laser tag area for our nimble players.' Nimble players? We're in our sixties, seventies and eighties. How nimble do they expect us to be?"

"It sounds as if they're courting a younger crowd."

"They can court them elsewhere. If we wanted to live in a multi-generational neighborhood, we would have bought houses elsewhere. We moved to a senior community that would meet our needs, not be a mini amusement park for people going through a midlife crisis. Offer them a pill or something."

"Maybe they'll listen to you at their next meeting."

"Good luck with that. Now what do we do? Those general meetings are useless. People show up with all sorts of petty complaints. The last time someone complained about the choice of flowers in the median by the Bell Road entrance. And before that, it was the shower temperature at Beardsley Rec Center."

"What about—"

"Wait! I haven't finished. At the same meeting, a woman complained about coyote poop on her street. What did she expect? A wildlife leash law?"

"I'm afraid you and your friends will have to find another way to voice your objections. Maybe a letter to the editor."

"Don't be ridiculous. No one reads them except for Cecilia. We need to get the board's attention and there's only one way to do it—We'll stage a sit-in at the administration center. Hit back first!"

Hit back first?

"You'll what?"

"You heard me. I need to call everyone. If we don't act now, next thing you know, that board will turn the club rooms into speakeasies and install giant waterslides at our pools! It's a matter of saving the integrity of our community. Besides, those strobe lights they have planned will give poor Gloria a migraine. And poor Bud on her team. He can barely get the ball down the lane as it is. You know I'm right, Phee."

"Mom, I—" But it was too late. She ended the call.

CHAPTER 5

That was yesterday. By nine fifteen the next morning, my mother called to tell me the sit-in plan was "in the works," and that Gloria called. Not needing a complete rendition of her morning, I tried to end the call but it was useless.

"Some sort of photo shoot is going on at the bowling alley. Gloria said the place was teeming with photographers but it was a press thing. Not a dead body."

"Uh, that's good, I suppose." *I don't have time for this.*

"No, it's not good. The Wainwrights are there, father and son in all their glory, pontificating about their plan to modernize the bowling alley. They were speaking to the morning leagues. Trying to drum up support for their project. They even brought a huge rendering of their proposal according to Gloria. Oh, Kenny was there as well. Not about the presentation or the tournament. He left his bowling glove there a few nights ago."

"Thanks for the info. I really need to get back to work. And do not include me in your sit-in. That's the last thing I need. Our office is busy enough."

"It's that body they found in Surprise, isn't it? The news anchors have been very cagey about it."

"Because they don't have the details yet. Like the victim's name. You know how that works. They have to contact next of kin first. And go through all the proper channels before they can release information. Not like your crew. They release scuttlebutt like a belch."

"It's not scuttlebutt when more than one person has heard it from a different source."

"No, that's rumormongering. Listen, I'll talk to you later. I really have to go."

With that, I ended the call and took a deep breath. It was early in the day but I was still drowsy. Marshall and I had stayed up late last night so he could tell me about the missing sibling case and his take on the suspicious death in Surprise. It was past midnight by the time we called it a night.

One thing was evident. Since the victim was indeed a Sun City West resident, and our detectives were more than familiar with the community, it made sense for them to pick up the reins. The fact that they had an ironclad consulting contract pretty much cinched the deal. Unfortunately, that meant my mother would be plaguing the office day after day to find out if the killer had been apprehended.

With the exception of the Maricopa County Sheriff's Office, only the four of us in Williams Investigations knew that the guy had been strangled. But that information wouldn't stay put for long. Once it leaked out, there would be no turning back. I could almost recite the questions from the book club ladies.

"Is it a serial killer?"

"Was it a robbery gone wrong?"

"Was the victim a secret agent?"

"What about the witness protection program?"

"Was the bowling roster a hit list?"

I cringed at what was to come and made up my mind in that split second to do anything I could that would keep my mother focused on the bowling alley dilemma. At least that didn't involve murder. Only mayhem. Especially with her cockamamie sit-in plan.

Then there was Gloria's situation. I hoped Rolo would be able to home in on the perpetrator before the scam had escalated. It had only been a day since I contacted him, but given the myriad of "assignments" he juggled, I knew I'd have to wait my turn.

Dizzy and somewhat disturbed at the thought of my mother and her cronies going off the deep end, I walked into the outer office to make myself another coffee. As I approached the Keurig, I caught a side glimpse of a tall Asian woman on her way out the door.

"Wait," I called out, thinking it was Lydia, but it was too late. It certainly looked like her, but by the time I got to the entrance, the woman crossed the street and got into a car. I glanced at the digital clock on our wall and remembered that Augusta had a dental appointment for nine thirty. If it *was* Lydia, why wouldn't she have called me?

Please don't tell me I'm making stereotypical conclusions about people based on nationality.

Rather than wait and see, I shot off a text to Lydia: *Waiting to hear from Rolo. It should be soon. Will keep you posted.*

I figured if it *was* her and she didn't find anyone in the outer office, because I'd forgotten to leave my door ajar, she would let me know.

Back once again to my spreadsheets, I barely heard Augusta return. Not until her voice, along with Nate's, carried into my office.

"Can't believe I chipped a tooth. I told the dentist to put some Bondo on it or something so I could get back to work."

"I take it he or she filled it with an enamel paste or something." Nate's laugh made me smile.

"Or something. Anyway, it may turn out that I'm a night grinder. Don't know why I'd be grinding my teeth. It's not as if I have any issues."

"I think it has more to do with sleep patterns and genetics."

"Nothing that a good shot of bourbon or rum before bed wouldn't cure."

"If you say so. Listen, I need you to fax Rolo and have him call me. He's got my burner number."

"The eight thirty appointment? Mrs. Lanne?"

"Yep."

"Shall I tell him what it's about?"

Then more of Nate's laughter. "You sure are sneaky, Augusta. If you must know, she's worried about a family member getting scammed out of money."

"People need to wise up. If it sounds too good to be true, it is. Hang on. I'll get Rolo to call you."

I heard Nate's footsteps as he walked back to his office. Hmm, another scam. Must be I didn't hear Mrs. Lanne leaving either.

Curious to see if Augusta knew more than what she let on, I stepped out and smiled. "Fun at the dentist?"

"Until the bill comes. Must be these choppers are getting old because he thinks I'm grinding them. Fat chance."

"Say, you didn't happen to see Mrs. Lanne when she arrived, did you?"

"Sorry, no. I was probably halfway to Surprise by then. Mr. Williams said he'd take care of it. Didn't want to bother you. Why? Was it important?"

"No. Just curious."

"Me too. Gotta call Rolo. We can catch up later and compare our bets. This time I think we both might have lost."

I grinned. "That's why I don't gamble."

"Well, there's one bet I'm willing to make. If you ask me, that nippy little murder in Surprise is going to turn out to be the tip of an iceberg that no one will be prepared for."

"Yeesh. What makes you say that?"

"The fact that Bowman and Ranston couldn't wait to pawn it off on us. Oh, don't get me wrong, they'll be working the case, too, but only from the sidelines. I think they already know who the victim is. That's why Mr. Gregory is meeting with them and a rep or two from the Surprise Police Department as we speak."

"Uh, yeah. He mentioned a meeting but not about the victim's ID."

"Mark my words, this is only the beginning. Mr. Williams got the intro yesterday and today Mr. Gregory gets Act One."

"Thanks, Augusta. That's about as reassuring as a forecast for a hailstorm."

"Anytime."

By midmorning, Nate had joined Marshall in Sun City West and I was pretty sure Augusta's take on the situation was spot-on. That meant I needed to act fast regarding the bowling alley fiasco, but I got sidetracked when Rolo called me back.

"Must be scam week at your office, huh?" he said when he phoned me at a little past three. "Got Nate's message via his sentry. You don't think she'd want to come work for me, do you?"

"Absolutely not! What did you find out?" I was breathless and anxious for an answer.

"Nothing yet where your boss is concerned. Still need an IP address from him. As far as your friend goes, it's as ugly as it gets. I tracked down her contact to an office building in Lagos, Nigeria, but that's only for starters."

"Starters?"

"Much better off if it was a cyber-café but this operation smacks of a 24/7 deal with government ties. Hey, it's a poor country and scamming is probably one of the better ways to make a living. But I don't think we're dealing with your everyday scammers."

"Uh-oh."

"You got that right. Additional links take me to Sao Paulo, Brazil. No surprise there, except for one thing. The government ties I mentioned are joined at the hip with key industries in—get this—housing and urban development. It's like an octopus with its tentacles everywhere."

"Can't Lydia's mother just drop off the internet for a while?"

"Sure. But even if she does, these criminals may come after her in another way. Finances, home title, that sort of thing."

"Why? Why on earth would they do that to a senior citizen in a retirement community who's most likely living off of a pension and social security?"

"Could be a mix-up in identities. That happens, you know. Or, maybe Lydia's mother is not who everyone thinks she is."

"Oh my gosh. This is awful. You'll have to explain all of this to Lydia. I wouldn't know where to begin. But maybe you should leave off the last part."

"No problem. Get me the burner number and I'll expect a call."

"Thanks, Rolo."

"Remember, intermittent fasting with Keto overtones."

"Sure." *Just translate that to gadgetry money.*

I didn't have the heart to call Lydia. At least not right there and then. I figured I'd text her again to see when she'd be home after her shift and I would stop by. Preferably when her mother was out. Even if I had to arrange that myself.

Then, a minor epiphany. If I could get my mother to invite Gloria over on some pretense, then I'd be able to talk freely with Lydia.

Oh my gosh! This is worse than I thought. I've become my mother!

CHAPTER 6

I kept rehearsing what I'd say to Lydia. I couldn't very well tell her to call Rolo without providing her with a little bit of reassurance. And for that, I had to be there when she placed the call.

By three forty-five, I was as edgy as ever, but a phone call from Shirley changed everything.

"Phee, honey, I'm sorry to bother you at work. That's why I called your cell."

"Is everything all right?"

"Yes, yes. Fine. Well, sort of. I really didn't know where else to turn. Frankly, your mother and I are worried about Gloria. She's been so distracted lately. And when we do get together, she can't stay away from that phone of hers for more than five minutes. Even Kenny noticed at the last bowling night. Said she spent half the time looking at her phone and had to be reminded it was her turn. I know it's not my business but something's up. That's for sure."

I can't break confidentiality but I can skirt around it.

"Um, how does she seem when she's looking at the phone? Worried? Anxious?"

"No, that's just the thing. Sometimes she smiles to herself, other times she chuckles. Then she excuses herself for a few minutes and comes back. You know what I think?"

Uh-oh.

"She's on one of those gambling sites. Lordy, that woman's going to lose all of her money. First, they lure you in with lots of little wins, and then—BOOM—your bank account is down to zero."

"Have you or Mom mentioned it to her?"

"No, we don't want to be buttinskis."

Since when?

"Maybe just ask how everything's going."

"That's exactly what we're going to do tonight. Your mother and I are going to the Homey Hut with Gloria on the pretense of trying their gluten-free orange almond cake. But that's not why I called you. I wondered if there was some way you could find out for us. I would be heartsick if Gloria got addicted to online gambling."

"See how tonight goes, first. Maybe segue into discussions about people who gamble online or start relationships online."

"Oh, I doubt it's a relationship. Gloria was married for over forty years before her husband passed. And it isn't as if she hasn't caught anyone's attention. I watched her bowl once, and the men were ogling all over her. No, I think it's the gambling thing for sure."

We should only be that lucky.

"I'll see what I can do but keep me posted. I wonder why my mother didn't call me about this. Usually she calls over the tiniest nitpicky things."

"I'm sure she'll get around to telling you, but right now she's working the phone tree and the emails about staging a sit-in to protest any changes to the bowling alley."

"I pray it will never get off the ground. Literally! A sit-in? The only sitting that crew does is in their recliners or, in Herb's case, at Curley's Bar. And between the two of us, it will take the Sun City West Fire District Response Team to hoist half the women up from the floor when the sit-in is over!"

"Maybe they'll come up with a better idea."

Or not.

"Let me know what happens with Gloria, will you?"

"Absolutely. And thanks for listening. I wouldn't have bothered you if I didn't think it was important."

"I know. Just don't jump to conclusions. Okay?'

"Okay."

The thought of my mother and Shirley messing up things as far as Gloria was concerned was the least of my problems. But her ludicrous idea of a sit-in made my stomach churn. I pictured Streetman in his tote going ballistic if anyone came near him, and Essie in her "kitty-carry" sweatshirt hissing and yowling. Then again, my mother had recently purchased a multifunction travel system for the dog and cat at a cost of most compact vehicles. And to think, as a baby I was in a fold-up stroller that would fail all safety standards today.

Apparently Lydia wasn't the only one who noticed her mother's unusual behavior. Gloria had managed to get the full attention of my mother and Shirley. Rather than put it off until the end of the day, I phoned Lydia and kept my fingers crossed it wouldn't go to voicemail.

Thankfully, I caught her at a good time.

"Phee! Did your friend find out who's behind this so-called romance? I'm on a ten-minute break so we have to talk fast."

"Um, he did have some information and he'll explain it to you. Can we meet after work at the same Starbucks? That way, if you have any questions I'll be right there."

"That's awfully nice of you. Do you think maybe a 'cease and desist' letter would help?"

Like offering someone a paper towel to clean up a mudslide.

25

"Uh, er, we can talk about that later. I know you have to get back to work. Same here."

"Okay. Thanks again."

• • •

"Judging from the look on your face," Marshall said when I walked into the house after meeting with Lydia, "things didn't go too well once Rolo broke the news."

I kicked off my shoes and gave him a hug. "She's beside herself. In addition to worrying about her mother being duped for money, she's now concerned about what else that criminal group may have in mind."

"The first thing she needs to do is get her mother off that computer. Or at least delete the perpetrator from her Facebook friend list and her email. Block it in no uncertain terms."

"I know that, and Lydia knows that, but Gloria may not believe her."

"She needs to emphasize how dangerous this is. Especially if they can get into her bank accounts."

"Rolo already told Lydia to have her mother change passwords and speak with a banker about security. She doesn't have to provide explicit details, only a concern that she may be hacked."

"I'm not telling her what to do, but she may want to move her monies into different institutions so it's not all in one place. Then again, these criminals have intel that's unbelievable."

"I'm afraid Gloria will be embarrassed about this and do nothing."

"She's not the only one. Nate's dealing with a similar case. Lots of seniors being taken advantage of because that generation happens to be more trusting than the rest of us."

"Maybe my mother and Shirley will have better luck and get Gloria to tell them what's going on."

"Telling them is one thing. Getting her to sever all ties with this guy is another."

"I know. Lydia plans to 'have the talk' with her mother tonight. Wants to step in before her siblings find out. She said she'd call me tomorrow or the next day."

"Okay. That's the best you can do for now."

"There *is* good news, though. Rolo was able to disrupt the connection between the initial server and Gloria's computer. However, he said it won't take long before that cyber-enterprise reconnects. They've got their tentacles everywhere."

"Sounds like our buddy will be doing interference for a while."

"Uh-huh. But he loves that stuff, as well as the kitchen upgrades."

Marshall chuckled as we headed to our own kitchen.

"Any word when that victim's name will be released to the media?" I asked. "What did Bowman and Ranston find out?"

"You mean what did *we* find out in conjunction with the Surprise police?" Marshall laughed. "Guy's name is Orlando Fleish. Home address is Sun City West. We'll speak with the neighbors and see what they can tell us."

"What about the rec card activities?"

"Bowman's already on it. Tracked down every place the guy frequented in the last three months."

"And?"

"Your mother won't like this—the library, the bowling alley, and the fitness center near her house. Now she'll be concerned about a killer lurking there."

"What else is new?" I rolled my eyes.

"The guy simply could have been at the wrong place at the wrong time. Anyway, he was in the service in 1964 so his fingerprints were on file. That helped. No record of convictions and no living next of kin. Maybe his residence will provide some clues. Bowman said his name will be released to the media tonight, along with a photo from his wallet in the hopes that someone will come forth with information about him."

"I know what will come forth—my mother and her merry band of gossipers. Good grief. I never thought I'd be saying this, but I'm going to give her sit-in a thumbs-up. If nothing else, it should keep them away from any real trouble. I mean, how dangerous could a sit-in to protest that bowling alley plan get?"

"It's your mother's friends, honey. Need I say more?"

CHAPTER 7

I braced myself for a phone call from my mother once the morning news came on, but I didn't expect it before the sun came up. I reached over and grabbed the landline hoping not to wake Marshall.

"Phee! Lucinda just woke me up. She knew the man they found dead in Surprise. It was the one who gave that presentation at her church about life-care communities. Cecilia was there too. His name is Orlando Flesh or something."

"Fleish."

"You heard the news too?"

Oops.

"It's not as if Lucinda knew him, Mom. She happened to attend a function, that's all."

"And *he* happened to have the registration list from her church. Just like the bowling roster. Of course, that may explain it. He was fishing for clients. Still, it's unnerving."

"I don't think that's a reason for concern. If anyone in Sun City West was at risk, the sheriff's office would notify them. And, um, speaking of risks—*I can't believe I'm doing this*—are you still going through with that sit-in plan of yours to squelch the bowling alley proposal?"

Marshall tossed the covers off and sat up. His grin was ear to ear and I turned away for fear of laughing out loud.

"As a matter of fact, we have it all planned. Myrna and I intend to mention it on our radio show as well. Louise made flyers and Kenny said he'd distribute them at the bowling alley today. Oh, and get this! Your aunt Ina called that reporter from channel 10. What was his name? Justin something-or-other."

"Not Justin. Tim Justin. Justin's the last name. And I can't believe she called him. She doesn't even live in Sun City West."

"According to your aunt, New Media Entertainment's plan is contagious. She's concerned they'll transform the Grand into the next Las Vegas hot spot."

"Oh brother. So, when does this catastrophe take place?"

"A week from today. At nine in the morning. We should have a decent crowd of protesters considering the bowlers, our book club, and the pinochle crew. Plus, Herb was going to speak with the Men's Club and Wayne said he'd let the auto restoration club know. Not to mention all those sewing groups Shirley is in, plus the clay club and bocce. Goodness. But that's not the best part."

On no. Here it comes. Streetman and Essie are going to be dressed up for the sit-in.

I held my breath and waited for my mother to continue.

"In order to coordinate the bowlers, Kenny thought it would be a good idea to chat with them at Lizard Acres Pub after tomorrow night's league games. Unless you and Marshall have plans, you should stop over. Saturday nights are always packed. That means we can garner a larger crowd for our sit-in."

"I don't think—" Then I stopped myself. I imagined that with a large crowd, we'd be able to overhear snippets of information regarding Orlando Fleish. It might turn out to be useful for Nate and Marshall since they were stuck with that case.

"I don't think that's a bad idea. I'll run it by Marshall in case he's got something else going on."

"On a Saturday night?"

"It's not a nine-to-five job. The office has been swamped with clients and investigations have no off-hours."

"Fine. Let me know."

"Will do. Gotta run or I'll be late for work. By the way, and not that I'm asking for him to be involved, but I was surprised your radio host cohort, Paul Schmidt, hasn't shown up with the guys."

"Paul's at Lake Havasu. Largemouth bass fishing with Mini-Moose from the billiard room and a few buddies of his who live there. He's supposed to be back in time for our murder mystery and fishing show. If not, it will just be Myrna and me. We know about fish. We cook and eat them. Did I ever tell you how popular that radio show is? Myrna and I are still scratching our heads. At least we have our own show once a week without references to fish or bait."

I gulped. "Uh-huh." *And please don't tell me who Mini-Moose is. I can only imagine.*

The *Murder Mystery and Fishing Show* was the result of an accidental scheduling mistake when the local Sun City West *Mystery Hour* on KSCW, featuring my mother and Myrna, collided with *Lake Fishing with Paul*, and neither of them agreed to give up their slot. So, the listeners got an earful of mystery and fish stories all rolled into one. It resembled a casserole that featured seafood, ground beef, and tuna, yet the audience loved it. I still cringe.

"Thanks, Mom. Really do have to get going. I'll catch you later."

Marshall couldn't help but laugh. "You asked for it, hon, when you mentioned Paul."

"I know. But he's usually in the thick of things, like moths around a lightbulb."

"So, Lizard Acres tomorrow night, huh? I take it it's the *Happy Days* version of Curley's Bar."

"Pretty much. It's the Sun City West senior hotspot. And it beats snooping around in the dog park. You overheard my mom. The place will be packed and we'll be able to overhear conversations about Orlando. Face it, if he made a presentation at Lucinda's church, then he must have targeted other houses of worship. Kind of like a captive audience."

"And you're thinking one of those captives might have done him in?"

"I'm thinking it's the perfect place to find out. Or at least pick up some decent leads."

"You've got my vote. Track down a killer and save the bowling alley from entering into the twenty-first century. How can we possibly turn down this invitation?"

"I've never been in the place but it's hard to imagine a bar in a bowling alley. My mother tells me they have entertainment as well as Wii Bowling and even a trivia night. Of course, she's never been there, either, but Myrna went once with the bocce club when they offered a special on drinks."

"And?"

"That's all I know."

Marshall stretched and got out of bed. "We're up early thanks to your mom. I'll wash up and get breakfast going or we can grab something at Starbucks for a change."

"Starbucks cappuccino sounds way better than a Keurig pod. Glad our bathroom has two sinks."

"Heck, I'm glad the house has two bathrooms."

And with that, we readied ourselves for Starbucks and work.

● ● ●

When I told Augusta about our plans for Lizard Acres, she lifted her glasses, rubbed the bridge of her nose, and said, "Does *lizard* refer to the clientele or is it something else?"

It was a little after nine and I had just completed some invoices when I took a break for more coffee. "Before 1960, it was a cattle ranch and train stop. Got its name when one of the ranch owners said the land was 'only fit for raising lizards.' At least that's what I've been told."

"And look what it's raising now—septua-, octo-, nona-, and cente-narians."

"Shh! The word is *senior*."

"Hey, the secret's safe with me. I've already bought my ticket for that ride."

"Marshall and I think we can pick up some information about Orlando

Fleish. You know those folks. They'll be buzzing about it. Especially since it's been on the news. No mistake about it. They used the word *murdered.* Meanwhile, I'm trying to keep my mother occupied with that bowling plan. You know how she gets when there's been a murder within a ten-mile radius of her house."

"Only too well. Mr. Williams said the deputies are looking into the man's background along with him and Mr. Gregory, but I suppose you already know that."

I nodded and Augusta continued. "Meanwhile, Mr. Williams is off on a minor case and should be back soon. Uh-oh. That's our burner phone ringing. Must be Rolo."

As Augusta tapped the screen, I waited a few seconds in case the call involved Lydia. The expression on Augusta's face never wavered, giving me no indication of what Rolo had phoned about. Then, "Hang on. Phee's standing right here. You can tell her."

The phone all but shook in my hand as I took it. "What's up?"

"Don't you guys ever communicate in your office? No reason to get a second call from your boss about that IP address. I already took care of it. Well, as much as I can do right now."

"Huh? I don't understand."

Augusta tilted her head, straining to hear.

"The IP address. The one in Lagos. I got his message but if you ask me, you guys are tripping over each other."

"Hold on a sec, Rolo." I looked at Augusta. "That scammer case Nate's working on, did Mrs. Lanne give a full name?"

"Just a minute." Augusta pulled up something on her screen. "Mrs. Sue-Lynn Lanne. That's all it says."

"Rolo, I think there are two different clients, although Lydia's not really a client, just an acquaintance."

"Two different clients and one IP address? Whatever. Just try to get it straight."

"Let me know if you find out anything else."

"I'm always finding out everything else. Keep those burners close."

When the call ended, I stretched my neck and took a huge sip of my coffee. "I'm not a betting person, but I think Sue-Lynn Lanne and Lydia Wong have more in common than scammer cases."

I pulled out my cell phone and sent Lydia a text: *Call me ASAP RE: S.L. Lanne.*

"Rolo's mystery is about to be solved in record time. Or, as soon as Lydia checks her messages. Hey, here's one bet I'm willing to make—Your Mrs. Lanne is Lydia's sister and somehow, she found out what their mother was up to."

"That's the trouble with families. Everyone keeps everything to themselves as if they were guarding trade secrets. All that drama. It wasn't until I was in my forties when I found out my great-aunt Helga had three husbands before Uncle Klaus."

"Divorced?"

"Kicked the bucket."

"Oh."

Just then my cell phone pinged and it was a text from Lydia: *She's my sister. Oh no! I'm dead meat. Will call you when my shift ends in a half hour.*

I sent back a thumbs-up, only I didn't think there was anything she'd cheer about.

Then, a second message appeared. This time from my friend Lyndy, who learned how to keep things short and to the point. *Can U meet at NW coffee after work? Rumors abound.*

With Marshall running a late schedule, I texted back that I'd be there by five thirty. Lydia would just need to muster the courage to deal with her sister and any of the fallout. I had to agree with Augusta. Much easier as an only child.

CHAPTER 8

Lyndy was already at NW coffee, a new spot for us, with a cup in her hand when I got there. Petite and brunette, she looked younger than her forties. Waving me over, she had a mischievous smile on her face. I pointed to the counter and she gave me a thumbs-up.

With my order in, I joined her and perused the place. Not quite as busy as the early morning hours, but this cozy coffee shop with its incredible aromas and welcoming modern décor did a booming business in our neighborhood.

"You piqued my curiosity," I said. "Spill it and then I'll ask what else is going on in your life."

Lyndy laughed and took a sip of her coffee. She and I had become good friends when I first moved to Vistancia. We were both single and spent our free time in the pool. As a recent widow, Lyndy moved out west to help out an elderly aunt and get herself a fresh start. The aunt also lived in Sun City West and rivaled my family for kookiness.

"When I said 'rumors abound,' I wasn't kidding." Lyndy widened her eyes. "And oddly enough, it was Lyman who clued me in."

"Lyman?"

"Uh-huh. And by the way, dating him is by far the best thing that ever happened to me, but I'll hold off on those details so we can get to the business of murder."

"I'm all ears. But honestly, I thought it would be your aunt who heard something. Her antennae are always up."

"Her antennae may be up but she hasn't gotten a signal. In fact, it's really bothering her that she hasn't picked up any gossip."

"Oh brother. So tell me what Lyman said."

"Not him. The guys on his softball team. They're a worse bunch of busybodies than the pinochle crew and book club combined. Anyway, it seemed that Orlando pressured a number of people to sell their homes and move into a life-care community. That's when one of them told him that if he didn't back off, the guy would wring his neck."

"And they think because Orlando was strangled, the guy actually *did* wring his neck?"

"They don't just *think* it, they have a bet going on to see how long it takes for the deputies to catch up with the guy. Seems he's a real hothead and it wouldn't take much to have him reach a boiling point."

"That's unbelievable! Why don't they just report what they know?"

"Because it's more hearsay than 'real say,' and the last time something like this happened, they were given the proverbial boot by the sheriff's office."

"Did Lyman know the name of the man who supposedly made that threat?"

"Yep. Harris Wainwright."

"Harris Wainwright? From New Media Entertainment? The guy who wants to turn Pleasantville into Las Vegas? *That* Harris Wainwright?"

"The very one. But like I said, it's all rumor. Still, there's always some truth behind the gossip."

"See if Lyman can get more concrete evidence of the threat."

"I'll do my best. By the way, what's this I hear about a sit-in? My aunt had a flyer on her coffee table."

"Ugh. It's my mother's brainchild, so brace yourself."

Then, I told Lyndy about the plan to let the rec center board know exactly how disgruntled the residents were and that Sun City West was a senior community, not a college campus.

When we finished our visit, we vowed to brave it and try the pool when the sun was out. Even if the temperature was frigid. At least the water would be warm and we'd have the whole place to ourselves.

When I got home, I checked my messages and voicemail. Sure enough, Lydia called. I wasted no time calling her back.

"Hi," I said. "Sorry I didn't get back to you sooner but I had to meet a friend."

"No problem." Lydia's voice was tentative. "I've been working up the courage to call my sister. She can be a bear at times and this will be one of them."

"Look, both of you have your mother's best interests at heart. Start with that and call me back. This is probably a good thing because the two of you can work in tandem."

"Until my brother gets wind of it."

"One thing at a time, okay?"

"Okay."

Marshall got in a few minutes later and recounted a recent conversation with the deputies as well as some progress on a minor case. "Don't know about you, but I'm up for ordering a pizza or anything that doesn't require work. I'm exhausted."

"Pizza it is." I updated him on Lydia as well as my conversation with Lyndy.

"Harris, huh? We'll need lots of evidence to go down that rabbit hole."

"I know. That's what I told Lyndy. And order any kind of pizza you want. From anywhere. I'm ready to chew my arm off."

The good news about living in our area was that we had plenty of choices and all of them delivered. With our stomachs full from a Pizza Hut special, we called it a night and prepared ourselves for what we imagined would be quite the show at Lizard Acres the next night.

I half expected Lydia to call me back but that never happened. Not until the following morning when I got into the office and had settled down at my desk. My cell phone vibrated and I instinctively knew it had to be her. Not that my mother didn't plague me on the cell phone, but the office line is usually her first choice.

"Hi, Phee. My sister didn't get back to me until really late last night and I didn't want to bother you. Turned out she had gotten suspicious of my mother's sudden fixation with the phone and when my mother was otherwise occupied, Sue-Lynn took a look at my mother's messages and emails. They were at her house in Chandler since they had a shopping day planned. Once my sister saw what my mother was up to, she contacted your boss and well, you know the rest."

"I take it your sister wasn't all that upset with the Facebook account you started for your mom."

"Oh, she was upset all right, but her mind worked like a machine. She was going to call me yesterday but got waylaid at work. She wants us to get Mom to meet with her banker, set up fraud alerts, and put a loan freeze on all her accounts. Just as Rolo said."

"And your brother?"

"Oh. Sue-Lynn and I agreed not to tell him anything until the bank situation is taken care of and we can be reasonably assured Mom will be safe from these cyber-criminals."

"When are you and your sister going to have the chat with your mom?"

"This afternoon, Sue-Lynn and her husband will drive over and we'll all go out to lunch. That way my mother is less likely to pitch a fit and accuse us of meddling while we're in a restaurant."

"Sounds like a good plan. Keep me posted."

"Thanks, Phee. I really appreciate everything."

And while Lydia would have to contend with her mother, Marshall and I would be on high gossip alert at Lizard Acres. Kenny assured us the bowlers would be out in full force as well as the regulars. But what he didn't count on was that Gloria had asked my mother and Shirley to meet her there as well.

Not that any of them were drinkers, unless you count cherry Cokes, Shirley Temples, and tonic water with lime. Still, it was a night out and a chance to hop on the rumor train.

When Marshall and I walked into Lizard Acres at a little past eight, the place was virtually humming. People throwing darts, people shooting pool, people laughing as they sat at the bar, and people milling all over the place.

"Um, look to your left, hon, but don't make it obvious. Isn't that your mother with Shirley and Gloria?"

I turned my head and—lo and behold—there was my mother engaged in an animated conversation. Gloria waved her hands in the air while my mom and Shirley nodded in agreement.

"Must be Gloria told them about her earlier conversation with her daughters and son-in-law," I said.

"Seems that way. Let's find Kenny and hope your mom doesn't notice us right away."

It took all of thirty seconds before Kenny approached us and ushered us to a fully stocked table with imported and domestic beers that the Lane Chasers seemed to be enjoying.

"In case you're wondering," he said, "having more than four or five players on a team is unusual and, well, overkill. But we didn't want to say no to anyone. And since the other teams didn't object, we decided to have seven players. Plus, seven is a lucky number."

I nodded, unsure of what to say. I had no idea about bowling regulations and hoped to avoid a long-winded lecture.

"Hey, everyone," Kenny shouted, "these are friends of mine—Phee and Marshall." Then, without pausing to catch a breath, he continued, "And this is Mary Alice, Fred, Erik, Cassie, and Bud. Bud's our best bowler, and believe it or not, he's legally blind."

"That's right," Bud chimed in. "Someone has to walk me to the lane and point me in the right direction. Then I take it from there. Last year, these hooligans pointed me the wrong way and I nearly wiped out the two tables behind us."

"I wasn't part of that adolescent behavior," Cassie said. "And neither was Gloria. Speaking of which, has anyone seen her?"

"Uh, she's in the bar area with my mother and another friend."

Fred looked at us and then back to his team. "Do any of you know what's going on with her? If she keeps up her losing streak much longer, she's going to be known as 'Gutter Ball Gloria.'"

"Probably trouble with her HOA. That stuff gets under your craw and stays there." Fred reached for a Michelob and took a swallow. "Help yourselves, guys. We've got plenty to go around."

Marshall and I thanked him but told him maybe later. *Or not.* Then the conversation shifted to the sit-in that was planned for this coming Friday. No doubt, the Lane Chasers would be there in full force along with the Desert Scorpions, the Day-Late-Dollar-Short Stars, and the Ball Busters.

"I didn't retire here to find myself in the middle of an amusement park," Mary Alice said. "If I wanted that, I could have moved in with my son and his family in San Diego."

"I left the city to get away from all that noise and those flashing lights. Lived my whole life in lower Manhattan. Don't need to be reminded every time I bowl." Fred took a slug of his beer and wiped his chin with a napkin.

"Do you think the sit-in will have any impact on our board?" Cassie made a half-hearted attempt at smiling but I could tell she was concerned.

"You never know. Boards are supposed to represent the people who voted them in." *In what universe?* "At least it will be a quiet sort of protest. I mean, everyone sitting and all."

"Is your mother bringing the dog?" Kenny looked directly at me and I was positive the color drained from my face.

"I'm not sure, but given past experience with these sorts of things, I'd say—"

"Phee and Marshall! You made it after all." My mother approached the table and skootched her way into the remaining few seats with Shirley and Gloria right behind her.

"We wanted to chat with the bowlers," Marshall said. "To get a better idea of their plight."

My mother smiled. "Good. Find out about Orlando Fleish." Then she eyeballed each of the Lane Chasers but made sure to speak extra loud when she looked at Bud. "Phee and Marshall work for Williams Investigations in Glendale."

"I've heard of your agency," Bud said. "No surprise they've got you on the Orlando case. Seems Williams Investigations has its hand in lots of MCSO consulting. If so, you may be interested in what I know about the late Orlando Fleish."

Marshall, who was seated directly across from Bud, moved forward and rested his elbows on the table.

Bud cleared his throat and wasted no time getting to the point. "He and the Wainwrights used to be in the same business development enterprise when they lived in Pocatello, Idaho. I know because I'm from the same area. Then they had some sort of falling out and went their separate ways. Didn't think I'd run into that crew of snakes and leeches again, but come to find out, they relocated to my own backyard right here in Sun City West."

CHAPTER 9

"Could you be a little more specific about 'snakes and leeches'?" my mother asked. "Are we talking white-collar crime or something that calls for a permit to carry?"

I shot her a look and she responded, "What? It's the state of Arizona, for crying out loud! Everyone has a permit to carry. Even if they never held a gun!"

I did a mental eye roll and waited for Bud to expound on the bombshell he dropped. Thankfully, I didn't have to wait long.

"The Wainwrights, in conjunction with Orlando, bilked people out of their savings with investment schemes that looked good on paper but weren't even worth the postage they used to mail them."

"Like Bernie Madoff in the 1990s?"

"On a much smaller scale, but yeah, like that. They were accused of attempted murder to silence a whistleblower but got off due to incompetence at the local police department."

Just then, Shirley poked Gloria. "Lucinda told us all about it. Lack of evidence. She follows those podcasts almost as much as her Telemundo episodes."

"Are you saying you think someone in our community murdered Orlando to get even for a bum investment?" By now I felt my pulse quicken as I waited for Bud's response.

"I'm saying it, but I can't prove it. I know he was in the senior life-care business as of late, but old grudges die hard. While you're scoping that out, you may want to do some homework on his past. Not all murders deal with recent events."

"I don't like the idea of someone in our community getting killed," Kenny said, "but if those Wainwrights are as slippery as eels, then we need to stop them now. If they wind up creating their futuristic bowling alley at our expense, I'm afraid Orlando's murder won't be the last."

Cassie, Mary Alice, and Shirley all gasped.

"Are you implying what I think you are?" Marshall asked.

Kenny nodded. "Yep. Got lots of unhinged and unstable people out there. We read about it all the time: *Cashier shot to death because they ran out of Marlboro Lights, Server punched in the jaw when she delivered cold French fries, Car run off the road when driver behind him thought the woman drove too slow.* Need I go on?"

"Speak of the devil," Erik said, "isn't that Harris in the corner over there, having words with the manager?" It was the first time Erik spoke and I detected a slight Southern drawl.

"Yeah, that's Harris all right, and Jonesy doesn't look all that happy." Fred stretched his neck to get a better look. "I'd like to be a fly in that corner."

"Lordy, that man is most likely telling the manager about his awful plan for Lizard Acres."

"Okay, folks," my mother said. Her voice was louder than usual and sharper. "Let's get down to business. We've got a captive audience here and we need to get out the word about the sit-in this Friday, just in case anyone missed it. Not everyone here is a bowler. Like I mentioned earlier, we'll be in front of the Welcome Courtyard all the way down to the bowling alley. It's a good way to get the board's attention."

"I take it you want us to go table to table and tell them?" Cassie asked.

"More like bar stool to bar stool," Fred said and laughed.

"I don't like approaching strange people by myself." Shirley looked at my mother and then at Gloria.

"The three of us will go together. The rest of you can do whatever makes you comfortable." She looked my way and smiled.

What makes me comfortable is leaving and going home.

After a few minutes of figuring out the logistics of who would walk where, our group split up. Marshall and I wove our way toward the corner where Jonesy and Harris stood. Their voices were muffled by the bar noise but we were able to make out a rather nasty threat from Harris—"Try to stop me and it will be the last thing you do."

I nudged Marshall. "I guess Bud's take on the guy was pretty accurate, huh?"

"And then some. Come on, might as well meander around and see what we overhear. That's what we came here for. The rest is gravy. Your mother's friends and the Lane Chasers seem to be doing a good job. Take a look."

I turned my head, and sure enough, that merry band of bowlers proceeded from group to group spreading the word as if it was a fifty percent off sale at the supermarket.

For the next half hour, I strained to overhear whatever tidbits of chatter I could, while Marshall did the same. By the time we pulled into our driveway, we were exhausted and on overdrive.

"What do you think about the chitchat regarding Orlando blackmailing Harris and Harris getting even?" I asked Marshall.

"It's as good a theory as anything else. Now all we need to do is substantiate it."

"Think Bowman and Ranston are making any headway?"

Marshall shook his head. "If they were, they wouldn't be counting on us."

• • •

My mother phoned the following morning, and for the first time, at a decent hour. We'd already had breakfast and were preparing to do some food shopping when I took the call.

"The sit-in is going to be a big success, Phee. Everyone we talked to said they'd come."

"Good. I'd say the evening went as planned."

"Not for Gloria. Well, the evening was all right, but not the earlier part of her day. She was accosted by both of her daughters, who thought she was being scammed by one of those lotharios who was after her money."

It was difficult for me to keep mum, but I had no choice. I figured if I let her talk long enough, she might come to realize Lydia and Sue-Lynn were right. "An online thing?"

"That's how it started. On Facebook, no less. And here's the kicker—her daughter set up Gloria's account. Anyway, she chatted with a nice widower who works on an oil rig in Louisiana."

"Doesn't that sound a little fishy to you?"

"Not everyone has a white-collar job. Anyway, the man hasn't asked Gloria for a single dime. He just wants to continue their friendship. Personally, these online things aren't for me, or Shirley either. But what harm is there in simply corresponding?"

"Mom, if Gloria gives away too much information, and that man turns out to be a scammer, she could lose a fortune. You read about this stuff all the time."

"Well, as it turns out, Gloria won't be corresponding with him. His Facebook account disappeared completely and her emails and messages aren't going through. She thinks her daughters blocked the accounts or something. Can they do that?"

"Um, I know you can unfriend someone on Facebook, and block them on other social media. Did Gloria come right out and ask them?"

"They denied removing his account but Gloria can't imagine what else could have happened. Anyway, she's beside herself. I suggested a fun sleepover for her, Thor, and my fur-babies. Also Shirley, since she's so attached to them."

I can't imagine anything worse than a sleepover with Streetman and friends.

"Seriously? A sleepover?"

"We have to do something to cheer Gloria up. We'll fit it in before or after the sit-in."

"Um, sure." *As long as I'm not invited.*

"Oh my goodness, Phee. I almost forgot. I'm joining your aunt and uncle at a new breakfast place in Peoria for brunch today. First Watch. Or was it Final Watch? Well, it was watching something. I'll have to give Ina a call. Anyway, you and Marshall are welcome to join us."

"Thanks, but we already had breakfast and plan to barbeque something later. Maybe another time."

"If you change your mind, give me a call. If your barbeque meat is fresh, you can always freeze it."

Advice from the mother whose freezer dates back to the Ice Age.

I thanked her again and ended the call before she had a chance to extol the virtues of freezing food.

"We can thank Rolo," I told Marshall. "Gloria's now incommunicado with that cyber-scammer."

"Let's see how long that lasts. From what Rolo's told us on other cases, these criminals move to other servers, other setups, other countries. It never ends."

"Maybe by then Gloria will have gotten over him." *Fat chance.*

• • •

Sunday was as enjoyable as it gets, but Monday morning rolled around way too quickly. We were up, dressed and at the office a few minutes after Augusta arrived.

"You just missed a call from Ranston, Mr. Gregory. Now that they've located Orlando's house, and spoken with his immediate neighbors, they need you and Mr. Williams to 'widen the net.' Those were his words. Hoping your schedules will allow you to do that. I don't suppose Mr. Williams will be any too thrilled when he gets in."

"Yeah." Marshall chuckled. "Interviewing the folks at Sun City West almost gave him hives last time. Something about being shown photos of eligible daughters."

"At least it wasn't photos of Streetman and Essie. My mother hands people her cell phone to see her photo gallery all the time."

"I need to talk with the deputies anyway. Phee and I picked up some interesting information on our victim when we went to Lizard Acres Saturday night."

Augusta's eyes widened and I quickly added, "I'll tell you all about it at break."

That said, I walked toward my office and Marshall headed directly to his. Nate arrived shortly after and the two of them took off for Sun City

West. With the fresh information about Harris and Jonesy's dispute, coupled with Bud's take on the Wainwrights and Orlando, I imagined those players left standing would be summoned in to chat with the deputies. Or, our guys if they were lucky.

The next day didn't yield much, except for my mother letting me know that Gloria and Shirley would be "camping out" at her place on Wednesday night with the dogs and Essie. In addition to eating and watching YouTube, they intended to make signs for the sit-in on Friday. Lucinda and Louise had already gotten a head start, and Kenny convinced his wife to get her decorative arts club to help them out with more signs. The very thought of the sit-in gave me the willies and I thanked my lucky stars it was a workday for me.

When Wednesday night finally rolled around, I held my breath that it would be uneventful. And for the first part of the evening, it was. Marshall and I made meatballs and spaghetti with extra toppings of mozzarella and ricotta cheese before plunking ourselves on the couch, too stuffed to budge.

"I think this is what a food coma must feel like," he said. "Good thing we can sleep it off."

And with those words, the phone rang. The food I'd eaten felt as if an anvil had lodged in my stomach. "I'll get it. It's probably my mother calling to tell me some cute thing Streetman did."

The second I lifted the receiver, I heard Lydia's voice. "Sorry to call your landline, Phee, but your cell went straight to voicemail."

"Oops. What's up?"

"My mother phoned Sue-Lynn and me from your mother's house. She was all but doing the Happy Dance. Her cyber-con artist is back. She heard from him a few hours ago. Talk about a line of malarkey. He told her there was a fire on his oil rig and that's why he couldn't reach her. Then he covered his sneaky tracks and said it was all hush-hush so that's why it wasn't on the news. Said they moved to another rig further out in the ocean and not to be worried if the communication goes dark. Lots of technical issues."

"Did she ask why it was such a secret?"

"She didn't have to. He told her they worked for a government agency and that if word got out about the fire, it would compromise oil and gas prices."

"Oh brother."

"Now what do we do?"

"Rolo already said he'd be keeping track of the scammer, or scammers in this case, and that he'll keep shutting them down in the hopes they move elsewhere to a different target. Meantime, keep a tight watch on your mom's bank accounts and investments. Also, the title to her house."

"Thankfully she has title insurance, but as far as anything else, it's definitely concerning."

"Keep me posted."

"I will. Hope I didn't ruin your night."

"Nah." *I'm waiting for my mother to do that.*

CHAPTER 10

After my call from Lydia, Marshall and I glued ourselves to the TV like a pair of slugs on a stick, too lazy to make a move. And then, simultaneously as if it was planned, both of our cell phones sounded. I already knew who my caller would be and took my time, but I heard Marshall say, "Hey, Nate, what's up?" before I answered my call.

"Phee! Herb's over here. It's a good thing we didn't get into our sleepwear yet. Not that it would matter. All of us have those long terry-cloth robes that are more blanket than robe, but—"

"Mom! Enough with the robes. Please don't tell me you called to let me know Herb stopped by."

"No. I wanted to let you know *why* he stopped by. They just evacuated Lizard Acres and the bowling alley. We heard a number of sirens but we hear them all the time. Too many speeders on RH Johnson and Grand. Anyway, Kenny called Herb from the bowling alley. What a disaster!"

"What disaster? A fire?"

"No. Worse. Lizards."

"I don't think I heard you clearly. Marshall's speaking on his phone and he's right next to me."

"I *said* lizards. L I Z A R D S. Lizards."

"I still don't understand."

"No one knows exactly what happened, but when they opened Lizard Acres this evening, the place was crawling with lizards. On the bar. On the tables. On the floor. And in Nomos Bistro, too. Of course, the bistro was closed since it's not open at night, but the cleaners got a shock when they went in. Lizards everywhere."

I looked at Marshall but he was too occupied with Nate's call.

"Are you listening, Phee?" The annoyance in my mother's tone was hard to miss.

"I'm just stunned, that's all."

"Kenny said there were all kinds of small lizards. They've got the fire crew over there, along with members of the Arizona Herpetological Society who will help catch and release them."

Just then I heard Marshall say, "What? Crickets? Didn't think they were around this time of year—*Pause*—Oh, pet shops. Got it."

Then, everything jelled at once as Marshall continued his conversation with Nate. "Why do they need us? We don't have any experience catching those things—*Pause*—Source of origin? I understand. Okay, I'll meet you in front of the bowling alley. It'll be priceless to see the look on Bowman

44

and Ranston's faces."

"Let me call you back, Mom. I'll just be a minute." Before she could answer, I ended the call. A practice I was getting pretty good at, I might add.

Marshall and I tripped over each other's words as we both conveyed the same thing to one another—someone let a bunch of crickets loose in the bowling alley complex and added to the fiasco by dumping a boatload of small lizards as well.

"Sounds like your mother heard about it, too, huh?"

"Yeah, she's got a front-row seat, plus 'breaking news' from Herb via Kenny. Tell me the real version."

"It's chaos over there. Not dangerous, just creepy and annoying. Oh, and it will involve the health department, too. The deputies need Nate and me to check with local pet stores regarding purchases of crickets and lizards. The stores are open until nine so we need to hustle. The fire department and the herpetological volunteers are gathering up the reptiles."

"What about the crickets?"

"Who knows? Maybe they'll open a door and let them scoot out. Of course, I imagine many of them were already dinner for the lizards."

"Ew. I don't want to think about it."

"Please tell me that your mother doesn't intend to go over there."

"She didn't say, but I doubt it. I mean, they evacuated the building. Can't very well bend everyone's ear at night in the cold February air. My bet is that more book club ladies show up at her house for an extended sleepover and marathon gossip fest. It'll be a first, that's for sure."

Marshall stood, grabbed his jacket from the closet and returned to give me a kiss. "I'll keep you posted."

"Do they think it was a prank?"

He shook his head. "No. Given the fact that quite a few people observed the verbal altercation between Harris and Jonesy, the deputies believe Harris might have been behind this crawling nightmare. Plus, it cost the bar quite a bit of business, not to mention the bowling alley. To make matters worse, everything will be locked down tomorrow until they get an all-clear from the county health department. Keep in mind, those lizards pee and poop, too!"

"Thanks. I hadn't thought about that, but now it will be impossible to get that out of my mind."

Marshall laughed, gave me another kiss and raced out the door. It was past ten when he returned, exhausted and hungry.

"I know more about feeding reptiles than I ever thought imaginable. Nate and I divvied up the list and went to all of the stores, including PetSmart, Petco, Pet Market and Pratts. Not to mention EJ's Reptiles."

"And?"

"Lots of grasshopper and cricket purchases but all were cash and no one seemed to remember who did the buying. No significant reptile purchases. The chain stores are forwarding their surveillance videos to MCSO, so I guess Bowman and Ranston can have some fun with that. Meanwhile, I'm starving. Any good leftovers? Or junk food? Or anything?"

"Lots of yogurt, granola, and cereal. Also leftover deli ham and cheese. Come on, I'll make you a sandwich."

It was eleven thirty by the time we crept into bed and I wondered if indeed Harris had sabotaged Lizard Acres to strongarm Jonesy. If that was the case, then he didn't count on the owner and cook at Nomos. Martha McMillan took over the bistro that she and her late husband owned a number of years ago. A no-nonsense former line server, she built the bistro up by catering to the bowling crowd. Given what I'd heard about her from the book club ladies, she wouldn't take well to a setup caused by unwelcome crickets and lizards.

"What's your take on this mess?" I asked Marshall before I turned off the lamp on my bedstand.

"If not Harris, someone sent Lizard Acres and the bowling alley a message. Let's hope that's all it turns out to be."

"For once, I agree with Bowman and Ranston. Gee, that's scary. Anyway, New Media Entertainment is the only enterprise I can think of."

"Unless it's personal. And if so, someone discovered a new scapegoat. Get some shuteye, hon. You'll need it. I have a feeling that things are going to escalate. Especially with that sit-in."

"Aargh. Don't remind me. That's the stuff that'll make me toss and turn all night."

"Join the club."

• • •

Augusta couldn't keep a straight face the next morning when all of us told her about the lizards and crickets at the bowling complex. The consensus from our guys and the deputies was that Harris wanted to deliver a clear message to the folks who ran the establishments there—"New Media Entertainment is about to change everything! Like it or leave it."

And while Harris was brought in for questioning at MCSO, our guys focused on their ongoing cases as well as uncovering more details about Orlando. By late afternoon, having chatted with the guy's neighbors, they uncovered a tidbit of information that promised to change the trajectory of the investigation. Namely, about Sherrille Wainwright, Harris's wife. The woman was presumed to be having an affair with Orlando. And not only did the neighbors mention it, a former waitress at Nomos by the name of

Doris told Nate about it as well.

"It was serendipitous really," Nate said when he and Marshall returned to the office at a little past four. "Doris, who goes by Dot, is a friend of the widow who lives across the street from our victim. She was there when we knocked on that lady's door. As soon as she heard why we were there, she opened up like a cooked clam."

"It's a regular Peyton Place over there, isn't it?" Augusta waited for me to finish getting my coffee before she approached the Keurig for her usual late afternoon "energizer."

I glanced at Nate and then Marshall. "What did Doris say? Does she think Sherrille killed her lover?" *Oh my gosh. This is straight out of my mother's mouth.*

"Whoa, slow down, kiddo. We can't really ascertain that they were romantically involved. It's still hearsay. *Believable hearsay*, but hearsay nonetheless."

"It gives us another motive to point the finger at Harris," Marshall said. "Not only business, but now, personal."

Just then, the phone rang and Augusta picked up the call. "Hold on a minute. Mr. Williams is right here." Then she mouthed to Nate and Marshall, "Ranston."

I held still, along with everyone else, waiting for a new shoe to drop. Thankfully, it didn't, but this case was just getting started.

"One mystery solved," Nate announced. "It seems someone broke into the small lizard breeding sanctuary at the Arizona Herpetological Sanctuary in Scottsdale on Tuesday evening and made off with coolers full of the reptiles. The volunteers and workers who showed up at Lizard Acres had no idea it was their lizards. None of them worked in that part of their building so they were clueless."

Augusta furrowed her brow. "You mean to say no one realized they were missing until yesterday? Back on the dairy farm, we'd notice if the eggs were gone in the chicken coop. Hmm, they probably had their faces glued to their phones."

"If it was Harris," I said, "I wonder how he'd know about those lizards."

"I'll tell you how he'd know." Augusta couldn't wait to spout off. "It was on channel 3 last week—fun places to take the family during midwinter break. Kids love those slimy, crawly things."

"Apparently, so did our perpetrator." I rolled my eyes. "Now what?"

"The usual. Forensics at the sanctuary and in the bowling complex. Interviews ad nauseum and the deputies latching on to Harris as our guy." Marshall stretched his shoulders back and half-heartedly shrugged.

"What about the evidence? Reliable evidence?"

"They'll find it," Nate said, "or they'll make a darn good stab at it."

CHAPTER 11

I woke up at three in the morning with every nerve on high alert. Not a terrific way to begin a Friday. It was impossible to get back to sleep. In less than five hours, my mother and most of the West Valley would be converging on the Sun City West Recreational Center for their sit-in. Okay, fine. Maybe not the West Valley, exactly, but enough clubgoers, bowlers, curiosity seekers, and pot stirrers to ensure that it would rival anything last seen in the late sixties and early seventies.

Marshall rolled over, propped an elbow under his pillow and leaned his head on it. "I can't sleep either."

"The sit-in?"

"Nah, I'm used to that stuff. I suppose it does make sense that Harris would want Orlando out of the way, especially if he had anything on the Wainwrights that would jeopardize their media deal. And then the business about the wife. Two solid motives. But it feels too easy. And that makes me think we're overlooking something."

"I know what you mean. Same deal with Gloria and her cyber-romancer. I know Rolo will be diligent and stay one step ahead, but where does it end? And Gloria refuses to take off the proverbial rose-colored glasses."

"That's something her kids will have to deal with. Meanwhile, we should try to catch at least another hour or so of sleep. I say we give it a try, and if not, we head over to Wildflower Bread Company for an early breakfast."

"Heck, forget the sleep, let's head over when they open."

Needless to say, when Marshall and I showed up at the office, it was with full stomachs and some bakery treats.

"Looks yummy! Thanks! Must be my lucky morning," Augusta said. "By the way, Mr. Williams will be a few minutes late. He had to pick up some food for Mr. Fluffypants. That parrot eats more than all of us put together."

"And talks more, too," Marshall said and laughed. "Nate's a good sport to foster him for his aunt."

"Um, speaking of good sports," Augusta went on, "he said you guys had a full schedule but wondered if Phee wouldn't mind attending that sit-in for the purpose of—"

"Losing my mind?" I winced.

"For seeing if you find out anything about Wednesday night's fiasco. The health department's going to do a walk-through this morning and if the facility passes the inspection, then everything can open at one o'clock."

"But—" Then I looked at Marshall. "Did you know about this?"

"Guilty as charged, but I figured you'd take it better if Nate asked."

I saw that slight crease on the side of his lips and had to laugh. "Both of you owe me. Big time. At least my workload's manageable."

"We wouldn't ask you if it wasn't." Marshall put his hand on my shoulder and gave it a squeeze.

"Like I said, you owe me."

At eight fifteen I headed out the door and drove to the rec center on RH Johnson Boulevard in Sun City West. Over and over, I told myself this would be a quick protest of sorts and by ten, everyone would head to Bagels 'n More to commiserate.

If only.

When I pulled into the driveway on 138th Avenue between the supermarket and the rec center, the parking lot was packed. So packed that I had to find a spot adjacent to the gas station. I told myself how beneficial walking was, but even I didn't believe it.

It was a quarter to nine and the sidewalk from the upper end by the Welcome Courtyard and social hall, all the way down to the lower end by the bowling alley, was completely taken up with lawn chairs and a full crowd. All that was needed was a parade and a few food trucks. The weather was unseasonably warm for midwinter, low sixties and full sunshine, which probably accounted for more residents and lookie-loos.

I watched as the throng moved in slow motion, some folks holding picket signs, others holding small dogs. In that split second, I knew without any uncertainty Streetman was somewhere in this crowd. I prayed he was in his stroller and not cuddled in my mother's arms, where he was apt to bark, snap, and who knew what. Then again, he did those things in his stroller, but at least he was contained. Until he bit through the mesh. It would be a disaster any way I looked at it.

Then, the inevitable. Tim Justin, with a photographer a few feet behind him, made the rounds like a politician in an election year. I tried to catch snippets of conversation as I scouted for my mother but the words were garbled. Spotting Cassie, Fred, Bud, and Eric a few yards away by the arch that led to the Rec Center Administration Office in the Welcome Courtyard, I elbowed my way toward them.

Apparently the Lane Chasers were pretty organized. All of them had signs with messages that said "Nix New Media Entertainment," "Keep Sun City West for Seniors," and "We Dare You to Card Us."

Not sure how this event would unfold, I knew I'd have to find my mother if I wanted an answer. Behind me, I heard a loud voice with a familiar greeting—Hey, cutie! Glad you could make it!"

"Herb!" I turned to see him and Kenny right behind me. "Do you have any idea where my mother is?"

"Yeah. She's down by the bowling alley. I spotted Myrna, Shirley and Cecilia too. I imagine the rest of the ladies are floating around here somewhere. Oh, look—it's KPHO channel 5 over there in their truck. Channel 10's already here."

Kenny gave Herb a high five. "That'll do it if they cover the story right. Senior citizens bullied to take a backseat in their own community."

As I glanced around, I noticed a number of signs that read "Stop Bullying Seniors," but I also noticed something else. A small crowd was gathered around Harris and Jonesy, and had it not been for two sheriff's deputies who walked over, the tension might have escalated.

"Thanks, guys. I'll try to find my mother."

It was a veritable folk-fest for lack of a better description, but at least it was somewhat organized with signs and chairs facing toward the admin building. With any luck, I figured I'd be back at my desk within the hour. The press would cover the story, the residents would speak their minds, the board would reconsider, and all would be well with the world. *Fat chance!*

In retrospect, I should have expected things to go topsy-turvy because, in my entire experience with this senior community, that's exactly what happened. Still, when I spied my aunt Ina clad in jeans and a long poncho, guitar slung over her left shoulder with a paisley green and yellow guitar strap, my first reaction was that of amusement.

I figured she'd relive her hippie days and lead the sit-in with a few rounds of "Kumbaya," maybe a Dylan song or two, and "We Shall Overcome." Yep, she'd get the sit-in underway and then everyone would disperse, mission accomplished. *If only.*

Before I had a chance to make my way over to her, I heard my mother's billowing voice. "Phee! I thought you might have parked near the supermarket. That's why I walked up to this end. What a wonderful crowd! The women are by the bowling alley and isn't that—Oh my goodness! It is!—Your aunt Ina is thundering her way toward us. I can't bear to watch. She's knocked into a few people with that old guitar of hers."

"I think she took the word *sit-in* seriously."

Then, along with the Greater Phoenix area, I heard my aunt's voice. "Harriet! Phee! I got here as soon as I could. Looks like I'm right on time. I couldn't schlep my own lawn chair *and* the guitar, so I'll need to borrow your chair, Harriet. I thought a few choice protest songs would set the mood."

"I think our presence and the signs pretty much say it all," my mother said, "and we didn't plan on any speeches, just a sit-in."

"It's not a sit-in without songs. Where are you camped out?" My aunt looked around and my mother pointed to the entrance by the bowling alley.

"Streetman is in his stroller," she said, "and Shirley is keeping an eye on him. Please, Ina, just a song or two."

My aunt waved her off and proceeded to nudge and elbow her way to where the book club ladies were seated. I gave my mother a look that said "This could be bad," but all she did was shrug. As the two of us followed my aunt by at least five paces, I noticed reporters with microphones interviewing members of the crowd.

Then I zeroed in on something else. Blake Wainwright stood against the building wall between the courtyard and the bowling alley. His arms were crossed and he was deep in conversation with a well-built middle-aged woman whose pixie cut in highlighted shades of blond set her off from the crowd.

"That's Sherrille Wainwright," my mother said. "One of the women pointed her out to me a few minutes ago. What do you make of that conversation?"

I gulped. "I don't know. She's Blake's mother. They could be talking about anything."

"She just pointed a finger at him. I doubt it's good."

"Forget Sherrille. One of the reporters is talking with Aunt Ina. Oh no! Shirley motioned her to your seat next to the dog's stroller. Now the reporter is holding out the mic."

"Your aunt can't hold a tune."

And then, as if to prove my mother right, Aunt Ina began to belt out a chorus of "We Shall Not Be Moved."

"Pete Seeger is probably spinning in his grave," my mother grumbled.

Two seconds later, it didn't matter. Apparently lots of people knew that song and everyone seated near my aunt started singing. A mish-mosh of raspy voices, squeaky sounds, and notes that were so far off tune it was unimaginable. Unimaginable and contagious. Within minutes, the voices rose from the bowling alley all the way to the Welcome Courtyard. If any prospective homebuyers were in the vicinity, they'd be headed to Tucson.

Then, the worst. Streetman began to howl. A long, loud, thunderous howl that made me wonder how such a small dog had the lung power to produce such a noise.

"At least the dog is singing in tune," someone remarked as they passed by my mother and me toward my aunt.

Then, Aunt Ina played "This Land is Your Land," but with her own lyrics, "This lane is my lane, and only my lane." I figured the bowlers would chime in, but the dogs beat them to it. Streetman had set off a doggie howl fest that was virtually unstoppable. From tiny Yorkies to Labs, retrievers, and shepherds, the dogs lifted their heads in the air and bayed as if they were werewolves during a full moon.

The noise was deafening. But worse yet, the sound set off a number of shock/impact sensors in the cars that were parked in the area. First one car, then another, and another. The more noise, the more impact sensors going off.

"Stop singing, Ina!" my mother yelled, but it was too late. People began scrambling for their cars, creating a maelstrom in the parking lot. Worse yet, no one really knew if it was their car or someone else's responsible for the noise.

The human-interest story that sent the reporters to the rec center had now turned into breaking news. Photographers snapped shots of people making their way to the cars. Some with walkers, some with canes, and others carrying lawn chairs. Within minutes, the posse arrived but they were powerless to do anything about it.

"Think we got the message across?" my mother asked me and the book club ladies as we stared at the parking lot.

"I know I did. Next time Nate asks me to do him a favor in Sun City West, I'm going to come up with an excuse."

CHAPTER 12

"I'm sorry I couldn't pick up any intel from the sit-in," I told the guys later in the day when they had returned to the office. "No sooner did I get there when catastrophe struck in the form of my aunt Ina reliving her hippie days. Add one tone-deaf guitar player to a neurotic dog and well, you can only imagine."

"We didn't have to imagine." Marshall rubbed his temple. "It's been streaming on YouTube all day."

Wonderful. Next thing you know, Aunt Ina will want to do a podcast.

"I did see Harris's wife, Sherrille, getting into it with Blake, though. Of course, that could've been anything. Anyway, since the sit-in turned out to be such a failure, my mother's now considering something else from the same playbook. She said if nothing else, it might take Gloria's mind off of her cyber-romancer."

Nate shook his head. "Depending on what she has in mind, it might very well cause us to lose ours."

"I always keep my head on straight, Mr. Williams," Augusta said.

"Good, we'll need it."

And while Augusta's head was on straight, the same could not be said for my mother or her friends. In the few hours that had passed from the fiasco at the rec center to the latter part of the day, her crew had gotten together at the Homey Hut for a super early-bird special. While there, they concocted more "action plans" to thwart the "nefarious and inhumane" treatment of senior citizens.

"Changing the scope and venue of the bowling facility is not inhumane," I told her when she called at precisely quarter to five. "It may be *unwelcome*, and possibly callous, but not inhumane."

"We need to emphasize how distraught we are," was her response.

"Creating a spectacle won't get you anywhere."

"We'll see about that. Anyway, Gloria's team is part of something called a red pin game. They take the regular bowling pins and swap out a few of them for red ones. Then when someone knocks down a red pin, they get extra points. I think. She wants us to attend her game next week."

"Have fun."

"At least Gloria isn't beside herself anymore, now that she and her male friend are back in touch."

Not for long.

"Uh-huh. I'm heading home. Have a good evening."

"Call me if something develops."

Lamentably, it was *film* that developed by way of a video taken by one of the reporters for KPHO during the sit-in. Unbeknownst to me, the reporter had gotten ahold of Harris and questioned him about his development plans. That exchange hit the seven p.m. news and gave Sun City West residents something more to complain about.

In no uncertain terms, Harris made clear his intent. And it went beyond the bowlers, the drinkers, and the eaters to include the billiard players. Up until that minute, the billiard hall, which was adjacent to the bowling alley, had been immune to the New Media Entertainment proposal. And the lizards. But following the brief TV interview earlier in the day, Harris explained his futuristic vision for a billiard hall that would feature projection mapping technology. He went on to explain that the billiard hall would have an augmented reality system whereby sensory projection, in the form of sound and light, would bring the game to new levels.

It came as no surprise when my mother called us at eight. "The pinochle crew is pitching a fit. I just got off the phone with Herb. He wants us to help make posters. The men plan to picket in front of the rec center on Monday."

"What? You just held a sit-in and you saw what a disaster that turned out to be."

"That's only because your aunt Ina just *had* to bring her guitar and relive her youth. I'll make sure Louis hides it before Monday."

"You're going to join them?"

"We can't very well let them down. Of course we're going to join them. And don't worry. Streetman and Essie have a spa day booked at the Glamorous Groomer for Monday. Both of them will have baths and get their nails trimmed."

"I hope you told them to use a falconer's glove for the dog."

"Honestly, Phee, just because he snaps occasionally when he's stressed doesn't mean he's necessarily difficult."

"Mom, he's *always* stressed. Listen, try to talk Herb out of it if you can. Tensions can escalate and who knows what can happen next."

"Other than some yelling and the usual finger-pointing, I think everything will be fine. The board will finally hear us and give a thumbs-down to Harris and his company."

"Don't get your hopes up. Those boards can be very fickle."

"Once we get their attention, they won't have much choice but to nix the project."

And if they don't, I won't have much choice but to listen to the grumbling that will follow.

• • •

Thankfully, the weekend was uneventful with the exception of Nate and Marshall pursuing leads on Orlando's demise, along with the deputies, and Lydia calling me on Sunday night to let me know her mother was even more *obtuse* when it came to her online romancer.

Both Lydia and Sue-Lynn were poised and ready to do whatever else it would take to prevent their mother from falling deeper into a bottomless trap. Even Rolo was stymied, but not for long.

"Remember those Whac-A-Mole games?" Rolo asked me when I called. "It's like that. Only this setup is more extensive. Tell your boss and your friend that I'm working on a more permanent solution and to hang tight. And by the way, I've got a good handle on the Wong bank accounts. I'll alert you if anything changes."

That was Sunday night. By the following week, everything changed.

Sure enough, Herb's crew, in conjunction with the bowlers, the pool players, the Men's Club, and anyone who wanted something to do on a Monday morning, held their picketing event. And on short notice, too.

Once again, I was asked by my boss to "drop by" for a few minutes and listen in. He even offered to pay for my lunch, so Augusta ordered the He-Man's Sub from the deli for me. I figured Marshall and I would have it for dinner too.

Not to be left out, the book club ladies decided to attend as well. The demonstration was without the fanfare of last Friday's debacle but that didn't stop Tim Justin from showing up to interview the picketers.

The not-so-merry band of picketers stood in front of the administration building with signs that read "Our Pool Hall is not a Science Experiment!" and "Who Do You Think Pays the Dues?" I figured they'd last an hour at best and I could return to the office. Ha! So much for dreaming.

Harris and Blake both arrived on the scene, but with their own signs, touting New Media Entertainment's design for the future.

"You can't be here!" Herb shouted to them. "It's Sun City West property and picketing is only for residents. And only with prior approval from the rec center. I had to wait my butt off on Saturday morning to get the okay."

"Easier to beg forgiveness than get permission," Blake yelled back.

And then words flew like Canadian geese on their way further south. But that was only the beginning. The pièce de résistance came when Paul showed up with Mini-Moose. It was like seeing double.

Mini-Moose was the manager of the billiard room and had taken a few days off for fishing, leaving the establishment in the hands of the monitors on duty. But as soon as word got out as to what happened with the lizards and crickets, he and Paul drove back to "protect the territory." At least that's what Herb told my mother.

J. C. Eaton

Tim Justin had just finished chatting with two women and I rushed toward him. We hadn't spoken since our last encounter at the Automotive Restoration Garage and I hoped this situation didn't begin to rival that one.

"Hi! Nice to see you again. Guess it's always something, here. Huh?"

"Hey, good to see you too, Phee. Yeah, this is turning out to be more than a one-off when it comes to feature stories. If you want my opinion, 'Don't ruffle the feathers of seniors.'"

"No kidding. By the way, have you picked up any news about Orlando Fleish's murder?"

"Strangled, but that's all we know. I figured your office and MCSO would have more on it by now."

I shook my head. "It's a slow process. Lots of suspects and the list is growing."

"Chances are I'll be doing a story on his connections, including the Wainwrights and Milton Winkle."

"Who?"

"The guy goes by the nickname Mini-Moose. He manages the billiard room."

"Right. Paul Schmidt's fishing partner."

"And Harris Wainwright's former accountant, before he retired to run a pool hall."

"Whoa. That's news. Any hanky-panky?"

"That's what I'm about to find out."

"Keep me in the loop, will you? Like last time. And I'll do the same."

"Got it."

An instant later, there was a loud clang. I turned to see a metal trash can, now rolling into the parking lot, having been knocked over. Mini-Moose ran after it and returned it to its spot under a mesquite tree. Then I watched as he thundered a few feet to where the Wainwrights stood.

"I'll see to it this deal won't go through," he shouted. "And no amount of rolling garbage cans is about to stop that."

"The wind must have gotten too close to the trash, and your picketers. Hard to tell the difference."

With that, Mini-Moose grabbed Harris by his shirt and all but lifted him up off the ground. "This isn't over by a long shot. Find another community to go after, will you?"

The exchange only worsened with a series of expletives and the occasional gestures that didn't require any explanation.

Tim Justin aimed his cell phone and started snapping photos. "Drat. Should have brought a photographer with me. Oh well, this will have to do. At least they'll look good on digital."

By now the picketers crowded around Harris and Mini-Moose with

56

shouts of "Leave our cue balls alone," "Seniors Rule," and one "Hang 'em High."

It was only when the posse arrived that the group was directed to disperse for "causing a disruption to the rec center."

As the pinochle crew and the ladies made their way to the parking lot, I heard my mother shout, "Call me later, Phee."

Then I heard another voice. It was directed at Harris and it all but echoed in my ears. "If you're not careful, the garbage can won't be the only thing rolling around."

I looked back at Mini-Moose and saw that he was smiling. Not a little grin, but a wide smile that spelled trouble in my book.

CHAPTER 13

"I see you made it back from the picket line unscathed," Augusta said when I returned to the office midmorning.

"Unscathed maybe, but not unhinged. What a sideshow! Harris and Blake crashed the party with their own signs touting New Media Entertainment. That was enough to get Herb's hackles up, and then, to top it off, a guy who goes by Mini-Moose was there since he runs the billiard room and doesn't want any interference."

"By interference, you mean the new technology, right?"

"That, and who knows what else. Anyway, Mini-Moose and Harris got into a verbal altercation that could have escalated but only went as far as Mini-Moose grabbing Harris by the shirt."

"Whoa. Sounds more than verbal."

"It pretty much stopped when the posse showed up. Except for the threats and expletives. Worse than kids needing to have the last word. Did I mention Mini-Moose is a friend of Paul's?"

"Oh, that would explain it."

"Wait. There's more. Tim Justin from channel 10 showed up to get information for a feature article and caught the whole thing on his cell phone. I hate to say it, but I think the situation will worsen if the board doesn't drop the idea of changing everything around."

"I've never known those boards to change their minds once they get an idea in their heads. And that goes for our own town board back in Wisconsin. Not a single dairy farmer on the board yet they thought they knew everything there was to know about the industry."

I was about to say something when the phone rang and Augusta picked up. I held my breath that it wasn't my mother. Then I remembered she had to go to the groomers to pick up Streetman and Essie. Relieved, I gave Augusta a wave and trotted off to my office.

At a little past noon, my He-Man Sub arrived from the deli along with one for Augusta. As we chomped on them in the break room, with the door open wide in case clients dropped in, I gave her the update on Gloria's cyber-romance.

"Rolo will make sure the guy disappears again, but he'll only bounce back with a new line that Gloria will fall for."

Augusta wiped her lips with a napkin and took another bite of her sub. "Long as the family keeps tabs on her banking and finances, it'll be okay. He'll lose interest and move to another target. Or should I say, *They'll* lose interest. Those crooks never work alone. It's a cyber-network of flimflam men or women."

"At least Gloria has her bowling to keep her occupied. Her team is playing in a Red-Pin-No-Tap event tomorrow when the lanes open at noon. Thank my lucky stars it's a workday."

"They used to have red pin days back home. When the pin landed in the head position, everyone went crazy. It was a really big deal. Of course, that was when we only had three channels on the TV and if it rained, it would knock out two of them. Bowling was the only excitement. Especially since the only movie theater was fifteen miles away."

"At least Mankato was more exciting. We had two movie theaters."

"Well, I'm sure you'll hear all about it from your mother and her book club."

"Don't remind me."

As it turned out, Augusta was right. I *did* hear about the Lane Chasers' red pin game the next day, and it wasn't exactly what I expected. Or anything else for that matter. I had just eaten a bagel and cream cheese for lunch and finished it off with a swallow of Coke. That's when my cell phone vibrated and the bagel became a lead sinker in my stomach.

"What's up, Mom?"

"I wanted to let you know that Gloria's game won't start on time. The machine that brings the pins back up is jammed. They'll be getting off to a late start so you can still catch some of it if you drive right over after work."

Why would I do that?

"Can't you and the women cheer her on without me?"

"She needs all the support she can get. Not so much for Kenny. He's oblivious to everyone around him when he bowls."

"I think that's the way it should be. Listen, I have to get back to work. Wish Gloria good luck." And once again, I ended the call at breakneck speed.

A half hour later the phone vibrated again with a call from my mother. *Now what?*

"I could see the legs, Phee! Legs belonging to a dead body! Legs! Here, talk to Shirley!"

"Mom, I—"

"Oh Lordy, this is the most awful thing. Myrna screamed out 'legs' and then we all looked but it was too late. We saw it. We saw it. You can't unsee something like that!"

"Like what? Like what, Shirley?"

"Legs!"

"Uh, please put my mother back on."

"It was a dead body, Phee! I mean, it *is* a dead body! Gloria is hysterical and so are Cassie and Mary Alice! And Shirley just turned ashen."

"What about Myrna?"

"She's still screaming about the dead body."

"What dead body? What are you talking about? Are you still in the bowling alley?"

Then I heard shrieks and all sorts of unrecognizable sounds. I took a breath and tried again. "What's going on?"

"It's horrible. It's emblazoned on my brain. Worse than Margaret Hamilton's black and white socks in *The Wizard of Oz*."

"Whose black and white socks? I'm not following any of this."

Just then, Augusta tapped on my door and walked in. "Got a body in the bowling alley at Sun City West. Bowman called for Nate or Marshall or both. Said he texted them but hadn't heard back. Oh, hold on. The phone's ringing again."

With that, Augusta went back to the outer office and I resumed my conversation, if you could call it that, with my mother.

"Augusta got a call from Deputy Bowman. Okay, they found a dead body at the bowling alley and it doesn't appear to be natural causes. That must be what all of you saw. I imagine they'll cordon the place off and have everyone remain for statements. Just stay calm."

"How can anyone stay calm? And isn't that what everyone's been telling you?"

"Everyone's been yelling about legs."

"That's because it's what we saw. And legs are attached to bodies. And don't even begin to tell me someone had a heart attack. It was no heart attack. The body was jammed into the mechanism for the pin return. So much for mechanical failure. Cecilia left to see if she could sneak out some holy water from her church. Of course, I don't know if they'll let her back in here, or even out of here. We'll see."

"I take it the entire book club is there?"

"Except your aunt. Tuesdays are her massage days at Corta Bella."

"Listen, MCSO requested help from Williams Investigations. Nate or Marshall or both should get the message and will be there as soon as they can. Like I said, stay calm, and whatever you do, don't call anyone or spread any rumors." Then a thought crossed my mind. If the book club ladies were there to cheer Gloria on, then some or all of those chatty pinochle men would be there, too.

"Um, is Herb there?"

"Herb, Kevin, Wayne, and Bill."

Yep, the entire cast of the latest Marx Brothers movie.

"I don't suppose you have any idea who the victim is, do you?"

"I saw legs, Phee. Legs that belonged to a dead man. Then the monitor ushered us into Nomos and that's where we are. Oh, hold on a second, will you?" And then, to someone, "Yes, make that a double order of fries."

"You're ordering food?"

"All of us are. It's the only way to handle our stress. Gloria's terrified the body might belong to one of the men on her team since no one has seen Erik or Bud."

"The body could belong to anyone. Stay put. I'll call you back."

"We have to stay put. A deputy none of us recognized showed up with one of the posse and we were told to remain here."

"Okay. Stay put and don't let your imaginations go wild."

I got off the phone and took a breath before chugging the remainder of my Coke. "Any word from the guys?" I asked Augusta.

"Yeah. A few seconds ago. You were still talking. Mr. Williams texted me. He and Mr. Gregory were on their way back here from meeting with Blake Wainwright at the request of Deputy Ranston. You'd think those two deputies would stay on the same page. Sometimes it's as if the left hand doesn't know what the right hand is doing."

"Try a dozen hands, and each of them outdoing themselves as far as rumormongering. My mother and her friends are in the thick of it at the bowling alley. So much for red pin bowling. Aargh. I hope I don't wind up having to deal with her pets."

"I'm tapping my Smart News app for Sun City West. Might as well find out what they're telling the public."

I waited while Augusta fished out her phone from her bag and tapped the app. She crinkled her nose and looked at the screen. "Deceased male found at bowling alley in Sun City West. Cause TBD. Bowling alley will be closed until further notice."

"Guess that's half the puzzle. It's a guy. Or *was* a guy. Of course, my mother said as much, but you never really know with her."

Just then, a text came in from Marshall: *At SCW bowling alley. Body discovered in one of the lanes. Will keep you posted.* It was followed by a screaming emoji, a heart and a hug. Go figure. I texted back: *My mother and crew are at Nomos. Beware.*

"Nothing more I can do. Except to call my mother back, and I plan to hold off for a while. Boy, I've never looked forward to delving into spreadsheets as much as I do right now. It may be the only time I get some peace and quiet."

"Enjoy it while you can. I think all of us are going to be gifted with a free pass to Sun City West's version of the Fast and Furious Coaster Ride at Universal Studios."

CHAPTER 14

Augusta wasn't kidding when she made that remark. At a little past two, I got another text from Marshall and Augusta got a call from Nate. The coroner's office removed the body and a forensics team was fast at work in the bowling alley. The victim's name, found on the man's driver's license, was not to be released to the public pending verification and notification of next of kin. The only information provided to the news media and the public was that the man was most likely in his sixties.

"That could be anyone in your mother's community," Augusta said.

"Yeah. Let's pray it's no one she knows."

"Viewing audiences in the Greater Phoenix area will all know about the discovery. Mr. Williams said the place was crawling with reporters. Not so much that a dead body was found, but the circumstances. How does someone wind up in a pin-return mechanism?"

"Guess that's something for the forensic crew to figure out. But I'll bet money on one thing."

"What's that?"

"The book club ladies will move to Bagels 'n More to discuss it further once they're allowed to leave the premises. Trust me, this grim discovery will take on a life of its own."

"And more interviews for the guys."

"Yeesh."

Too bad I wasn't a gambler because I nailed it right on. My mother phoned at a little past four to ask me why I hadn't gotten back to her, and to let me know that Erik and Bud showed up so the body didn't belong to either of them. Then she said everyone would be meeting at Bagels 'n More at six in order to "unwind."

I explained that I didn't have any more information and that I'd be doing my unwinding at home.

"Call me if Marshall finds out anything."

"Mom, even if he did, it would most likely be confidential."

"It will be. Just you, Marshall, and me."

And anyone within a five-mile radius.

"Enjoy your evening. And keep in mind, it could have been an accident." *Who was I kidding? No one falls into a pin-return machine.*

"Not with all those deputies taking down our information. Good thing I have Streetman for protection."

Oh no! She's going to start in with Streetman.

"Yes. Absolutely. Talk to you tomorrow."

"Or sooner if you learn anything."

My head spun when the call ended, but that was only the beginning. It would spin like a top by the time the week was over.

Nate texted Augusta a few minutes before five and told her to lock up. He'd be stuck in Sun City West coordinating his schedule with the deputies. Ditto for Marshall, who shot off a similar text to me: *Home by seven. I'll eat anything. Xoxo*

Then another text. This time from Lyndy: *My loony aunt phoned me at work. Said there was a dead body in the bowling alley. Don't know how she finds out this stuff. What's up?*

I texted back: *Male. Found in pin return. Ew! Will call you when I get home.*

"I'm going to stop by BoSa Donuts on my way in tomorrow," Augusta said. "I have a feeling we'll all need a sugar fix by then. I'll get some apple fritters, too. Might as well add a healthy option."

I laughed as we both headed out the door. Ironic that I told my mother not to let her imagination go haywire when mine was doing exactly that. I tried not to get ahead of myself but it was impossible. The moment Marshall set foot in the door, I blurted out, "Do they know who it was?"

"So much for easing into the evening." He gave me a hug and took his jacket off. "Unofficially, yes. Of course, the coroner's office will need to verify and go from there, but between you and me, and our office, it was Harris Wainwright."

I gasped. "Oh no. Any chance it was accidental? Maybe he got too close to the mechanism."

"Not unless he followed Orlando's lead and strangled himself. According to the coroner's initial observation, that was the preliminary, and unofficial as of now, cause of Harris's death. Pretty clear-cut ligature marks. Naturally it will need to be substantiated by the postmortem and the usual tox screening. Then there's the bizarre part—whoever did him in managed to get the body into the pin return. And wouldn't you know it? The security cameras weren't working. A little fishy in my book."

"But the coroner will be able to pinpoint the time of death, right?"

"Time of death, yes, but not the timeline for the actual event. Right now, there's no way to tell if the murder occurred on the premises or if the body was dumped there, much like Orlando's situation."

"It's really loud back there by the pin return from what Herb told us. Mini-Moose once gave the guys a tour. Herb said it's louder than ten F-35s. Harris could have been strangled back there." I gazed off and tried to collect my thoughts. "Did the sheriff's office determine exactly how his body got stuffed in there?"

"They presume it took two people at least. And one of them had to climb a few steps on a metal ladder. Still, lots of open space to shove a body. And Herb was right about the noise. The killer or killers could have shut off the lane machine while the other nineteen machines were still running. Anyway, MCSO sent in additional forensic techs to scour every inch of the place. Looks like bowling, billiards, food, and bar will be shut down for the interim."

"That's not going to bode well with the community."

"Better than two unexplained murders that involved Sun City West seniors."

"How are you and Nate going to be involved?"

"The usual way. Interviewing the folks who were at the bowling alley beginning the night before. Bowman and Ranston will be doing the same. And since Nate and I have a connection to your mother and her friends, the deputies will be handling those interviews."

"Lucky them. My mother will take out photos of Streetman and Essie, and who knows what the other ladies will do."

"Like I said, lucky them."

"Then what?"

"Depends on what evidence the techs uncover. We'll be making connections and following up with the usual gumshoeing."

"You *do* realize that with two unexplained deaths by strangulation, residents are likely to think there's a serial killer loose."

"Oh, believe me, the deputies are well aware of that. All of us need to work fast, once the coroner's office reaches its conclusion. From family members to Sun City West bowlers, and rec center managers, we've got a never-ending pool of suspects."

"Soon to be followed by a never-ending supply of theories."

"At this point, I'll welcome anything. Come on, let's grab dinner, whatever it may be."

• • •

The following morning took a different turn for me, and it had nothing to do with the recent homicide at the bowling alley. I was in the shower when Lydia called but I listened to her voicemail over my morning coffee. "This is horrible, Phee. My mother called to let me know that her online love interest plans to visit her. He told her that communication was spotty due to his new location that did not have good internet reception since it was so far out in the ocean. There's more. Much more, and it's scaring the daylights out of me and my sister. Call me. Thanks."

"I've got to call Rolo," I said to Marshall. He rinsed his coffee cup and put it in the strainer.

"Lydia?"

"Seems Gloria's online lothario hasn't given up."

"Those crooks rarely do once they believe they've got a gullible party at the other end of the chat. Hey, sorry to rush off but we need an early start. I'll catch you later, hon."

He gave me a hug and a quick kiss before reaching for the jacket he'd left on a chair and darted out the door. "Drive safe!"

Knowing how wackadoodle Rolo had become about us having to call him on burner phones, I was glad Augusta had given me one to use. My fingers tapped at breakneck speed and a few seconds later, I heard Rolo's raspy voice.

"Don't you people ever sleep in? I was up until three. Lots of deep diving in the murky underground."

"Well, put on some scuba gear because Gloria Wong's prince charming hasn't given up. Lydia left me a message. The imaginary guy told Gloria he plans to visit her."

"I figured as much. Tell Lydia to sit tight. I'll speak with her, too. Listen, this is usually how these scenarios play out. The cyber-scammers tell their victims that they're ready to meet in person and even go as far as to give them information about when their flight will be arriving. Then, a week or so before, a disaster will strike. Either a death in the family or some unforeseen circumstance that will mean the visit is postponed. That's the *good* scenario."

"What's the bad one?"

"That's when they tell the victim that something terrible happened to their bank account and it is now frozen. They'll tell the victim that they got hacked, or that their credit cards were stolen and since they're out at sea on an oil rig, it will take forever for a new one to arrive. Then, they ask the victim to wire them money. And all the while in between, they keep telling the victim how much they can't wait to meet in person because they believe they're destined for this 'one time love.'"

"I can't believe Gloria would fall for that. But Lydia says she's convinced the guy is the real deal."

"These people are experts, Phee. Academy Award performances on email and dating sites. And they have a believable answer for everything. Look, I won't kid you. I imagine they're frustrated because I've been able to disrupt them. But only temporarily. Still, they'll want to wrap things up with Gloria quickly and move on."

"What are you saying?"

"Whoever is communicating with her will use all their finesse to get her to send him, or her, money. Like I said earlier, Lydia and her sister need to get Gloria to stop communicating with him."

"I understand."

"Good. Because there's one more thing. Remember when I told you that the operation bounced from Lagos to Sao Paulo? And that I found government ties in this country to housing and urban development?"

"Uh, yeah. I guess."

"Well, I found a location a bit closer to home. Maybe too close for comfort but I'm thinking it's most likely part of a server farm."

"Where? How close is too close to home?"

"Las Cruces, New Mexico. The communications bounced through Las Cruces as well. I've got an IP address."

"That's a physical address. We can nail that lousy perpetrator."

"Not exactly. It's an internet protocol address. It's what other computers use to find yours. But it *does* have to go through a server. And servers have providers."

"So there is a way to track it down?"

"A complicated, extensive way and what I discovered may only be a blip and then—poof!—gone. Onto the next IP address."

"That's not the greatest news."

"It never is."

CHAPTER 15

When I got off the phone with Rolo, I hustled to get to work, postponing my call to Lydia until I could take a break. Once I was inside the office, Augusta informed me that Sherrille Wainwright identified Harris's body last night. That tidbit was on a phone message she retrieved for Nate and Marshall.

"You'd think those deputies would be more conversant with texting by now," she said. She pointed to the large box of BoSa donuts and grabbed a strawberry glazed one. "Mr. Williams and Mr. Gregory headed straight over to the posse office. Good thing they don't have appointments until later in the day."

"Did the message indicate anything else? Do they think she could be a suspect?"

Augusta shook her head. "Nope. Just one sentence. Short and sweet. Oh, and there was a call for you, too. From Paul."

"Fishing Paul? I wonder what he wanted."

"As long as he doesn't want to come in. Last time it took me two wash loads to remove the fish smell that permeated my clothes."

I took an old-fashioned donut and laughed. "I'll keep you posted."

"Watch out he doesn't open a new can of worms."

As my computer booted up, I returned Paul's call. No sooner did I say hello when he got right to the point. "Mini-Moose is on the chopping block. He helped out with that very pin mechanism at the bowling alley a day before that body was discovered and told me he thinks he accidently dropped his key chain down in there."

"Then how did he drive home or get inside his house?"

"The key chain was more of a lucky charm. Just a plastic moose but it had sentimental value."

Sentimental value and now possible evidence of the whodunit.

"Did he tell anyone? Report it missing?"

"No. He figured he'd check it out himself but then, well, you know. Some guy comes up dead and that key chain all but screams, 'I did it.'"

"Tell Mini-Moose to call the sheriff's office and let them know. No sense jumping to conclusions right now."

"I suppose you're right. That body could belong to anyone. Mini-Moose probably didn't even know who the guy was."

Uh-oh. Thanks to the shirt-grabbing incident during Monday's fun-filled picketing, we can cross that thought off our list.

"It will take more than circumstantial evidence to convict someone."

"Convict? Do you think my buddy is going to be arrested?"

"That's not what I said. Look, just have your friend contact the sheriff's office. Okay?"

"Okay, but if he is arrested, I want Williams Investigations to find out who the real killer is."

"They're already working on it, in conjunction with MCSO. And you know our guys, they won't rubber stamp anything."

"No, the press will beat them to it. Hmm, maybe I can help during our radio show. Okay, thanks. Catch you later."

He ended the call before I had the chance to stop him from making a huge mistake on the air. Then, a worse thought came to mind. Was this his *Fishing with Paul* show or the shared *Murder Mystery and Fishing Show* with my mother and Myrna. If it was the latter, then there would be no end to the extent of damage that could be caused.

I immediately phoned my mother and took a slow, deep breath. "Hi, and no, I don't have any more information about the bowling alley incident."

"You mean the dead body."

"Yes. That. But I got a call from Paul, who's concerned that his friend Mini-Moose may be implicated because he helped out with that pin retrieval mechanism and may have dropped his key chain there."

"He should notify the deputies."

"Yes, yes. I told Paul the same thing. Then he told me he might try to fix things up over the air during his radio show. I don't have to tell you what a disaster that would be. Especially if it's the shared show with you and Myrna. Is that taking place during its usual slot?"

"You mean our *Mystery and Fishing Show*?"

"How many mystery and fishing shows are there?"

I shuddered to think about it. That combined radio show was certainly one for the books. I still get shudders when I recall tuning in to that first disaster on the airwaves. Talk about mess-ups. And egos. When Paul's lake fishing show and Mom and Myrna's cozy mystery program crossed paths, it should have ended there. But oh no! Rather than resolving the issue like adults, they talked over each other on a hodgepodge of topics that blended into each other. Bait and elements of suspense. Lake trout and character development. Not to mention best fishing holes and prominent authors. It was a fiasco. Only the community didn't see it that way. They loved it! Loved it so much that now all three of them got to share a combined show.

"The schedule got changed for this month. Myrna and I will be on next Monday, but all three of us picked up a show for Friday. Remember how deadly Vernadeen Stibbins's sewing show was? Well, *Cooking with Lucille* is a million times worse. Makes you want to run right out the door to the nearest McDonald's."

"What does that have to do with anything?"

"Let me finish. Seems Lucille Whalen got food poisoning with her own recipe for gluten-free dumplings. She's still recuperating. Her time slot was given to us. Eleven a.m. You can listen to it while you work."

Or pass.

"That's the reason I called. Whatever you do, don't say a word about the investigation. Paul is only going to muddy the waters if he mentions Mini-Moose and anything else. It would all be rumor and speculation. Things will get out of hand and will compromise the investigation."

"Myrna and I know when to be discreet. But we can't put a muzzle over Paul. That man blurts out whatever comes to mind. Like a belch after a big meal."

"Then turn off the mic. Seriously. The three of you could unwittingly start a frenzy. Especially the way rumors spread around here."

"We can't very well spread any rumors until we know who the body belonged to."

"Nice try."

"Call me if you hear anything. And don't worry, Myrna and I will be very circumspect during our show."

Words to live for.

"Okay, thanks."

"By the way, did I mention Gloria told me her online interest is planning to be here for Valentine's Day? Something about wanting to wine and dine her."

"It's a scam, Mom."

"It won't be when he shows up at her door. He asked her to let him know which hotels are near here so he can make a reservation."

"Like I said, it's a scam."

"She says it's like music in her ears."

"Tell her to get earbuds and go to YouTube. Remember, no mention of the body. Love you!"

It was worse than dealing with my daughter, Kalese, when she was in junior high. At least I could monitor what she did, unlike my mother.

Friday was the day after tomorrow and I knew by then Harris Wainwright's name would be plastered all over the news. His wife already identified the body so that meant next of kin had been notified. I also knew that once it became common knowledge, it would take on a life of its own. What I hadn't counted on was that the sheriff's office would have a different suspect in mind, and all because Paul couldn't keep his mouth shut. Just like the largemouth bass he raved about on his fishing show.

I reached for my pile of invoices when I decided to get it over with and call Lydia back. Then I could concentrate on work. It must have been one of her days off because she answered after the first ring.

"Phee! Thank goodness you called. I just spoke to Rolo. Yesterday my mother got a delivery of flowers from her online Romeo. It was a local delivery so I phoned the florist but all they could tell me was that the transaction was made from a gift card with no name attached. And no way to track it down. A gift card! You and I know what that means. Some other sucker sent that cyber-scam group a gift card and now they were using it to lure my mother into doing the same. Or worse. Rolo was insistent my mother drop all communication with the guy but that would be like trying to pull a steak out of Thor's mouth."

Or anything out of Streetman's.

"Aargh." I gulped. "I tried to explain this to my mother but she thinks it's on the up-and-up. And before you say anything, I already know that the guy told her he'd be visiting her for Valentine's Day. My mother couldn't wait to share that news."

"That criminal is dangling a carrot in front of my mother and I'm scared to death of what she might do. It's like she's lost her marbles. I can't even figure out how he got her home address. They only communicated online."

"Easy. Sun City West is a small community and I'm pretty sure she's the only Gloria Wong."

"Of all times not to live in San Francisco. I remember one of my aunts telling me there are more Wongs in the phone book than Smiths."

"Rolo will continue to disrupt the communication but knowing him, he'll take it one step further. He hates these cat-and-mouse games so he'll undoubtedly figure out a sting. The only trouble is, I have no idea how long that will take. Or if it's even feasible."

"I have another idea. It's crazy, but so is this mess."

"What?"

"I find another love interest for my mother. Even if I have to pay someone off to pretend."

"From what the book club ladies said, there were lots of men interested in Gloria, but she wasn't interested in them."

"I know. So I create a new online interest."

"I'm not sure, Lydia, that could turn out to be catastrophic. Hold off for a few more days. And do all you can to get your mother to ignore the communication."

"Okay. I'll try for now. But Valentine's Day is coming up soon."

Complete with Streetman and Essie in matching heart design outfits!

CHAPTER 16

"Hurry up, Phee," Augusta said. "It's almost eleven and your mother's radio show will be on the air any second. We'll take an early lunch hour. Good thing the deli delivered our sandwiches already."

"Only because you told them to," I said and laughed. "For sure the timing's good. The men are out interviewing all those folks from the bowling alley and I checked the calendar. Their appointments won't start until one."

"That radio show is such a hoot! It's become a high point of my week."

"And a real nail biter for mine. Especially since every news station in the valley announced it was Harris's body they found in the bowling alley. We heard it last night on the ten o'clock news. I suppose there's no chance my mother missed it. And even if she did, Myrna and Paul would have heard."

"Well, hold your horses, we're about to find out."

And so began my Friday morning. Minutes later, while digging into a ham and Swiss sandwich, I heard my mother's voice. And Paul's. And Myrna's.

"Good Morning, Sun City West, and everyone in hearing range. I'm Harriet Plunkett and this is the morning mystery and fishing show with—"

"Me! Paul Schmidt at your service. Offering you all the best tips for lake fishing in Arizona and selecting the kinds of bait that will—"

"Keep you up all night begging for more. Yes, that's the joy of reading cozies with Harriet and me. Myrna Mittleson. With two t's."

"So far so good," Augusta whispered.

"Give it a minute."

A minute? They didn't need thirty seconds.

"We're going to do something different this morning," my mother said. "We just learned how to take calls from listeners so we're going to open up our program to you. Ask us anything about murder and mystery."

"Or fishing. Or bait. In fact, I wanted to talk about using bubble gum for bait. It never fails. There isn't a fish around that doesn't like bubble gum. That's right, you chew it and stick it on the end of a hook and then—"

"Snuggle up with a book in your hand, in your favorite chair and begin to—"

"Throw it into the water and wait until—"

"You find out who the victim is so you can—"

"Reel that sucker in and then kill and gut it with a filet knife. Because you can't strangle a fish. Not like those recent bodies that were found."

71

"SHH! Paul! You weren't supposed to mention that. Forget you heard Paul, everyone. He was referring to the bodies that were found in Surprise and our very own bowling alley."

"Oh hell no!" I shouted. "I can't believe this."

"I can. Pass the mustard, Phee. And keep your fingers crossed the station manager doesn't cut to a commercial or take them off the air."

"The station manager only does the paperwork. No one is there except those three big mouths."

And then, the saga of Orlando's and Harris's homicides unfolded like a classic suspense novel, only much worse when two words were mentioned— *serial killer*. I covered my mouth and fixed my eyes on Augusta.

"Cat's out of the bag now." Augusta raised the volume on the device. "Might as well brace ourselves for the rest."

"I'm praying no one is listening. Maybe they still think it's Lucille's cooking program."

Then the office phone rang simultaneously with a text on mine. Augusta and I eyeballed each other before she stood and answered the extension in the break room. Meanwhile, I stared at the series of angry, crazy emojis from Marshall.

"So much for wishful thinking, Phee. That was Mr. Williams. The radio was on at the posse station and everyone in there heard the show. Won't be long now until the Boston Strangler has a revival in Sun City West."

"I will personally point him or her to the three throats who were responsible for this mess!"

Augusta took a large gulp of Coke and continued to munch on her sandwich. "Shh, I think the Q and A is about to start."

"Good morning." My mother's voice was chipper. "And to whom do we have the pleasure of speaking with?"

"Teresa LaPinta. I've lived in Sun City West for twelve years and this is the first time anyone's been strangled. What's the plural for 'anyone'? Because there were two of them. My neighbor thinks it was a jealous wife."

"Hold on a moment, will you?" And then, "Myrna! What was that book we all read where the woman was having an affair with her husband's friend and then the husband wanted to divorce her but they had a prenuptial agreement and so she murdered the husband by strangling him with her heavy-duty yarn."

"I remember that. She never *did* get to finish the sweater she was knitting."

"Oh my gosh!" I poked Augusta's elbow. "This is awful."

"I think it was called *Knit One, Kill One*. Or was it *The Deadly Loop*?"

"No, it was *Killer Cable Stitch*. I'm pretty sure," Myrna said.

Then Paul spoke up. "Fishing line is an excellent tool for strangulation.

And I'll bet that's what happened to those two. Did they ever say what they thought the material was?"

"Forget the material. I wonder what the motive was." Either my mother had lost her senses entirely, or she had no idea how much this speculation would damage the investigation.

Then, the next call. This time Paul picked up the phone line.

"You're speaking with Paul. What kind of fishing do you have on your mind?"

"Um, fishing for answers about those murders, I suppose." It was a woman's voice but she didn't give a name. "I heard Orlando and Harris narrowly escaped prison in Idaho a number of years back. The snowbirds who live behind my house told me as much. They're Idahoans. That's a funny sounding word, Idahoans. Isn't it?"

"I went trout fishing in Bear Lake in Idaho not too long ago. Trick is to get there before sunup." Paul ended the call and within seconds a new caller was on the line. This time a man.

"Hey, you can call me Bentley. It's not my real name but I'm not about to give anyone my name over the air. I wanted to let you guys know that I live down the block from the late Harris and guess what? A giant U-Haul just left the place. Just saying . . ."

"Give me that phone, Paul!" I heard my mother shout. Then, "Mr. Bentley, this is Harriet. Are you saying you think the wife had something to do with the man's murder?"

"I said I saw a U-Haul. You figure it out."

And with that, Bentley was off the air.

Augusta and I looked at each other without saying a word. I rubbed my temples and remained still for a few seconds before I could muster the words, "I know what's coming. It's an invitation to snoop on the late Harris Wainwright's wife. A lovely hand-embellished invitation to pry, poke, pester, and spy on that woman on the off chance she turned out to be a black widow."

"I'm not quite sure you'd call it a black widow, Phee."

"I call it 'cease and desist' before it even starts, but you know my mother and the book club ladies. Once they get an idea in their heads, it's like a seed that will eventually turn into a beanstalk. I only hope they have the good sense to let the deputies and Williams Investigations do their job. Oh, who am I kidding?" I buried my head in my hands and listened as the show continued.

"Well, mystery and fish listeners, that concludes our phone-in portion of the program. Now we will continue with our cozy mystery feature of the week—Lynn Cahoon's *Five Furry Familiars*. A delightful story that takes place in Magic Springs, Idaho, where—"

"Orlando and Harris were nearly incarcerated," Paul announced. "And speaking of Idaho, did I mention crappie fishing? Heard Hayden Lake was a good spot for that."

"We're talking about Lynn Cahoon's novel, Paul," Myrna said.

"And I'm talking about crappies."

"You can say that again."

Thankfully, the time was up and the show ended. Whatever wishful thinking I had regarding the listening audience dissipated the second Deputy Ranston phoned for me. I had already returned to my desk and had just completed some account reconciliations when Augusta forwarded the call.

"I had to take a fistful of Tums a few seconds ago, Mrs. Kimball. Gregory. I had my radio on in the car and heard your mother's program. I don't even want to know my partner's reaction. Anyway, please do me a favor and inform her to refrain from, from . . . whatever you call this!"

"I'm as shocked and dismayed as you are." *Actually, more like disturbed and aggravated but shocked and dismayed sounds better.*

"You *do* realize what this means, don't you?"

"I, um . . ."

"It means we'll be getting all sorts of calls from every nincompoop and nutcase in the area who thinks they're the next Sam Spade. Then, the frenzied calls from all those loonies who are now convinced we have a serial killer on the loose. All I can tell you is to please try to keep your mother at bay."

"Uh, sure. Oh, and about what that guy said on the air—Are you going to check it out? About Sherrille and the U-Haul?"

"Right now, the wife is not a suspect. And there's no law against renting a U-Haul. Our investigation remains in its preliminary phase. Interviewing and gathering evidence for both murders."

"Okay. Well, have a nice day."

"Same to you."

If only.

CHAPTER 17

I poked my head out of my office for a split second and announced, "Deputy Ranston is not pleased with my mother's on-air interference."

Augusta looked up from her computer screen and tilted her head to move her bifocals farther up. "No surprise there. Is he going to look into that U-Haul comment?"

"Not on your life. But I have to admit, it does leave all sorts of speculation. Okay. I'll bet you a dollar my mother's going to act on it."

"Ha! I'll double it! Only you'll be the one acting on it."

We both laughed but in the pit of my stomach, I knew she was right. What I didn't know was how soon it would take for one of my mother's "plans" to jell.

It was a little before two when I got her call.

"I'm at Shirley's house, Phee, and the most awful thing happened. Herb called me when Kenny called him to tell him that Mary Alice was escorted to the posse office by Deputy Bowman. She phoned Kenny so he would let the bowling team know."

"They probably want to question her, that's all."

"They would not have brought her in separately. Besides, your office is questioning people. I wanted to let you know in case something develops."

"Um, which one was Mary Alice? The short gray-haired lady with the floral top or the one who was built more like Myrna?"

"Like Myrna. Only more muscular. And she carries her weight better, too. I think she works out at Kuentz when she's not knitting or bowling. That's what Gloria told me."

"Nice to know. I'll get back to work now."

I rolled my eyes and resumed my bookkeeping. An hour and a half later, another call came in. Same source. Same drama.

"You said to let you know if something develops," my mother said. "That's why I'm calling. Mary Alice is now an official person of interest in Harris's death."

"What? How? Based on what evidence?" *Because the deputies don't listen to hearsay or even real-say.*

"They found the same kind of string in the pin-return machine that was used to strangle Orlando and Harris. It matched the dimensions the coroner measured around the victims' necks. Only it wasn't string. That's what Kenny told Herb. Mary Alice was allowed to make more phone calls."

"I hope she called a defense lawyer instead of her bowling team."

"Actually, Gloria called me and Mary Alice needs a recommendation from your office."

I took a deep breath and held it as long as I could. I'd read somewhere it was a good tension-relieving practice. "I'll have Augusta phone you with our list. And what did you mean when you said 'it wasn't string.'"

"It was yarn. Robin's egg blue yarn. Very, very popular. And they found a good long string of it wrapped around the basket that brings the pins back up. Herb sent me a video of one from YouTube. The basket reminded me of how our milk bottles used to get delivered when I was a girl."

Oh no! Please don't tell me I'm going to have to relive my mother's "growing up in Mankato, Minnesota," days.

"Mary Alice always knits when it's not her turn to bowl. And, according to Gloria, she was working on a blue blanket."

"It's circumstantial evidence. And preliminary at that. The lab will need to determine exactly what kind of yarn—wool, acrylic, cashmere, you name it. Then, the dimensions. It's not as easy as it looks. Shirley can tell you that. She's in all those sewing, knitting, crocheting clubs."

"Mary Alice is convinced the deputies will go to her house with a search warrant. And what's she supposed to do? Hide all of her skeins of yarn?"

"Like I said, it's circumstantial. What possible motive could she have?"

"I don't know. But I do know someone who does have a motive—Sherrille Wainwright. And here's where you come in."

"On no. Not on your life."

"Listen a minute. Sherrille was most likely seeing Orlando and then her jealous husband did him in and dumped the body. Then, she got even and murdered him. This is a very common plot on Telemundo. Ask Lucinda."

"I don't have to ask Lucinda. And whatever it is that you want me to do, forget it."

"Phee, this may be the only opportunity we have. If we don't prove Sherrille did it, because she's really the only one with a motive, then we're left with a serial killer. We have to poke around."

"What do you mean 'poke around'?"

"We need to find out if she has any of that robin's egg blue yarn in her house. We already know that a huge U-Haul left the place. But people usually only rent those things for big-ticket items like furniture and electronics. They save the little stuff for last. Now is our time. We need to act fast. I can't very well do this on my own."

"Good. Then don't do it. That's why we have a sheriff's office. I'll have Augusta phone you with the list of criminal defense attorneys. Although I think it's a bit of an overreaction right now."

"It's not an overreaction. Besides, parking is a nightmare downtown by the Fourth Avenue Jail. Of course, the nearby restaurants are good, so—"

"Okay, then. Talk to you later."

By the time this ends, I'll be the one who needs a defense attorney.

I resumed working when something nagged at me and compelled me to call my mother back.

"It's me again, Mom. One quick question. How did the deputies know Mary Alice was knitting something with robin's egg blue yarn? Someone must have tipped them off."

"Ah-hah! Now I've got your attention. *That* someone was most likely Sherrille. Or someone at Lizard Acres the night we met the Lane Chasers. Someone who knew Sherrille. This is just like those Telemundo plots. They start out simple, husband cheating on wife, wife cheating on husband, and then—Bam!—they get tangled up like a phone cord."

"You may be on to something. I'm not sure. And one more question. Does Sherrille knit? Or crochet? Because if she doesn't, then scoping out her house for blue yarn would be a waste of everyone's time."

"I knew it! You're on board! I'll call Shirley to see if Sherrille is in any of those sewing and knitting clubs. Then, I'll call the girls so we can plot our strategy. Then I'll let Herb know so he can assist if we need him."

"Whoa! Hold on! I didn't say I was on board."

"You implied it. That's all that matters."

"It's one thing to have Shirley look into club lists. It's a crime to snoop around in someone's house by nefarious means."

"Not if a door was left open. Or a window. Or a garage door that opened with one of those universal remotes. It's entering. Not breaking in. Hmm, I'm not sure about the garage door."

"I'm not sure about any of this. Just sit on it, okay? Nothing crazy. We can talk tonight."

"That's more like it."

When the call ended, I stared straight ahead. Stunned that we had this conversation. And while my mother did come up with a logical sequence for murder, I knew it would involve an illogical and most likely tooth-chattering, nerve-racking action plan that would defy all sense of reason.

And worse, she'd drag the dog into it. I shuddered and tried not to think about it. Instead, I resumed my orderly and sequential work with numbers that added up and sequences that made sense.

At four, I got out of my chair for a much-needed break.

"Do we still have any donuts left?" I asked Augusta.

"New box of Entenmann's. They're in the cabinet over the sink in the break room. Boy, we really went through the ones from BoSa."

"We may be going through more than that before long."

"What makes you say that?"

And then I told her.

"I'll print out a list of defense attorneys for you, too, Phee."

CHAPTER 18

Between the interviews for the Bowman-Ranston investigations and the minor cases that Nate and Marshall had picked up, they didn't get back to the office until four thirty.

"Any donuts left?" were the first words out of Nate's mouth and I heard them all the way from my desk.

For the second time in a half hour, I left my seat and walked into the outer office. With not as much as a greeting, I blurted out, "Mary Alice was brought in for questioning and my mother is devising a plan."

"We know," Marshall said. "About Mary Alice. And I'm afraid to ask about the other part."

"My mother's pretty well convinced someone ratted on Mary Alice to take the heat off of Sherrille. That is, if Sherrille is a knitter, or crocheter. She's having Shirley look into it."

"As long as the looking doesn't involve breaking any laws. The deputies believe they've got this under control. The investigations are in their preliminary stages, hon."

Nate took a giant bite of the chocolaty donut and grabbed a napkin. "It's that thick icing that makes these things irresistible." Then he looked at Augusta and me. "Not that I put any credence into Telemundo plots, but even the deputies have a suspicion the murders were related. Old business grudges."

"So now what?" I asked.

"We continue the questioning and the deputies continue analyzing the evidence."

"My mother's right. This will take forever."

Augusta laughed. "Think of it as a slow-moving storm. Then again, don't! Those things may take forever but they do the most damage."

The last thing any of us needed was a tempest moving at glacial speed. Especially in a community that was prone to overreaction. But all I could do was keep a level head and put the pieces together as they wafted my way. At least that's what I told myself. Until I got swept into that storm through no fault of my own.

• • •

Thankfully, the following day was Saturday and I was off that morning. Lyndy and I planned to check out Home Goods, Barnes & Noble, and Hobby Lobby. Then lunch at First Watch. Unfortunately, those plans never got beyond Barnes & Noble when a call from my mother interrupted us.

Lyndy had just handed me the latest Jess Loury novel to peruse when my phone vibrated and my mother's voice could be heard well into the children's section.

"How fast can you drive to Pyracantha and North Crown Ridge Drive by Hillcrest Golf Course?"

"Why?" And then, before she could answer, I already knew. "Is that where the Wainwrights' house is? Don't tell me you're snooping around."

"Not anymore."

"What do you mean?"

"I told Myrna she'd never fit under the new fence the golf course installed, but would she listen? Heavens no! Now she's caught under the fence and doesn't want to make a scene."

"She probably has already. There are a zillion golfers out there."

"And they're all golfing. No one is watching us. We're way out of range. They won't even go after stray balls out here because of the little creek that's really a drainage swamp."

Lyndy put a hand over her mouth to stop from laughing.

"You better hope Sherrille isn't watching you from a window."

"That's why you need to drive over here and help get Myrna out. And don't tell me to call the fire department. It would be way too embarrassing for Myrna. That's why I didn't call Herb. Only Shirley and Lucinda."

Terrific. Shirley and Lucinda. Just what we need.

"I don't know how I'd be able to get Myrna out. Couldn't she just wiggle around and break free?"

"Are you going to help or not?"

Lyndy nodded and gave me a thumbs-up before turning away and laughing.

"Fine. Figure twenty-five minutes. Twenty if traffic is light."

"Take the El Mirage turnoff and then Beardsley to Meeker. Much faster."

"Is the dog with you?"

"In a manner of speaking."

"What's that supposed to mean?"

"I let him down for a potty break and he's on the other side of the fence in the Wainwrights' backyard. He's on a leash but refuses to come back. Occasionally he sniffs at Myrna. She's petrified he's going to pee on her."

By now, Lyndy was doubled over and had to step away. I could see tears rolling down her cheeks and I tried not to laugh as well.

"Fine. We're on our way."

"Marshall is with you?"

"No, Lyndy."

"Good. Myrna wouldn't want this to get out."

"Believe me, Marshall would be the last person to spread the news. See you in a bit."

"Forget shopping," Lyndy said. "This may turn out to be much more fun."

"Seriously? You want to join me in this, this . . . I don't even know the word for it."

"Debacle?"

"Works for me."

Lyndy returned Jess Loury's book to the shelf and said she'd get it online. Five minutes later, we were in my car and headed to Sun City West.

"Do you really think your mother and her friend would have broken into Sherrille Wainwright's house to look for robin's egg blue yarn?"

I nodded as I drove. "Yep. They've done worse. Don't even get me started. And Streetman! I hardly know where to begin. He's like Houdini with four paws."

"That's Pyracantha on your right," Lyndy said as I drove down Meeker from Beardsley.

I made the turn and then another one onto North Crown Ridge Drive. "I have no idea how to access Sherrille's backyard. Hold on, I'm calling my mother."

"Put it on speaker. I don't want to miss anything."

"You're almost as bad as Augusta."

"A woman after my own heart."

The phone rang once and my mother took the call. "Where are you? Myrna may wind up with neuropathy after this. She says her legs are getting numb."

"Tell her that's temporary. Listen, I'm on North Crown Ridge. How do I find you?"

"Oh goodness! My fault. I should have explained. You need to drive to the dog park. Not the little one where my Streetman goes, but toward the big dog park in the back. Go in and walk to the first covered awning. In the corner are some boulders with flat tops. Not very high. Climb the boulders, go over the brick fence and into that yard. No one has lived in that house for years. I know, because Louise told me. She knew the former owner and the place is in probate."

"You and Myrna climbed over boulders?"

"They weren't high. She held Streetman and then passed him over to me."

I turned to Lyndy and whispered, "Are you getting this?"

"And then some."

"Listen, Phee, once you're in the yard, there's an opening in their brick fence. Just go through onto the golf course and stay close to where the houses are. Sherrille's house will be about the same distance as my house is to Herb's."

Nothing like Minnesota measurements. Go to the green house. Make a right. Then turn at the house with the ugly statue in front . . .

"I'm still not sure what we're going to do to help Myrna."

"You'll figure it out."

I ended the call, drove to the dog park and looked around. "We're lucky. Not many people here this time of day. For some reason, they all arrive at the crack of dawn. See? Lots of parking."

Lyndy nodded. "Come on, girl, let's get this fiasco over with. Maybe we can still salvage some time for a decent lunch out. Uh-oh. Don't look now, but isn't that Paul, your fisherman friend, on that golf cart? It sure looks like him." We had just peered over the boulders and were ready to make our first move.

I stretched my neck for a better view. "Whew. You scared me half to death. It's not Paul. Paul's hair is scragglier. And I've never seen him wear anything in solid colors. We lucked out. Just a look-alike. Let's get moving."

We were over the boulders in no time and through the opening in the brick wall. "Look straight ahead! That's my mother waving us down."

"She's really waving. Frantically! Must be Myrna's legs have gone numb or something."

Lyndy and I walked as fast as we could over the sandy, rocky part of the golf course until we reached my mother and Myrna.

"Tell Myrna to hang on," I shouted.

My mother rushed toward us. "Forget Myrna! My Streetman slipped out of his collar and went straight for the house! The patio door was open and he got inside!"

And in that moment, I knew Lyndy and I wouldn't be eating lunch at a nice restaurant. We'd be lucky if someone tossed us a bag of chips before the day was out.

"He's in the house? You saw him go in?"

"That's what I said. I yelled to him but he didn't hear me."

"Trust me, Streetman heard you all right. He just ignored you."

Just then, Myrna called out, "I can't stay like this forever. Give me a pull or push or something!"

"You and Lyndy go over there and help Myrna. I'll sneak into the house and retrieve my little man." My mother started for the patio when I grabbed her sleeve.

"You can't just mosey in there. The dog is probably fine, which is more than I can say for their house. Does he still have those territorial marking issues?"

And you better hope they don't have expensive carpeting.

"Not in a while."

"Good. Listen, I have an idea. First, we get Myrna up and out. *If* we can figure out a way to extricate her. Then, we skirt around to the front of the house and knock on the door. Tell Sherrille, or whoever answers, that our dog ran into their backyard. Chances are they've already seen him in the house."

"Then what?" My mother furrowed her brow. "We won't be able to do our snooping. I have a better idea. Myrna and I will go through the patio door while you and Lyndy knock on the front door. All you have to do is keep Sherrille's attention and get Streetman. Meanwhile, Myrna and I will poke and pry around a bit. Open a few drawers, peak into closets . . ."

"More likely knock over stuff or worse yet, break something valuable. You know what Myrna's like. She was born with the clumsy gene."

"Shh! She'll hear you."

I turned around and saw that Myrna still hadn't budged. Then, as I approached, I realized why. The V portions of the chains at the bottom of the fence had gotten looped into Myrna's underwear. Her pants were pushed down but her drawers were being held up by the fence links. One wrong move and everything would rip to shreds.

"Don't crawl or do anything, Myrna," I said. Then I turned to Lyndy and my mother. "One of us needs to unloop the material from the fence chain while someone else holds the fence in place or it will move."

"I'll unloop it," Lyndy said. "You can hold the chain links steady."

Both of us got down on our knees and within a matter of seconds had freed Myrna from bondage. Unfortunately, neither of us thought we had the physical strength to hoist her up from the ground.

"Crawl on your hands and knees, Myrna," my mother directed.

"If I could crawl on my hands and knees, I would be doing that. I'm not an ex-Marine!"

"Maybe if we each grabbed one of Myna's arms, we could lift her," Lyndy offered. "What's the worst that can happen?"

A hernia? "Sure, why not?"

I took a deep breath as Lyndy and I bent down and tried to lift Myrna from under her arms. No luck.

Suddenly my mother let out a shriek, "Snake in the grass! Snake in the grass!"

In that second, Myrna was up on all fours and we quickly helped her stand. Next thing we knew, she had darted at least ten yards in front of us, all the while screaming, "Where is it, Harriet?"

I gave my mother the snake eye and muttered, "There is no snake, is there?"

"You have to do what you have to do. And now I have to rescue my Streetman."

CHAPTER 19

"Is that snake near me, Harriet?" Myrna's voice was more of a shrill.

"It darted away. You're safe."

I poked Lyndy and kept my voice low. "It's February. Not a single snake in sight. They're underground by now."

She giggled as we approached Myrna.

"Okay, Mom. You and Myrna go around front and Lyndy and I will sneak inside from the patio." *I cannot believe I am doing this.* "Keep whoever answers the door occupied. Chances are the dog will go right to the front door when he hears you. You *did* bring treats, didn't you?"

"I don't go anywhere without them. He needs to be rewarded. Or bribed. Like now."

I did a mental eye roll and didn't say anything.

"Hold on a moment." Myrna brushed off her clothing and fumbled in her purse for a small mirror. "I want to make sure my hair didn't get too mussed."

"It's fine," we all shouted at once. I put my finger to my lips and pointed to the side of the house where I thought my mother and Myrna should walk. "Um, on the off chance that no one answers the door, go around back and wait by the patio but don't come inside. Just in case."

"You're getting worse than those deputies, Phee." My mother took Myrna by the arm as Lyndy and I crept toward the open patio door like cat burglars.

"I've done this before," I whispered. "Search around someone's house. Only I had permission. This is—"

"I know. Against the law. Then again, you could say you were distraught over the dog and didn't want him to cause any damage to the place."

"Very believable. Works for me."

The slider moved seamlessly and we slipped inside to find ourselves in a finished patio room complete with a gas fireplace, a wall-mounted TV, patio table and chairs, as well as a wicker sectional couch. Seconds later, we heard the doorbell ring, followed by barking.

"It's a Pavlovian response," I whispered. "It's not even his house."

"Uh-oh. Listen closely. It's two dogs, not one."

I froze. This was all we needed. Streetman to interact with another dog, knowing how unpredictable he is.

"I don't understand it," I said. "Someone should be answering the door."

We strained to hear sounds other than the dogs but there weren't any.

84

"Maybe Sherrille is out and forgot to close her patio door. It happens."

"You're probably right. Come on, let's have a quick peek at the places where someone would stash knitting yarn."

The next five minutes felt like fifty as we sifted through drawers, closets, and cabinets in every room except the master bedroom. That door was closed and something told me to leave it that way.

"No sign of robin's egg blue yarn," Lyndy said, "or any other yarn for that matter."

Just then we heard a rustling sound and a woman's voice. "Quiet, Zuri! Mommy is resting."

My hand flew to my mouth in the fastest reflex reaction ever. *Rats! She's home.* "We've got to grab Streetman and get the heck out of here. Fast!"

I looked around for the dog and found him making amorous advances toward Zuri, a cute fluffy gray dog, about his size. *This is all I need.*

Wasting no time, I launched myself at that little chiweenie and scooped him up. Then I raced toward the patio slider, where my mother and Myrna stood. I don't know what was louder—the pounding in my chest or the quick breaths that came out of my mouth without warning. "Here, grab him and go!"

Lyndy was at my heels as the four of us ran around the house to the sidewalk in front. "Act nonchalant," I said. "Let's pretend we're all taking the dog for a walk on this nice winter day." Then I added, "Hope you're satisfied, Mom. Our search was a bust. No yarn whatsoever. Unless it was in her bedroom, and we didn't go there. The door was closed and we played it safe. Good thing, too, because she's home."

"I know. Myrna and I looked in the window when we walked around the side of her house. You can rule out an affair with Orlando."

"What do you mean?"

"I mean, how many affairs can one married woman have? Because the man in her bedroom is none other than Jonesy from Lizard Acres."

"What? Are you sure?"

"We're both sure," Myrna said. "It was Jonesy all right. No doubt about it."

Lyndy and I exchanged glances but didn't say a word. Then my mother continued.

"You know what that means, don't you?"

I shrugged, expecting her to use words like *harlot* or *trollop*, or my personal favorite, *strumpet*. "Um, actually, she's no longer a married woman," I said. "Maybe the merry widow, but a consenting adult. And what did you mean by insinuating there's something else to be concerned about?"

"Think about it, Phee. With Jonesy keeping her bed warm, she couldn't have been involved with Orlando. That means there was no connection between Orlando and Harris as far as a love interest gone wrong and a motive for murder. If the husband was going to do away with anyone, it would have been Jonesy."

"Maybe Harris killed Orlando over that former business interest." Lyndy looked at me and then at my mother and Myrna. "Some old grudges never die."

"Maybe Harris and Orlando weren't the only ones carrying a grudge. We need to find out more about Jonesy."

"Not if it involves another escapade like today's mess. You're lucky your dog didn't do any damage to that house. And by the way, you can count me out of whatever you come up with."

"We have to eliminate the possibilities, because if we don't, then there's only one explanation for those murders—a serial killer loose in Sun City West. Worse yet, a serial killer with a penchant for knitting yarn. That cinches it."

"It doesn't cinch anything!" I was adamant. "And stop saying 'serial killer.' We have enough rumors going around."

"Fine. We'll take a pause from our house surveillance. Right, Myrna?"

I held up my palms and stretched my fingers. "Take a pause?"

"According to Gloria, who heard it from Kenny, the rec center is reopening the bowling complex tomorrow night. Just in time for Sunday's weekend wind-down at Lizard Acres."

Lyndy elbowed me as we walked. "Did they get all the lizards out of there?"

Myrna immediately jumped in. "From what I've heard, they did. But a few of them cropped up inside the bowling balls and at Nomos. I know someone who works for the cleaning service. She's applied for a transfer to another activity building."

I looked at my mother and Myrna. "Let me guess. You're going back to Lizard Acres tomorrow night because today wasn't enough for you."

"I haven't planned that far ahead."

"Well, don't! I can picture the both of you tailing Jonesy and making a scene with your comments."

"It's called gathering evidence."

"Gather something else. Preferably someplace else. In daylight."

"Ah-hah! So, you *are* worried about a serial killer."

"I didn't say that."

"I suppose we'll just have to reconvene tomorrow at Bagels 'n More for Sunday brunch. Just the book club ladies and some of the pinochle men. Your aunt and uncle will come too. Louis likes their kippered herrings on

Sunday."

"Wonderful." I tried not to wince, but Lyndy sure did.

As we got to the entranceway by the auto restoration building and walking track, Myrna nudged my mother. "Does Phee know about Gloria's Valentine's Day visitor?"

I rolled my eyes. "Yes, I know. And trust me, he won't show up."

"Not according to Gloria. He asked her to give him the names of nice motels in the area so he can make a reservation."

"He's bluffing. And *he* most likely is a cyber-scammer."

"He sent her flowers. Isn't that so, Harriet?"

My mother nodded. "Flowers and then chocolates from Harry and David. Only a real person would do that."

"Then maybe Gloria's 'real person' should give her the details of his flight from wherever to Sky Harbor Airport."

"He already has. He's flying out of Mobile, Alabama, directly to Phoenix. Gloria has the details."

And I have indigestion.

"What airline? Did she say?"

"He's going to be using a corporate jet from his oil company. They allow employees to do that."

I'll bet.

I really wanted to tell her about Rolo's cyber-investigation and the fact that both of Gloria's daughters had sought out help from Williams Investigations, but I couldn't breach client, or in my case *personal*, confidentiality. Instead, I tried to use reason, but that was turning out to be futile.

"And one more thing, Phee. If Gloria's online interest was a cyber-romance scammer, then how do you explain the flowers and chocolates?"

"Wire transfers from stolen monies, gift cards, that sort of thing."

"I guarantee you'll change your mind when he arrives to sweep Gloria off her feet on Valentine's Day."

Or we'll be sweeping her off the floor when he's nowhere to be found.

Suddenly, Streetman gave his leash a yank and all but knocked my mother to the ground when he saw the dog park.

"I'll have to take him in there," my mother said, "or he'll get agitated."

"He's already agitated. And what's he got in his mouth?"

My mother took out a cheese treat from her bag. "It's the only way to check."

The dog opened his mouth, snapped at the treat, and swallowed it in a nanosecond. In doing so, a man's gold wedding band dropped to the ground.

"That explains why he didn't bark at anyone when we walked here," my mother said as she picked up the ring and studied it. "He must have found it on the floor when he got into Sherrille's house. He's never gotten over his habit of retrieving small objects and hiding them in his mouth. Hmm, there's a date inscribed on the back of it but nothing else."

"What are you going to do, Harriet?" Myrna looked at the ring and then at the dog.

"I can't very well return it. It has to be Harris's, or maybe it's Jonesy's, but Jonesy isn't married. It can only mean one thing. Sherrille murdered her former husband but took his ring off first. Or last, as the case may be."

"That's really a disturbing thought," I said. "And if she was the one responsible, she couldn't have worked alone."

Myrna looked at the ring again. "Maybe you could mail it back to her. With a little note. Something that says, 'We know what you did in the bowling alley.'"

I flinched. "That's not a note. That's a threat! And a very bad idea."

My mother put her hands on her hips, clutching Streetman's leash around her fingers. "I have a better idea. We'll just have to go to Lizard Acres tomorrow night after all, in order to find out who that ring belongs to."

Lyndy's eyes were like saucers. "How would you do that?"

"We'll need a plan. A carefully crafted plan that we'll devise tomorrow at brunch. For all we know, that ring could be Orlando's and then it wouldn't just be his gold ring, it would be evidence."

CHAPTER 20

I had a hard time believing Sherrille was the kingpin as far as those murders were concerned, but her behavior certainly indicated a marriage gone awry. And while my mother and Myrna were convinced the ring was evidence, I was positive Bowman and Ranston wouldn't concur. They were fixated on Mary Alice and *their* ironclad evidence of her robin's egg blue yarn.

If nothing else, I felt a certain sense of urgency in vindicating the poor woman, even though I'd only met her once. And true, she was only a person of interest, but that designation had been known to change in the blink of an eye.

I looked at my mother. "Brunch, huh? Maybe Marshall and I will join you after all. But please—no badgering him for information on the investigation."

"I won't badger him. But I can't speak for anyone else."

Just don't speak at all.

"Fine. Lyndy and I have to go." I grabbed Lyndy by the wrist and nearly yanked her in the opposite direction of the dog park.

"Nice seeing you again, Harriet and Myrna," she said as we power walked to my car.

"Same here!" they shouted, but by then we were at least ten yards away and moving fast.

"That was a quick turnaround," she said as we got into my car. "You usually try to avoid those get-togethers at all costs."

"I know. But something about those particular murders keeps nagging at me. And I'm worried my mother won't quit her meddling. Especially since Gloria is on the bowling team along with Kenny. Which reminds me, they're going to reschedule the Red Pin Bowling Event once they reopen. Given all that's happened, I expect to get a royal invite from them."

"Look at it this way, it's a chance to keep snooping. So, any kippered herrings for you tomorrow?" Lyndy broke out laughing.

"Ugh. Thanks for the reminder. I plan to sit as far away from Uncle Louis as possible."

When Marshall and I finally had a chance to unwind at night, I told him about my foray into Sherrille's house and my mother's discovery of a gold wedding band in Streetman's mouth. Unlike me, he was nonplussed. "Knowing these situations with your mother, I would have expected worse. Much worse. But still—entering someone's house like that? Better hope they don't have you on video."

It was as if a slight shock wave went through me. "You're the detective. What do you suggest we do? Other than wait for my mother and her friends to come up with some ill-thought-out and disturbing plan."

"Fess up. More or less. Best bet is to have your mother and Myrna call Sherrille and explain that they were walking the dog when he pulled free and ran around her house and got inside through her open patio slider. Then tell her that when she got home, she realized the dog had a gold wedding band in his mouth. Tell her not to go into details and ask when she can return the ring."

"I suppose that's the most logical solution. And if Sherrille is involved with those murders, it might unnerve her enough to trip up."

"Or lay low. Either way, it's the best option I can come up with."

"Let's hope my mother sees it that way."

"I'll give her a nudge at Bagels 'n More tomorrow."

"Don't sit near my aunt or uncle. Two words—*kippered herring.*"

Marshall's expression rivaled the scream emoji and we both laughed before heading off to bed.

• • •

When we arrived at Bagels 'n More the next day, I spied two seats in between Cecilia and Wayne and immediately made headway toward them. Shirley flanked Cecilia on the left while Herb sat at Wayne's right. Also gathered around the two connected rectangular tables were the other book club ladies as well as my mother, Gloria, and Bill. A few seconds later, Aunt Ina made her grand entrance wearing black leggings, a long furry tunic, and a hat that looked as if Omar Sharif was the last one to wear it during the filming of *Doctor Zhivago*.

"Where's Uncle Louis?" I asked.

"On his way. He had to park the car in the next county. Honestly, this restaurant needs to expand." Just then, Kevin and Kenny walked in.

Kenny rushed over and announced, "My wife is at my mother-in-law's house for some sort of Valentine's Day card making and I got a reprieve. Also got Kevin to give me a ride." Then he looked at Gloria. "Did the rec center get in touch with you about a date for the red pin event? I didn't get an email."

Gloria shook her head. "All I know is that it will be held after Valentine's Day. And that's coming fast. At least they're reopening the place tomorrow. We really need the practice." Then she looked down at her iPhone and I could have sworn I saw her blush.

"Did they get all the lizards out?" Shirley looked up and down the table.

"*That*, or they'll be all dried up," Herb said and laughed.

"That's a horrible thought. Imagine reaching for a bowling ball and finding a dead lizard in one of the holes." Lucinda shuddered.

"Could be worse," Kenny said. "Could be a brown recluse spider. Those things hide everywhere."

And then, the horror stories started. Who was bitten by a spider. Who was stung by a wasp. Who had an encounter with a snake. And finally, who had survived a bat in their hair. It was like watching a tennis match with my eyes darting all over the place. Thank goodness the waitress arrived to take our orders and get everyone centered on the one thing they had in common—eating food.

"They have tomato herring, Louis," my aunt announced. "You should get an order with the onions. It's on special today."

My uncle nodded and the waitress jotted it down, followed by a flurry of frittatas, eggs prepared in more ways than imaginable, bacon, ham, turkey sausage, pancakes, muffins, waffles and bialys. The orders were never-ending and on separate checks. Then, the waitress pointed to a credit card reader on the table.

"This is new for us," she said. "You can all pay separately using our credit card device." She then demonstrated how to use it and I thought I'd lose my mind. It was as if she was in the midst of teaching a college calculus class. A zillion questions. A zillion comments. And a zillion complaints about "why can't we go back to the good old days with pencil and paper bills?"

"Don't worry, everyone. I'll walk you through it," I said. "It's pretty easy." Then again, I forgot who I was dealing with.

Marshall shot me a look and I knew what it meant—add another half hour to today's brunch.

When the meals arrived, everyone dove in, and it was only when the last bread crumb was consumed that the conversation gravitated to Orlando's and Harris's murders.

I told my mother and Myrna not to say a word about yesterday's fiasco and thankfully they listened. However, that didn't stop them from brainstorming ideas to "find out who's really behind the murders before one of us gets the next-in-line ticket."

"There's no sense getting everyone rattled," Marshall said. "The deputies know what they're doing, but these processes take time. That allows for an arrest to stick."

"What about poor Mary Alice?" Gloria asked. "She was so distraught when I spoke with her last night that she said she wanted to quit the team. I convinced her it would only make things look worse, so she agreed to stay on."

"Darn good thing," Kenny remarked. "She's the only one who can get two consecutive strikes, and can convert any split."

"I'm not sure what any of that means," Cecilia said as she added more sugar to her coffee, "but I'm glad she's not leaving."

Gloria leaned across the table. "You'll have to come to one of our practices. And naturally to the red pin event. That is, if we're still left standing." Then she sighed. A long, drawn-out sigh.

Wonderful. The newest drama queen to enter the scene.

Not to be outdone by Gloria's last comment, my aunt just had to stick her nose in. "Those murders simply *have* to be connected, otherwise it lends credence to the theory of a serial killer."

And then, another voice in the crowd. One that I hadn't expected.

"All of you are forgetting someone who really had a motive to murder Orlando, and that's Martha McMillan, the owner of Nomos Bistro." It was my uncle Louis, of all people. He had finished off two plates of herring and was now enjoying his coffee.

"Huh? What do you mean? And how do you know? And why didn't you say anything?" The questions kept rolling out of my mouth like ice cubes from a freezer dispenser.

"Martha's late husband used to play the clarinet. He was in a number of valley gigs with me. The two of them wound up losing a fortune on one of those life-care communities that Orlando represented. Seemed they had to deed their house to the community in order to live in the life-care community, but once they did, they were suckered into paying a fortune each month. A fortune they didn't have, and when they tried to get out of their agreement, it was denied. So much for 'modern aging' in luxury. More like bilking seniors out of their lifelong earnings."

"That's horrible," Lucinda remarked.

"That's not all. The stress finally got to her husband and he died of a massive heart attack. Since *that* changed the agreement, they settled with Martha but not nearly enough to compensate for the loss of her home. Now I understand she's living in a one-bedroom condo somewhere. If that's not motive for murder, what is?"

Marshall looked at me and then at my uncle. "We did speak with her, but no red flags were raised."

"I would expect not. The woman's got a hide of leather and she wouldn't be foolish enough to let on," Louis said.

"I'll convey this to the deputies. Thanks. And please, everyone, don't use the words *serial killer.* Not yet anyway."

"Ah-hah!" my mother exclaimed. "I don't know about the rest of you, but I'm upgrading to one of those new strobe light Screamers. My Streetman can only do so much."

So much damage. She left out that part of the equation.

CHAPTER 21

"That still doesn't explain Harris's demise," I said. "Martha didn't have a beef with him, did she?"

My uncle shook his head. "Not that I'm aware of, but maybe these are two separate incidents. Two different killers."

"And what?" Louise asked. "Both of them found robin's egg blue yarn on sale? No, it has to be one person. One person, who, for all we know, could be right under our noses."

"That's why we need to move fast." My mother reached for the carafe of coffee and poured herself a cup. "Lizard Acres will be open tonight and we need to be there."

Oh no! The ring! She's going to mention the ring.

I stood and walked behind my mother. Then I shook her shoulder and whispered, "Um, I really need to speak with you about something."

"Can't it wait?"

"No, I'll be quick."

"Fine."

She stood and I turned to the table to excuse ourselves. "I just remembered something urgent. About the cat. We'll just be a minute."

As we walked toward the ladies' room, my mother kept asking, "What about the cat? What about Essie?"

"Shh! Not Essie, but I had to say something. Listen, whatever you do, don't mention the ring. Okay? Bad enough you and Myrna are in deep doo-doo over this."

"You were there, too."

"Don't remind me. Look, you were going to snoop around at Lizard Acres over that wedding band but now you can't. Not without pointing a target on your backs."

The exasperated look on my mother's face was hard to ignore.

"However, you can ask around about Jonesy's martial status as well as other players. That should get us somewhere."

"I suppose."

"Good, let's go back to the table."

"What if someone asks about the cat?"

"Tell them I was concerned about vaccinations. I guarantee you won't have to say more."

At least I was right about one thing. No one was interested in the cat. In fact, the conversation moved on to what everyone had planned, or in this case, *didn't*, for Valentine's Day.

"Louis is taking me to Cooper's Hawk in Surprise for an elegant dinner," my aunt said. She was followed by Kenny.

"Oh rats! I suppose I'll have to take my wife somewhere. Well, it won't be Cooper's Hawk. Maybe a pizzeria or Mexican place."

"None of us have plans," Lucinda said. She tilted her head and looked at Shirley. "Do we? I always forget these women outings unless I write it down."

Shirley shook her head. "No, nothing planned."

"Then let's do something!" My mother all but jumped out of her seat.

Gloria fiddled with her napkin before speaking. "Um, I might have plans."

"What kind of plans?" Myrna furrowed her brow.

"With a gentleman friend. I don't have the details yet but he plans on visiting here."

"I didn't know you had a gentleman friend," Cecilia said.

I shot my mother a look and for once, she took the hint. "What do all of you say to us going out to Chef Fabios on Pleasant Valley Road. I'll call and make reservations. And if they're booked up, then how about Sardella's pizza on Eighty-third? They're fabulous!"

"Cut to the chase and let's do Sardella's," Herb said. "I've been hankering for one of their meatball and pepperoni pies."

It was like watching a head count but everyone finally decided on Sardella's at four o'clock on Valentine's Day. Four p.m., because, as Bill put it, "We need to beat out the other old coots and get there before the younger crowd shows up."

I thought Marshall would split a gut.

"What about you two?" Louise asked.

Marshall and I looked at each other like deer in the headlights. "We've got plans, but thanks anyway," he said. "That was nice of you to consider us."

All in all, the brunch didn't turn out to be the disaster I expected but I had no idea what would ensue during my mother's jaunt to Lizard Acres that night. I kept my fingers crossed that it would be uneventful. *Fool that I am!*

• • •

At a little before eight, my mother phoned to let me know that Jonesy was single and wanted it to stay that way. At eight forty-three she called back to let me know that Mini-Moose overheard her and told her that if she was interested in dating, he would be open to that.

At eight fifty-nine, Shirley called to let me know that Mini-Moose caught my mother off guard and now my mother can't remember if she gave Mini-Moose a thumbs-up or down.

"Good grief, Shirley," I said. "Tell her to approach him again and say that she was so flattered but that she does not want to be dating at this time."

"What's with all the phone calls?" Marshall asked. "Is everything okay? And please don't tell me we need to drive to Lizard Acres."

"No. My mother just needs to get her social life under control before I wind up calling Mini-Moose Pop."

• • •

I was never so happy to see a Monday roll around as I was the next day. At least it wouldn't involve the book club ladies or Herb's pinochle crew. Unfortunately, it involved far worse.

Nate popped into my office shortly after we opened and plunked down in a chair. "Rolo called a few minutes ago. Not good news. Marshall's out on a case so I'll fill him in later."

"Is it about Gloria?"

"Oh yeah. It seems the toggling of IP addresses involved a rather complex setup. And it was a decoy, for lack of a better word. According to Rolo, whoever orchestrated this was not only a technical wizard, but a diabolical one as well. What Rolo originally thought to be Lagos turned out to be a ruse."

"I'm not sure what all of that means."

"What it means is that he can't get a handle on the real IP address. Not yet anyway. Not that it matters, but it might."

"What do you mean?"

"Rolo suspects the operation is taking place in this area, but that's not the concerning part."

"What is?"

"Gloria Wong wasn't a random romance target. It was deliberate. That much he was able to find out. The guy's got a number of reliable buddies on the dark web. A veritable 'den of thieves' if you will, but loyal to each other. Go figure."

"Does he think they're after her money? Because they'll be sadly mistaken. Gloria is a retired office worker and her late husband was an optician. Middle-class citizens. Not millionaires by any means."

"I know. Sue-Lynn gave me the rundown. Her mother has a modest pension and social security. Enough to retire to Sun City West but nothing to write home about."

"What about the brother? Or her extended family? Lydia really didn't say."

"Neither did Sue-Lynn. That's why we need to get them both in here to go over this. I'll have Augusta set it up. Listen, I know Lydia contacted you since you were acquainted with her mother, and you're helping out as a friend. Sue-Lynn hired us. And Rolo's doing the legwork. Might as well pull this all together. This may be one of those cases that turns out to have some nasty teeth attached."

"As long as they're not Streetman's." I looked at Nate and we both laughed. Then I told him about the brunch yesterday but Marshall had already filled him in.

"We've got a long laundry list of suspects on those two murders, but at least the interviews are done. Bowman and Ranston believe Mary Alice may be the culprit regarding Harris's death, but they're not a hundred percent certain."

"Good. Because they're a hundred percent wrong. Who else is on the A-list?"

"Depends on the victim. Martha McMillan stands out for Orlando as well as Harris. Sherrille and Jonesy may be running a close second on him."

"What about Mini-Moose? He was positive that his key chain would point right at him."

"He was smart to notify the deputies ahead of time. But he does have a motive. Harris's enterprise would have changed the billiard room into a dizzying display of technology that requires a skill set most seniors don't possess."

"So now what?"

"Now we continue our investigations."

CHAPTER 22

With the guys out on cases, Augusta and I ate take-out gyros in the break room while keeping an ear out for any walk-in clients. It had been a relatively quiet morning so I was able to concentrate on my work without any interruptions, but that changed once lunch was over and I had returned to my office.

My mother phoned to let me know she and Myrna drove to Sherrille's house to return the wedding band.

"How did it go?" I asked. "And Streetman had better not have been with you."

"No, I left the fur-babies at home."

"Good."

"Sherrille was home when we got there and I must say, she was stunned."

"Like *relieved* stunned or furious stunned?"

"Kind of surprised but not upset. Said she sometimes forgets to pull the slider all the way so it really wasn't the dog's fault."

"What about the ring?"

"She said it belonged to Harris and that he had taken it off to get it resized but never got around to it."

"I suppose that's as good an excuse as any."

"Phee, I'm positive she's his killer. When she answered the door and let us in, she was wearing an old, ratty-looking sweater. In robin's egg blue!"

"That doesn't make her Lizzie Bordon."

"The sweater was frayed on the bottom and long strands of yarn hung down. And I mean, *really* frayed. She probably cut off some of those strands and used them to murder those men."

"Interesting observation, but inconclusive. Still, I'll let our guys know. As far as Bowman and Ranston are concerned, they'd need substantial evidence to search her house."

"They just need the sweater. All we have to do is figure out a way to get our hands on it."

"Oh no we don't. Absolutely not. The ring was one thing. Any other 'takeaways' will land us in lockup. Forget it."

"Maybe we can come up with a better plan."

"What's with the 'we'? I am not coming up with a plan to swipe a sweater. End of discussion. I've got to get back to work. Glad everything worked out as far as the ring is concerned."

Ten minutes later, she called back. "We don't have to swipe the sweater. All we need to do is take a small scissors and cut off a piece of the yarn to see if it matches the one the forensic crew found in the pin-return mechanism."

"That's even worse, Mom. Forget it. Better yet, leave it where it belongs—with the sheriff's office."

My head spun and I prayed my mother and her book club wouldn't go off the deep end with this. Augusta was no help, either. She thought the idea had some validity and that someone needed to move at a speed that "wasn't glacial."

Then, a few hours later, the apex of our conversation.

"It's me again, Phee."

I looked up and tried to refrain from banging my head against the desk. "Uh-huh. What now?"

"Gloria's team is having a practice tomorrow night at six. It would be the perfect opportunity to scope out the billiard room. You need to do it. I can't. I'm avoiding Mini-Moose."

"I'd like to avoid him, too."

"Don't be silly. We can support the Lane Chasers and snoop around at the same time. Listen in on conversations. Find out about other motives."

I knew Marshall would have a late night tomorrow and it wouldn't be that much of a problem for me to swing by after work and grab a bite at Nomos. If nothing else, I could home in on the gossip and maybe even pry some information out of Martha.

"Aargh. All right. I'll grab a bite to eat at Nomos and stop by. Is anyone else going to be there other than Gloria and Kenny's team?"

"Shirley, Myrna, and Herb. Everyone else has plans."

Or they'll make some. "Fine. See you then."

• • •

Marshall and Nate had a late meeting on Tuesday night with Bowman and Ranston to review the timelines of the murders and peer into the schedules of the key suspects. That meant I would have more time at the bowling alley for Gloria's practice and my prying.

The place was full when I walked inside and I quickly realized lots of teams were practicing, not just Gloria's. Kenny waved me over but then put his palms in the air. "You can't walk any farther without bowling shoes. You need to stay on the other side of the white line. If you want to move closer, you'll need to rent shoes."

"I'm fine where I am."

"We're just getting started," he said. "Erik and Cassie are on their way. Take a seat and watch."

"I'm going to get a sandwich at Nomos and I'll be back. Have fun."

With that, I left the bowling alley and went inside the bistro. While the place wasn't particularly busy, about half the booths were taken and the waitress scurried about. I hoped a second one was somewhere in the wings.

Nomos was a casual, welcoming spot with lovely teal cushioned booths and sparkling white granite tables. It had a recent facelift that gave it a modern yet cozy feel. The sign on the counter said "seat yourself" and I did just that. A few seconds later, the waitress appeared and asked what I'd like to drink.

"I'll make it easy for you," I said. "Coffee and a BLT on wheat toast."

"Fries, sweet potato fries, or coleslaw?"

"Coleslaw. Thanks."

While I waited for my order, I looked around the place. Directly across from me were three women who looked somewhat familiar. Most likely acquaintances of the book club ladies. I took out my iPhone to check for messages and emails, when another woman, who had exited the kitchen, approached their table and greeted them.

"How are you handling everything, Martha?" one of the women asked. It was a small enough bistro so that I could hear every word.

"As best as could be expected. Lost business over that lizard nightmare, and between you and me, we're still finding some of them in corners. I'd like to get my hands on whoever pulled that stunt. And I have a pretty good idea."

Then she looked around and said, "Skootch over, Janice, I'll chitchat for a second."

I pretended to be fixated on my phone as I listened to every word.

"Do you think it was one of the Wainwrights?" Janice asked.

Martha lowered her voice but I still heard her. "It had to be. Those stinkers are trying their best to sabotage our businesses so we'll cave in to their demands. The rec board better open its eyes."

"Think Harris was murdered because of it?" another woman asked.

Martha nodded. "Very likely. He was a foxy scoundrel and that's saying it nicely. The three of them were lying, cheating, money-grubbing businesspeople. But Orlando Fleish definitely got what he deserved."

"We know," Janice said. "That reprobate cost you everything. And no one would blame you if, well, you were—"

Just then, someone opened the door to the kitchen and called out, "Martha! We need you for a minute."

"And no one would blame you if . . ." If what? You did away with him?

A second later, the waitress appeared with my BLT and I dug in. As I munched on my sandwich, I listened to the conversation across from my booth but it had reverted back to the Wainwrights with one of the women saying, "Two Wainwrights are still in the game, and if something doesn't stop them, this place won't be recognizable."

"I thought it was only the son," Janice said. "Blake? Right?"

"His mother, too. If you ask me, she's the brains behind their enterprise." It was another woman's voice. A different one this time.

"What makes you say that?" I looked over but I already recognized Janice's voice.

"Don't you know? Her family is from Nashville and they've been revitalizing eateries, bowling alleys, and amusement parks for decades. Why do you think the husband and son got into the business?"

"Hmm, just goes to show you . . ." The voice trailed off just as the waitress brought my bill to the table.

"Thanks," I said, handing her cash. "Keep the change. The sandwich was perfect."

I stood, smiled at the booth across from mine, then headed directly into the bowling alley.

In the back of my mind, I knew I had to talk with Marshall about their murder map and perhaps start one of my own. If nothing else, I figured it would keep my mind centered and focused. That, in and of itself, would help Williams Investigations and the deputies with those murders in the case that my map offered up something theirs didn't have.

Satisfied I had managed to eke out some information at Nomos, I walked through the sliding doors to the bowling alley, but instead of finding everyone in their lanes practicing, I saw a frantic frenzy of bowlers all but trampling each other on the way to the restrooms.

My first thought was food poisoning. My second was that they had better not have eaten at Nomos.

CHAPTER 23

"What's going on?" I shouted to no one in particular.

"A chemical reaction to something on the bowling balls," a woman shouted back as she followed at least eight or nine other women to the restroom. "We called the fire department and the EMTs are on the way."

"Phee! Where were you? What took you so long?" My mother thundered over with Shirley at her heels muttering, "Lordy, Lordy."

Then Myrna and Herb made their way to us. "It all happened at once," Myrna said. "Never saw anything like it. One minute people are lining up to bowl and the next, they're shaking their hands and scratching frantically."

"Like dogs with fleas." Herb chuckled.

"That's not funny. It had to be something they touched," my mother said. She reached into her bag and pulled out a box of doggie wipes. "I always keep these for Streetman. Here, everyone, take one and wipe your hands. It says doggie wipes but I'm pretty sure you can use them on people."

"Nothing starts to itch that fast," I said.

Myrna all but rubbed the skin off her knuckles. "It did here. One minute people are yakking and the next they're itching and scratching. I'm not taking any chances. That's why all the bowlers are running to the sinks. But I guarantee we'll be told its contact dermatitis. That's what my doctor says all the time. It's a medical term for 'I have no idea what it is.'"

"Not all the bowlers are at the sinks," Kenny said. "Some are okay." He walked up behind Myrna and reached for one of my mother's doggie wipes. "It's a stampede in the men's room. Pretty soon they'll be rinsing off their hands in the toilets because the sinks are packed."

"Lordy, that's an image I don't want in my mind." Shirley turned to the restroom doors and shook her head.

"What did you mean when you said some of the bowlers were all right?" I asked.

Kenny pointed to the racks of bowling balls that belonged to the rec center. "Only the folks who used the rec center bowling balls had that reaction. People who brought their own to the lane didn't. Can't believe of all days to leave my bowling ball in my wife's car. She's at Walmart and I'd never see the light of day waiting for her to get home so I decided to use one of the alley's balls."

Johnson Lanes turned into a madhouse with bowlers itching their hands and demanding answers from the poor monitor at the counter. The woman kept telling them she had phoned the fire department and asked that they please calm down.

Then, a booming voice as Mini-Moose approached from the billiard room. "What the heck is going on in here? Don't tell me you found more lizards."

The monitor started to explain but everyone spoke at once, and it wasn't until a half dozen firefighters and a few EMTs came into the bowling alley that they calmed down.

"We've been exposed to something toxic," one of the men said when asked by an EMT to explain.

"We've got a HAZMAT crew on the way," one of the firefighters announced, "so if everyone could just find a seat, we'll have all of you checked out. From what I'm seeing, it doesn't appear as if anyone is experiencing a life-threatening situation."

"I will if this itching doesn't stop!" Cassie yelled from her spot at the lane. "Darn it! Of all times to get my bowling ball resized. The holes were too small."

I pulled my mother aside for the second time in two days. "Shh. Think about it. Only the rec center bowling balls were tampered with somehow. Someone put something in the holes that would cause skin irritation. Gloria said she used a bowling glove and didn't have a problem. Then again, she used her own bowling ball. But still . . . I think whoever pulled the lizard stunt pulled this one. They're sending a message."

"Well, it's been received."

All of a sudden, we heard a blood-curdling scream. Like the kind in those silly horror movies, only there was nothing funny about this one.

"Help! I've been bitten by something inside this bowling ball! My hand's swelling up! Someone help!" It was Mary Alice, who was no longer being detained by the deputies since they needed more evidence to make their case stick.

All of the color had vanished from her face. In an instant, the EMTs rushed over, and next thing we knew she was given IV fluids, placed on a gurney and taken by ambulance to the hospital.

"She was probably allergic to whatever that stuff was," Herb said. "Probably has a nut allergy."

Myrna scowled at him. "That's for eating them, not touching them."

"Which bowling ball did she use?" the EMT who treated her asked.

Cassie pointed to the bowling ball, which was now back in the rack.

"Don't anyone go near the bowling balls," the EMT shouted. Then, he hailed over one of the firefighters and they used a small flashlight to peer into the holes. I stepped closer and heard him say, "Better leave it for the HAZMAT crew."

Shirley must have heard, too, because she grabbed my mother's arm and shook it. "Harriet, we may have been exposed to one of those Russian poisons. Sarin? Serotonin? Something with an *S*. You hear it all the time on TV."

"Pretty sure it's not a poison," the EMT shouted back. Loud enough for everyone to hear, lest Shirley and my mother start a panic. "It's a spider. Repeat, a spider. Not poison." Then he approached the firefighters and shook his head.

"Got to be a poisonous spider," Herb said. "Now the question is, did it get there by itself or did someone put it there?"

I kept my voice low as I responded to Herb. "I doubt anyone's going to walk around with a poisonous spider. But I've got to admit, someone sure put something in those bowling balls."

"If I wasn't so miserable, I'd be laughing," Kenny said. "Reminds me of putting itching powder on teachers' desks when I was in grade school. Someone probably did the same thing."

Nothing like putting old skills to work.

At that moment, a team of four HAZMAT workers came in and after conferring with one of the firefighters, began to sweep the area. Seconds later, Deputy Ranston appeared on the scene with another MCSO deputy and two posse volunteers.

"Looks like they're sending in the cavalry," Myrna said.

Not all of it. I wonder what's holding Bowman up?

As I watched the chaotic scene in front of me begin to normalize, I sent Marshall a text: *Trouble at the bowling alley. Irritant in bowling balls. Spider sent Cassie to hospital. Ranston here. Not Bowman.*

Marshall texted back immediately: *Stay safe. Bowman's with me. Will explain later. Don't touch anything.*

What started out as a simple hour or so at the bowling alley turned into a lengthy evening as all of us had to be checked out by the EMTs and give statements to Deputy Ranston, who was so flustered that he got one of the posse volunteers to take the notes.

When we were finally given the A-OK to go home, I had a pounding headache and my stomach was in knots. Worse yet, I wasn't sure what Bowman and Marshall were up to and that added to my anxiety. It wasn't until I got a phone call from Marshall at a little before nine that I finally knew what had happened.

"Sorry, hon. Couldn't share this right away. We've been tailing Blake. Bowman got intel and had reason to believe Blake was involved with Orlando's murder."

"When will you be home?"

"On my way now. Ranston phoned Bowman about the bowling alley.

One minute, murder, the next minute, a circus parade. Yeesh!"

"Don't forget Gloria's Prince Charming."

"Wouldn't dare. That's the other recreational hotspot of the evening. Nate's working on a broader outreach as far as the Wong family goes. I'm glad of one thing, though—our other cases are small and perfunctory, because these two are upstaging everything."

"Upstaging, huh? Must be Aunt Ina's been getting to you."

"Aunt Ina and the entire Sun City West community. By the way, how are we doing on ice cream?"

"Lemon-blueberry, toffee, and rocky road."

"Good. It'll be my three-course dinner."

CHAPTER 24

"I will never participate in a sport that requires me to stick my fingers into small holes where all sorts of creatures could be lurking," my mother said when she phoned me first thing in the morning. Marshall had gotten out of the shower and had already dressed when I took the call.

"You don't participate in any sport," I said.

"And that's why you don't see me getting carted off to the emergency room. By the way, I called to let you know that Cassie will be fine. Gloria called me. The forensic crew determined it was a wolf spider. Apparently very common but with a very painful bite. The hospital technician told Cassie that wolf spiders only bite if they feel threatened or if they find themselves touching someone's skin. And some victims can have an allergic reaction. At least Cassie didn't, but her finger is really swollen. She won't be able to bowl for a few days at least."

"It probably crawled into that hole in the bowling ball thinking it was a safe haven. I seriously doubt anyone would have put it there."

"Not like that powdery irritant. That was a calculated move on someone's part. Call me when your office finds out what it was. Not that I touched it, but I still want to know."

No kidding.

"Fine."

"And one more thing. Gloria told me the bowling alley has been cordoned off so the MCSO techs can check for any other potential hazards. That means the Red Pin Bowling Event is once again postponed. The bowlers need time to practice."

"Uh-huh. I've got to get ready for work so I'll catch you later. And please. Refrain from snooping around."

By the time I had gotten dressed and ready, Marshall had coffee on the table with two bowls of Raisin Bran.

"Your choice," he said. "Almond milk or two percent."

I reached for the almond milk and poured it over the cereal. "At least something healthy is going into my body. These lunches with Augusta need to tone down."

"Tell that to Augusta. Listen, Nate and I wanted to run something by you. You've been involved with these murder cases as much as the rest of us and we figured it might be a good idea to share our strategy for diving into the suspects."

"You mean creating a murder map."

"Of sorts. But our process has always been a bit different. Neither of us have appointments first thing this morning, so why don't we meet in Nate's office and share what we have."

"Has Augusta been bugging you about having me participate in investigations? Because I really love the bookkeeping and accounting that I do."

"No worries, it's just that you're more of an asset than you realize. You see things we don't. Sometimes we play by the rules so much that we overlook the obvious. And in Bowman and Ranston's case, they're so fixated on protocol that they tend to miss what's right in front of them. So what do you say? Nate's office at nine?"

I smiled. "Sure thing. But only for my own edification."

"Keep telling yourself that, Miss Marple."

• • •

"Deputy Bowman put a rush on that substance analysis," Augusta announced when Marshall and I stepped into the office. We had taken his car to work since I didn't need mine for anything during the day and he didn't have any late casework.

Marshall grabbled a donut hole from the box on the counter and shrugged at me before turning to Augusta. "Any idea when they'll have it?"

"He's hoping by midday. Holy cannoli! It's a regular amusement park over there, isn't it? Gives new meaning to senior living. Mr. Williams filled me in. He also told me there's a new consultant on those cases."

I widened my eyes and she laughed. "I'm referring to you, Phee. Have fun!"

A minute or two before nine, I rapped on Nate's door and he called out, "Come on in." He and Marshall were seated at Nate's round table with a mobile whiteboard in front.

"Welcome to old school," Nate said. "Dry-erase markers in red, green and blue. What more can you ask for? Oh, and if we need to print this, we'll take a picture with our phones. No sense driving us any crazier with new technology."

"Okay. Where do we begin?" I sat across from the board and waited for Nate to start writing. It reminded me of the last class I took in college, before PowerPoint presentations became the norm.

"I've always liked what I call the 'Richter Scale' approach when we narrow down suspects. In short, we write our list of names and then put bullet points next to each one. The more bullet points, the higher up the list they go. Then, we tackle them from the top down. Usually we're on target, but not always. Had a few surprises over the years but this tends to be a decent method. And we've been fortunate that Bowman and Ranston are comfortable following our lead."

"Ready to go?" Marshall asked.

"Absolutely."

Nate tossed him a marker and sat. Seconds later, Marshall had written two columns of names. One under the heading *Orlando* and the other under *Harris*. Orlando's column consisted of Martha McMillan, Harris Wainwright, Blake Wainwright, and Sherrille Wainwright.

Harris's column noted Mini-Moose, Mary Alice, Sherrille, and Jonesy.

"Now," Nate said, "we note not only who had motive, means, and opportunity, but whose motive was most compelling. As for means, yarn is pretty easy to come by, but opportunity could be tricky. That's where Bowman and Ranston come in. They're following timelines that they were able to establish via our interviews and the scant video surveillance around the bowling alley. That's what brought them to Blake and your husband's rendezvous with Bowman so they could see who Blake's contacts were. Unfortunately, nothing turned up."

For the next forty minutes, we discussed the motives that could have driven any of the players to commit one, possibly both, murders. All of us agreed that Martha's motive regarding Orlando was high on the list. He cheated her out of everything. Following Martha were the Wainwrights. "And just because Harris was found dead doesn't negate the possibility that he was the responsible party as far as Orlando's demise," Nate said. "To see just how Orlando's prior business dealings with the Wainwrights had any bearing on his death means diving deeper into their affairs."

"Makes sense," I said. "Seems like there's a lineup for him."

"The negative sentiment from the community was strong," Marshall said. "But negativity in general doesn't usually equate with murder. And in this case, we really don't know if it was a carefully calculated act or some sort of physical situation that got out of control. Harris's wounds could have been caused by the pin-return mechanism or a combination of an altercation and then the placement of the body. The autopsy report was inconclusive, unlike Orlando's. He wasn't murdered behind those bushes. He was dropped there. And there were no defensive wounds on his body. As for Harris, there didn't appear to be any sign of an altercation in the pin-return area, but we're not ruling it out. So noisy back there, no one would have heard it."

"I can understand dumping a body behind some bushes, but in back of the lanes in a mechanical room? Sounds like one of the book club's choice readings."

"It's easy access," Nate said. "According to the monitors, the back door is open so they can take out the garbage."

"What about prints?" I asked. "Was the forensic crew able to secure any?"

Marshall shook his head. "Nothing viable."

"Time to look at the players." Nate pointed to the four names on the board. "Starting with Mini-Moose, his billiard room would undergo such a transformation that it would be unrecognizable and would no longer serve the aging senior population. Same deal with Jonesy and Lizard Acres."

"But why would the deputies point to Mary Alice?" I brushed a strand of hair from my face and looked at the guys. They both answered at once— "Circumstantial evidence."

Then I mentioned the unfortunate incident with Streetman and the wedding band. "According to my mother and Myrna, Sherrille didn't appear all that broken up over her loss."

"You wouldn't happen to remember the date inscribed on the back of the ring, would you?" Nate asked.

"As a matter of fact, I do. It was July Fourteenth. Bastille Day. That's why I remembered it. Why?"

"Here's where it gets interesting. Don't take things at face value. Suspect everything. Sherrille said it was Harris's ring. Only one way to prove it. We need to find out if their wedding date was July Fourteenth. That's something Augusta can dig into for us. Anyway, back to our suspect list."

Marshall took a sip of his coffee and leaned back in his chair. "Rarely do suspects act alone, and in this case, it would be highly unusual, if not impossible, for someone to have accomplished the body dumping, for lack of a better term, by themselves. Whoever was responsible for one or both murders had help. That takes us to the next part of our process. In brief— connections."

"I think I see where this is going. If I've got it right, you start with the most probable suspect and look for any connections among the other suspects."

"Or anyone else," Nate said. "That's why Bowman followed Blake's whereabouts. But finding out who these suspects deal with isn't as simple as it looks. There's only so much internet and social media digging we can do. That's where nosing around comes in."

I moved further back in my seat and eyeballed both of them. "Please don't suggest the dog park. You have no idea how stressful it is to take Streetman there. He doesn't listen. He rolls in smelly stuff on the ground, pees in the water bowls, and worst of all, goes after the female dogs like a sailor who hasn't been to port in a year!"

Marshall laughed. "You can relax. We're not there yet, although I'm sure your mother is chomping at the bit to have you pick up the gossip from Cindy Dolton."

Cindy Dolton was Sun City West's eyes and ears when it came to discerning and passing along information. A polite way of saying *gossiping*. Only *her* gossiping had a lot of validity and without it, a number of murders would never have been solved. Plus, she had an adorable, well-behaved little white dog with no neuroses.

"Um, where do you go now?"

"Take a look at the names," Nate said. "Do you see any connections other than the obvious ones, like the Wainwright family members."

With my coffee cup in hand, I leaned forward on the table and looked at the whiteboard. "Unless the three managers are in cahoots—Martha, Jonesy, and Mini-Moose. Or, maybe just two of them."

"Bingo!" Nate crossed his arms. "Only two of them are business owners—Martha and Jonesy. Mini-Moose works for the rec center. Okay, what next?"

"Sherrille and Jonesy were cozying it up in her bedroom. I'd add those two."

"Fair enough. What else?"

I studied the board again. "Nothing sticks out, but a little social media probing on Facebook may point to friends, connections, and locations that could be helpful." Then I paused before continuing. "Actually, this is something my friend Lyndy and I are quite good at." Then I smiled at Marshall. "Not what you think. But we've snooped around on other cases as well."

He winked. "I know. We all know."

Nate stood, stretched, and pinched his shoulder blades together. "This is just a request. Would you be willing to have a look-see if your bookkeeping/accounting schedule will let you?"

"Estimated taxes are done. Invoices were sent and I'm working on account reconciliation. I'll have some time. And I'll need it. When we find friends, we look into friends of friends, and that's where the fun begins."

"Bowman and Ranston are looking into Blake but see what you can find out as well."

I crinkled my nose. "Did Augusta know about this?"

"It was Augusta who told us that 'Phee knows which rocks to pick up in order to find something good underneath.' I think that speaks for itself."

Thank you, Augusta. You're going to be buying me lunch for the rest of the week!

CHAPTER 25

"Y ou want me to help you do an internet search on Blake Wainwright?" Lyndy asked when I called her at lunch and filled her in on the latest news. "Isn't that something those deputies should be doing? Or your office, for that matter?"

"Oh, my office is on it, trust me. But Nate and Marshall think we know how to maneuver around Facebook and some of the other social media sites in order to root out stuff that would otherwise go unnoticed. Think of it as a comparative process."

"I'm thinking of it as a 'you owe me coffee at Starbucks' process."

"You've got a deal. What do you say we meet after work tomorrow? We can bring each other up to speed. Surely by now Lyman's been hearing tidbits from his fellow baseball players."

"For sure. They're worse than the henhouse gossipers."

"Good. I'll text you later. And thanks."

"No problem. This is far more exciting than medical billing. Too bad it's not a paying job."

"Maybe you can add it to your résumé."

"As what? Membership in the Snoop Sisters?"

"Okay, think of it as an internship. Or entry-level job."

"Nice try. See you at Starbucks."

No sooner did my call end with Lyndy when Augusta rapped on my door. "Got the fax from the lab on that substance in the bowling alley. What a hoot and a holler! It was itching powder! Itching powder! Haven't been around that stuff since elementary school. Here, see for yourself."

She handed me the fax and I read the words *Mucuna pruriens* and *rose hips*. "There's a notation on the bottom," I said. "It reads, 'Non-toxic irritant. Seedpod spicules from rose hips and legumes.' Guess that pretty much says it all. Someone's idea of a bad joke."

"Someone's idea of making life miserable so that a change in venue by New Media Entertainment would be a boon. At least that's my take on it."

"I never thought I'd be the one saying it, Augusta, but for once I agree with Bowman and Ranston. Blake may very well turn out to be our perpetrator of murder and now mayhem."

"Could be. But I wouldn't discount the wallflowers."

"The what?"

"You know. Those quiet, unassuming people who appear to sit on the sidelines and watch while they're really the ones orchestrating everything. Just saying . . . You may want to have another look at those bowlers."

Augusta removed her glasses and used the bottom of her blouse to wipe the lenses off. "See how they act around each other."

"I will if they ever keep that bowling alley open for more than a day at a time. MCSO has it cordoned off due to the itching powder."

"No surprise there. Hey, did Mr. Williams or your husband happen to mention the meeting this afternoon with Lydia Wong and her sister? Sue-Lynn Lanne."

"No, but we were busy going over murder suspects."

"The sisters are coming in at four and you're supposed to join them. I don't think they're going to take it too well when they learn their mother wasn't just a random senior citizen targeted by that scammer. Or scammers."

"You know what the worst part is? Those cyber-scoundrels have Gloria, Shirley, and my mother convinced it's the real deal and they won't believe anything we tell them."

"That's why those criminals are so successful at duping people. By the time the victims realize it, it's too late."

"Maybe not this time."

I hoped I was right, but I wasn't kidding myself. With Valentine's Day only a week away, that scammer would have to act fast. And apparently that was exactly what he was doing. At least according to Lydia and Sue-Lynn.

Nate and I met with the sisters in his office as scheduled. As expected, they were aghast when they learned their mother had been singled out.

"I've been sick over this ever since Mr. Williams told me," Sue-Lynn said. She fiddled with her bottled water, unscrewing and re-screwing the top.

"My mother is as obstinate as can be. She refuses to listen to me or my sister." Lydia looked at me and then Nate before continuing. "Can you tell us how she was singled out? What they're looking for?"

Nate explained what Rolo had told him about "fast dings" on servers that bounce with such speed that it's impossible to tie down a location. *That*, coupled with a bogus location, like the one in Lagos, Nigeria, made it even harder.

"But why our mother?" By now, Sue-Lynn must have worn down her fingertips with that bottle top.

"Most likely, mistaken identity. Or not." Nate took a deep breath. "Tell me, is your family in Fresno involved in a high-profile business? Shipping? Importing? Banking? Or politics?"

Lydia and Sue-Lynn locked eyes and didn't stir for a few seconds. Finally, Sue-Lynn spoke. "As you're aware, Wong is a pretty common name. And while I presume there are Wongs in all of those businesses, my brother owns an architectural firm that specializes in building luxury housing. The kind my sister and I can only dream about. You don't suppose they think *he's* sitting on a gold mine and that they'll be able to get a boatload of money through my mother, do you?"

Nate clasped his hands. "Quite possible. Has your brother been featured in any news articles or the like?"

Lydia slapped the palm of her hand to her mouth and sighed. "His company was featured in the *Fresno Bee*. Anyone in San Joaquin Valley probably read it."

"Give me a minute." Nate opened the door and called to Augusta, "Dig up the *Fresno Bee* and look under—" Then he turned to the sisters. "What's your brother's name and the name of the company?"

"Jay Wong Architects and Associates," Sue-Lynn said. "Jay is our brother."

"Did you catch that, Augusta? Jay Wong and Associates!"

"Got it, Mr. Williams!"

Nate returned to the table where we were seated and stretched his arms. "Now the fun part. Having a look-see if your brother and/or his business could have been mistaken for someone else. Similar names, similar businesses. Keep in mind, these crooks aren't stupid. They've got connections all over but mistakes are known to happen. I'll have my secretary look into it."

"Do you think our mother is in any physical danger?" Lydia's hands shook.

"As of now, no. But I would urge both of you, since you reside together, to keep doors locked at all times and keep the alarm system on if you have one. That's a general safety precaution. Whoever is at the helm of this is interested in one thing only—money."

"We do have a security system, thank goodness. Thor may be large but he's a pussycat when it comes to those kinds of situations."

"Okay, now the next step. I understand this so-called Romeo told your mother he plans on visiting for Valentine's Day. Expect some disaster to happen and a plea for money. Make sure your mother does not wire money anywhere or purchase gift cards for him."

"I think he contacted her this morning," Lydia said. "Just as I headed out the door to work. My mother shouted, 'It's going to be a wonderful Valentine's Day,' but I didn't have time to chat. I was already on a tight schedule. Oh my gosh. I should have stayed."

Sue-Lynn put her hand over Lydia's palm. "Don't beat yourself up. It wouldn't have made a difference. It's like she's in a cult or something."

"So what do we do?" Lydia looked at her sister and then at Nate and me.

"Do what you've been doing. Rolo will still keep blocking from his end, and when he tracks down the real IP address, which he will, he'll work to get it shut down for good."

"How?" I asked. "Malware and viruses can only go so far."

Nate smiled. "That's what they want you to think."

A half hour later, once the sisters had left, Augusta announced she had information for us. As soon as we walked into the outer office, she handed us copies of the *Fresno Bee*, dating back a few months to when Jay Wong's firm was featured as the Joaquin Valley's "Architectural Dream Team."

With words like *mesmerizing* and *priceless* as it referred to the style and the elements, it was no wonder Lydia said they'd never be able to afford what her brother's company delivered.

Nate studied the article and then asked Augusta, "Did you check to see if this was online too?"

"Absolutely. Online on all the news syndicates and on the publisher's website. Honestly, Mr. Williams, everything is online. Paper newspapers are going the way of the horse and buggy. Too bad, too, because I happen to use them for packing material. Do you have any idea how expensive packing material is?"

"Hadn't really thought about it. But thanks, Augusta."

I tried not to laugh as I walked back to my office. I expected Marshall to breeze in at any time, and sure enough, a few minutes before five, he did. He poked his head in my door and said, "A ten-minute meeting with Bowman that took an hour and forty-five minutes. He'd love to search Orlando's house for any clues to his murder, providing the beneficiary agrees. They don't have a warrant. All forensics did was to ascertain if the actual act was committed there and it was not."

"I take it the house is in probate."

"Nope. It was deeded to—get this, and I'm still wrapping my head around it—Cecilia Flanagan!"

"Cecilia Flanagan? From the book club? *That* Cecilia Flanagan?"

Marshall nodded. "She hasn't been made aware of it, yet. The fiduciary company handling the estate notified the deputies today."

"Why so late?"

"Because they weren't immediately notified. Let's just say the chain of communication when a crime has been committed takes on a life of its own. Anyway, the fiduciary company plans to contact Cecilia sometime tomorrow in order to set up a meeting with her."

"My gosh! I don't get it. When the women talked about Orlando, none of them said they knew him. And that included Cecilia. This is so odd."

"Trust me. It'll get odder yet once your mother gets wind of it."

CHAPTER 26

By early afternoon the following day, I hadn't received the call I was expecting from my mother. That meant one of two things. Either Cecilia hadn't phoned her, or the fiduciary company hadn't phoned Cecilia. I shrugged it off, figuring I'd find out before the end of the workday. With my new assignment of social media probing for Nate and Marshall, coupled with my usual workload, I was way too busy to think about it.

Then, at four forty-five, the call from my mother came in. Loud and clear.

"Phee! Cecilia called. You're not going to believe it. Not in a million years. She got a call from that fiduciary company on Stardust Boulevard and she's been deeded Orlando Fleish's house. His house! Not only that but all of its contents. Furniture, books, and who knows what. She didn't even know him. Only in passing when they ran into each other now and then at Sprouts. Can you imagine?"

"I, uh, er—"

"Go figure. Cecilia has a meeting with them tomorrow afternoon. From what they told her, the house is heavily mortgaged so she's not to expect much of a monetary disbursement if she decides to sell it. Unless, of course, she intends to keep the house and pay the mortgage, but why would she do that when she has a perfectly nice house as is."

"What about his will? Did the fiduciary company mention the will?"

"Yes. The will specified all of his monetary holdings go to Sherrille Wainwright."

"Holy cow! If that's not a motive for murder, what is?"

"Listen, Phee. No one is supposed to know about this. Cecilia only told us women in the book club. And we're not saying anything to the men. You know they can't keep anything to themselves."

I did a half eyeball roll. "What about the sheriff's office? Did Cecilia mention if they were informed?"

"No. She was too busy yammering about how this was going to eat up so much of her time. And worse yet, if it meant she'd have a target on her back because someone might presume she was in cahoots with Orlando and his shady business dealings."

"When does she get to see the house? Did she say?"

"She thought maybe she'd get a key tomorrow afternoon from the fiduciary company, but like I said, she was much more concerned about all the paperwork involved. Then she went on and on chastising herself for speaking with strangers at supermarkets."

"Mom, that house could hold an important clue as to who killed Orlando and why. And it's probably in Cecilia's best interests to find out."

"Why? Because you think she'll be next?"

"No, because someone is getting away with murder."

"If I find out anything else, I'll let you know. But like I said, Cecilia won't know anything until tomorrow afternoon. That's when we'll be going if she gets the key."

"*We'll?* What do you mean *we'll*?"

"Cecilia asked me to join her. In case she got flustered. That's why they always suggest you bring a relative or trusted friend with you to your medical appointments. One minute the doctor is telling you that you have colitis and you hear bursitis. That happens all the time."

I shuddered. "For everyone's good, please leave the dog at home. Okay? You don't want to be distracted." *Or worse.*

"Hmm, you do make a good point. I suppose my little man can manage for an hour or so."

I know everyone else will.

"Good. Keep me posted."

"And you do the same, Phee. Sometimes it's like pulling teeth to get information out of you."

"Only when it's confidential."

"Information is never confidential when it comes to your mother."

"Remind me to have that engraved on a keepsake."

"Very funny. Talk to you soon."

I sat absolutely still for the next few seconds trying to grasp what I'd heard. And while the Cecilia part of the equation made no sense whatsoever, the Sherrille part sure did. Maybe there was an affair with Orlando after all. Or maybe it was something else. But what?

It was going on five and I turned off my computer and walked to the outer office. Nate and Marshall planned to work longer and I was meeting Lyndy at Starbucks for our own social media probing. I rapped on Nate's door, told the guys what Lyndy and I were up to, and then asked Marshall to defrost something from the freezer or surprise me with anything takeout.

He winked and said, "Got you covered."

"Oh, almost forgot—this just in from the voice of the valley, my mother. Cecilia called her. Orlando left everything in his will to Sherrille. Were the deputies aware of that? Cecilia learned it from Orlando's fiduciary. And she's meeting with them tomorrow."

Nate sat upright. "We knew about Cecilia but Sherrille's windfall comes as news. Hmm, we can't very well reveal our source, but we'll nose around with Bowman and Ranston. Thanks, kiddo."

"Anytime."

• • •

Lyndy's hands were wrapped around a hot drink when I entered Starbucks. She was seated on the immediate left at one of those square tables in the corner, away from the hubbub. We'd both gotten used to seeking out the farthest spots from the counter so we could speak privately. Although, at early evening time, the place was relatively quiet.

"It's a hot chocolate with caramel," she said. "Positively decadent. Like drinking a Milky Way."

"I'll buy you the next one." I smiled. "I do owe you."

"When people talk about drinking their dinners, I doubt this is what they have in mind, but it works for me."

We both laughed. "Me too. I'm ordering the same thing."

"As promised, I did some digging around." The crinkles on the sides of Lyndy's dark eyes seemed to explode as she laughed. "Couldn't help it. The bad news is that Blake isn't on Facebook. Well, not directly anywhere. But Sherrille sure is. And her son, Blake, is all over the place in photos. One of them shows a birthday cake that read, 'Happy 29th Blake.' Then it showed the date—November 23. Get your drink and I'll tell you more."

"I'll order two."

Seconds later, I sat across from her. "I'm ready for Blake Part Two!"

"Fine. We know Blake's birthdate. November twenty-third or written as 1223. That may not seem like much but lots of people use their birthdates for passwords on computers, and even better, on their four-digit garage door openers or security systems. Then again, your guys would go through the right channels."

"Yeah, unlike my mother, who's decided to trade her role as armchair detective for something a little more physical. But hey, as far as getting into someone's house goes, we may have a ticket into the late Orlando Fleish residence."

"What do you mean?"

The barista called out my name and in a split second I retrieved our drinks and returned to our conversation. "I mean, he willed it to Cecilia Flanagan. And before you say another word, it's top secret for now."

Lyndy sat as still as a statue, her only movement the automatic blinking of her eyes. "I'm stunned. Were they acquainted? How come you never mentioned it?"

At that point, I sipped my hot chocolate and told her everything my mother had relayed to me. Including the part about not sharing the information with the men.

"No worries at this end. I trust Lyman, but if he slips, we might as well have your mother announce it over the air on that radio show."

"I won't know much more until Cecilia meets with the fiduciary tomorrow afternoon, but I'm hoping she gets a key and is amenable to having us look around for clues to his murder. Of course, knowing Cecilia, she'll want to sprinkle holy water all over the house first."

"Oh yeah. I forgot about that obsession of hers. Over the years she's probably taken enough to fill a few gallons."

"And then some." I sipped my hot chocolate and for a brief second landed in Nirvana. "Listen, we really need to get inside Orlando's residence. If Cecilia gets the key, I can convince her to let us look around for clues. Of course, that'll mean a regular circus with my mother there, but if you could join me, we'd be able to tackle this efficiently."

I took another sip of my drink and was sorry I didn't order the Venti size. "Face it, my mother and Cecilia will get sidetracked, looking at all sorts of stuff. I can hear it now, 'Look, Cecilia, a little jelly jar shaped like a lamb. I remember having a jelly jar shaped like a cat . . . '"

"I'd love to play Nancy Drew with you but it depends on the day and time. Lyman has theater tickets for this weekend and I've got a few appointments."

"I'll let you know if and when I know. Worst-case scenario, I'll be stuck sleuthing with my phone camera in one hand and Streetman in the other."

And while I was spared as far as the dog was concerned, my mother and Cecilia made up for it with their idea of scoping out the place.

CHAPTER 27

Nothing like walking into a sea of bad news on a Friday. The second I entered the office, Augusta waved me over. "Bowman just called. One of the bowlers, Mary Alice, was taken into custody regarding the murders of Orlando and Harris."

"You're kidding! I mean, I know you're not kidding, but—holy cow!—Mary Alice? What happened? Don't tell me they got the evidence they needed."

"The forensics lab finally completed their analysis of that robin's egg blue yarn. It certainly took them long enough. I could have knitted a king-sized blanket in that time. Anyway, they confiscated the yarn from Mary Alice and all of those tiny strands and threads found at the ends of the strand they obtained from the pin return were a perfect match."

I swallowed the little moisture I had left in my mouth. "That's undeniable evidence that the murder weapon, at least Harris's, came from her yarn. But it doesn't mean she was the one who cut it or used it."

"Tell that to the deputies. It'll be on the noonday news."

"What are Nate and Marshall doing? Marshall left an hour before me."

"Smaller cases and then a meeting with the deputies."

"This is awful. Once word gets out, those bowlers are really going to be distraught."

"They already are. You got a message from someone named Kenny. He asked if you could get your office to 'speed things up' because their team won't stand a chance in any of the tournaments without Mary Alice. Also added that she called him from the posse office to let everyone know."

"Terrific. Usually people placed under arrest call their lawyers. Ugh! I'd better see what my mother knows."

"That was the other message. She tried you at home but you'd already left and your cell phone was busy. Wanted you to know Mary Alice has legal counsel."

"That's a good thing." *I suppose.* "Augusta, there's no conceivable way Mary Alice could have committed both murders. Or even one. I don't get it."

"The deputies go by hard evidence and that forensic report is as hard as it gets."

"What about motive?"

"Maybe it wasn't hers. Maybe it was all about money. I'd be shaking that tree if I was interested in getting her off. Or on. As the case may be."

"Thanks, Augusta. That's very encouraging." I gave her the thumbs-down sign and she nodded.

"Always there to help. Do you want your last message?"

"Oh my gosh!! Not another message!"

"This one is from Lydia. Short and sweet. Here goes: 'A delivery of a dozen roses came early this morning for my mother. I phoned the florist when she took Thor out. No name. Paid for by gift card.' Then Lydia made a grunting noise."

"I'd make a grunting noise, too. Everything is such a mess. I'm going to the only place where the world makes sense."

"The donut shop?"

"No, my office."

I remained in my safe haven for the better part of the morning, focusing on spreadsheets and invoices. At eleven, Augusta popped in to ask if I wanted anything for lunch. We agreed on chicken and she raced out to Popeyes before I could even figure the calorie count.

Nate and Marshall didn't return until much later in the day, and by that time, I had gotten the only good news of the day—Cecilia had the key to Orlando's house on Huron Drive. It wasn't far from my mother or Herb, but far enough to prevent either one from walking over there for a sneak peek.

"Will the deputies get a warrant to search that house?" I asked the men once I had spoken with my mother. We stood by the Keurig waiting for Nate's cup to finish brewing.

"They have to have compelling evidence and they don't," Nate said. "The forensic team already determined Orlando wasn't killed there." Then he and Marshall exchanged glances and tried not to laugh.

Marshall took a step toward me and gave my shoulder a squeeze. "When does your snooping party begin?"

"I'm that obvious, huh?"

"And then some."

"Fine." I plopped my K-Cup in next. "First thing tomorrow morning. Before the women gab about it at Bagels 'n More. Although my mom and Cecilia both said they wouldn't divulge anything that had to do with Orlando's death. Frankly, my mother's expecting us to find a threatening letter, or something of that sort."

"That's what happens when you read all those cozy mysteries." Augusta took a bite out of her apple fritter and chewed slowly. Then she looked at the men. "I'd put Phee on overtime for tomorrow morning considering what she's going to be up against."

"No worries," I said and laughed. "I'm as curious as all of you and believe me, I want these murders solved as soon as possible, too. Bowling tournament or not."

• • •

As it turned out, I should have gotten triple overtime the following morning when I met my mother and Cecilia in front of Orlando's house at seven. With a Venti blond coffee cup in my hand, I braced myself for what was to come.

Cecilia unlocked the double security door and the main door, but before stepping inside, she sprayed holy water from a small bottle. "It's for cleansing," she said. "We don't really know if he was killed here."

"Yes, we do. The forensics team scoured the place for evidence and there was none that indicated he was murdered here. I think you, my mother and I can rest assured the murder was not committed in this house." Then I sighed and did a mental eye roll as we walked in.

The living room was straight ahead with a built-in media center, a leather sectional set and a large coffee table with inlaid turquoise. To the right was a dining area that Orlando had made into a small den with a side desk, La-Z-Boy recliners and a round ottoman. Off to the left was a large kitchen, complete with stainless steel appliances and a grayish white granite countertop. The stove looked as if it was there for show but the toaster oven still had a few crumbs.

Other than some generic paintings of the southwest and lovely horsehair pottery on end tables, the place looked as austere as could be. No indication of hominess whatsoever.

"This is odd," my mother said. "Usually, people have magazines and mail and all sorts of things strewn all over the place, but this looks like the last inhabitant was June Cleaver."

"I know what you mean." Cecilia opened the small pantry and stood still for a minute. "Would you look at this? He has the shelves labeled— spices, soups, rice, condiments and miscellaneous. And everything is on the proper shelf. Goodness! And I thought I was organized."

My mother was halfway down the hallway as Cecilia continued to ponder the pantry. Meanwhile, I tried to take it all in, figuring out the best approach to look for clues.

Then I heard a gasp and raced to where my mother stood. "Phee! Cecilia! Look at this hideous bathroom color. It's mustard green! Who paints a bathroom mustard green?"

"I thought something happened, Mom! Never mind the paint colors. We're not here to critique the place."

At that point, we gravitated to the master bedroom, and like the rest of the house, it was as plain and functional as could be. A queen-sized oak bed with matching chest and dresser and an oversize TV on the wall. More southwest art including a print of the Grand Canyon.

"Might as well check out the other bedroom," I said as I edged toward it. Then, as I swung the door open, my jaw literally dropped.

"What do you see, Phee?" my mother called out.

"Work! And lots of it! This room is stacked floor to ceiling with file cabinets."

"What about a bed?"

"Come in here and see for yourself. It looks like the back room in a medical office. There's a Murphy bed on the wall but his computer desk pretty much blocks it."

"Can you get into his computer?" Cecilia asked. "On all the TV shows, the detectives get in right away and find what they need."

Not a detective. Not a TV show.

"Um, not sure. Most people have pin numbers or security passwords."

Then again, I remembered hearing about computers with the passcode *Passcode1* so I gave it a try. No luck. Not that I expected it.

"In one of the books we read, the victim wrote her passcode on a Post-it and stuck it under the desk. Look under the desk, Phee," my mother said.

"No one is that idiotic, Mom, but sure."

I reached under the desk and could have pinched myself. Sure enough, I felt a piece of paper a good arm's length from my hand. Not a Post-it, but transparent tape holding it in place.

"Guess I was wrong. There *is* a piece of paper here. It says, "Uncle Ivan Eats Mushrooms At Eight Fifteen.""

"What the heck is that supposed to mean? Is that like 'The Crow Flies at Midnight'?" my mother asked. "Do you think Orlando was involved in something sinister?"

"Only his business. And no, hang on a second."

I turned on the computer and when it prompted me for the password, I typed "UIEMA815." Seconds later, I was in.

"How did you do that?" Cecilia asked.

"It's easier to remember passwords when you use a phrase. That's what Orlando did. Listen, we don't have time to go through everything but I'll download his Word and Excel files. I always carry a flash drive with me. We'll scan it for viruses and then check it out later. Meanwhile, let's each focus on an area and see what we find. Looks like these file cabinets have the keys in them so that makes things a whole lot easier."

My mother took a step toward the hallway. "How about if Cecilia and I look around the closets and the kitchen and you open up the files? It's cramped in this room with the three of us."

"Works for me."

"Do we have to worry about fingerprints?" By now, my mother was at the other end of the hallway.

"No, the property is Cecilia's and the deputies were informed we're going through it."

"Good. Last thing I need is to get hauled off. My poor Streetman would be beside himself."

Yes. My first thought as well.

CHAPTER 28

While my mother and Cecilia rooted through the rest of the house, it was impossible not to hear them.

"He used plain mustard. I prefer the spicy kind."

"These are horrible dish towels. Not at all absorbent."

"Look! Three sets of toenail clippers in this drawer."

It was like a trip to Goodwill but without money. I tried to ignore their commentary and instead focused on going through the file cabinets as systematically as possible. The first set contained monthly bills, organized by year and dating back fifteen years. I moved on. The next set were *National Geographic* magazines, sorted by year and dating back to the dinosaurs. Again, I moved on.

Then, I hit the mother lode. File folders were organized alphabetically by last name and each one contained information and notes about possible customers/clients who would most likely sell their homes and move into a senior life-care community. As I gazed at the names, I did a double take. One of them read, "Flanagan, Cecilia Marie."

I opened the file, expecting to see information regarding her potential as a client, but instead, it was a photocopy of a note from someone named Doris to Orlando and it read, "Single woman. Owned home for over ten years. Good potential." Underneath was a handwritten note from Orlando that read, "Cross off list. Do not contact." That was all. I stood for a moment and wondered if maybe Orlando had more than a casual interest in Cecilia and never pursued it. Not sure what to do, I removed the note from the folder and put it in my bag before returning the folder to its original spot. I figured I'd share the information with my mother and Cecilia once we finished, otherwise we'd be here all day pondering "Why Cecilia?"

The bigger issue was Doris. Doris who? The former waitress at Nomos? I thought I might glean more insight by checking out the other names and began in earnest to sift through the remaining folders. A half hour turned into a full hour with my mother and Cecilia going through kitchen cabinets, dresser drawers, and anything that opened. Their never-ending commentary played in the background like bad elevator music.

"He was a size medium underwear."

"These kinds of shirts went out of style in the seventies."

"Who eats spelt?"

Meanwhile, the other folders were curt and to the point. I had all but given up when I pulled up a folder with a sticky note to Orlando in it. The folder was for a woman named Denise Corey but the note inside was from

Doris. It read, "All but sealed the deal. Call her. I'm working late today at Nomos. Bowling tournament."

"Yahoo!" I called out to my mother and Cecilia. "Cut your 'Secret Life of Walter Mitty' short and get in here. I found something."

I told them about the file folders and how Orlando targeted certain people for his business enterprise. Then I revealed the Doris-Orlando connection. "She acted as if she didn't know him when Nate spoke to her at Sherrille's neighbor's house."

"They always do," my mother said. "I mean, what did you expect? She wasn't about to open up and tell you her dealings with him. She threw Sherrille under the bus. Then again, it was probably a quick trip."

I ignored the last part. "None of this means Doris was our killer, but she very well could have snipped some yarn from Mary Alice. Think about it. Those women always leave their knitting stuff at the booths when they use the restrooms. Real easy for a waitress to go over there on the pretense of cleaning up and then cutting off a thread while no one was the wiser. And who knows how long she held on to it."

Then I paused and took a breath. "Doris could have been in cahoots with someone. But the tough part is the motive. Not to mention the opportunity. We only have the means."

"How many file cabinets did you go through?" Cecilia asked.

"All but one."

"Maybe something's in that one. We still have time before everyone will be at Bagels 'n More."

"No problem. I'll have a look-see and the two of you can continue doing whatever it is you're doing."

Without a word, they marched out of the room and back into the master bedroom. I hoped Cecilia was right about that final cabinet yielding a clue into Orlando's murder but I wasn't optimistic. The first two drawers held packing materials and post office priority mailing envelopes so I was resigned to pulling up a big fat zero. That's when my eyes nearly bugged out of my head when I pulled open the third drawer down.

It only had four folders but they were stuffed full of printed copies of emails sorted by date with the oldest date on top of the pile. That made it easier to follow the timeline of his correspondence. But that wasn't the zinger. Three of the folders held very familiar names—Harris Wainwright, Sherrille Wainwright, and Blake Wainwright. The fourth name was Doris Tucker and it wouldn't take a soothsayer to figure out it had to be Nomos's Doris.

"I hit pay dirt!" I shouted. "You won't believe this!"

"You found a death threat?" my mother yelled from the kitchen.

"No, maybe something better." I grabbed the folders and raced to the kitchen. Cecilia stood in front of the cabinet by the sink while my mother was behind her, perusing a bottom cabinet. I put the folders on the counter and stepped back to show off my prize catch.

"Four folders. Three thick ones. Lots of info on our major players. This is going to take some time to dissect but maybe we'll get some answers."

Cecilia flipped over the folder on Harris and studied it for a second. "You're right. There's so much stuff in here. Do you think your office would be willing to go through it?"

With bells on!

"And how! With Nate, Marshall, Augusta, and me, we'll be able to tackle this in no time." *Not to mention Lyndy, if I bribe her.* "With any luck, we'll be able to find out what Orlando was up to and what might have gotten him killed. Listen, it's getting late. You two should head over to your bagel brunch and I'll let Marshall know what we discovered."

Just then, someone rang the front door and I went to see who it was, careful to only open the main door and keep the security door locked. A man in a dark sports coat and khakis held up his card. Behind him, I could see a magnetic sign on his car door that read *Hometown Realty.*

"Hi!" he said. "Are you the new owner? I'm Gus Matterson from Hometown Realty. Been living in the area for the past eight years. I heard the prior owner died under unfortunate circumstances and wanted to let the beneficiaries know that I'm interested in representing this property if you're in the market to sell it."

By now, Cecilia and my mother stood directly behind me.

"I'm the new owner," Cecilia said. "And I haven't decided what I intend to do about the property."

"May I leave my card?" Gus asked.

"You can slip it between the gratings on the security door." Cecilia pointed to the ornate design consisting of agaves and hummingbirds.

"I appreciate it," Gus said. He placed the card directly in front of me on the door. "And I'll be more than happy to show you a comparative list of properties sold in this neighborhood."

"Thank you. Have a nice day." Cecilia closed the door and pulled her black cardigan across her chest. "Buzzards! They certainly don't wait around for the body to get cold."

I watched as he drove off. "I don't suppose you've seen the last of them."

"What I want to see is an everything bagel with eggs, bacon, and tomato." My mother motioned for all of us to leave the premises and next thing I knew, Cecilia locked the doors and I was home free.

"I'll let both of you know what we find," I said. "But the office won't be open again until Monday."

"Since when do you need an office?" My mother gave me one of her looks and together with Cecilia walked to their respective cars. I clutched the folders to my chest and drove directly to the nearest Starbucks for another cappuccino reinforcement for my ride home.

With Marshall out on cases all day, I wasted no time clearing off the kitchen table and plunking open the file on Harris. The initial emails dealt with business transactions he and Blake were engaged in, along with Orlando. Succinct and to the point. Then, out of the blue, a rather telling email from Orlando, stating he would "let it be known to the authorities" if his share of the profits wasn't increased by forty percent.

"Let what be known?" I kept on reading the emails but from that point on, they morphed into a dissolution of their business. Pretty much what Bud had told us when we met the bowlers on Gloria and Kenny's team.

Exhausted, bleary-eyed and ravenous, I nuked the unhealthiest thing I could find in the freezer—stuffed apple pastries at a whooping five hundred calories each. *Fine, I'll walk fast for the next two days.*

Then, I phoned my mother since I knew Gloria would also be at Bagels 'n More, and with any luck, she would have Bud's phone number. Fortunately, I called at an opportune time, because their desserts had just reached the table and I was able to get the number without an interrogation.

That done, I phoned Bud and asked him if he remembered anything else about the situation in Idaho.

"Heck yes," he said. "It was all the news covered. *That*, and some sort of potato blight that would impact supplies."

"What can you remember? Who was the victim?"

"A contractor by the name of Clyde Olsen. From what I recall, he blew the whistle on them and sued their business for misrepresentation. Then he suffered an injury on the job that he claimed was deliberate. Someone sabotaged the job site so that the scaffolding would collapse. Clyde fell, broke both legs as well as an arm. The injuries were such that he could no longer work in the same capacity. It nearly ruined his family."

"What about his initial lawsuit?"

"He won that, but the compensation was minimal."

"Bud, between you and me, do you think the Wainwrights and Orlando were responsible?"

"Orlando was long gone but the Wainwrights for sure. But they got off. Same way big-deal politicians get off every day."

"Thanks. I appreciate it."

"Hey, hope you can make it to the Red Pin Bowling Event. Got an email about twenty minutes ago from the league president. It's being held the Saturday after Valentine's Day and the bowling alley will be open for practice after they oil the lanes. Hallelujah! Glad they decided not to hold it on Valentine's Day like they did a few years back. More crying women than you could shake a stick at, and more grumpy, sulking men. At least Lizard Acres pulled in a good business."

I immediately thought of Gloria and hoped she wouldn't become one of those sobbing women.

"Um, thanks again, Bud. I'll try to make it. By the way, what did you mean by 'oil the lanes'? Is that some sort of bowling expression?"

"Harrumph. I can tell you don't bowl. Bowling lanes need to be oiled. If the playing surface isn't right, the game's not right. And by oiled, I mean a synthetic substance. Don't go around thinking Crisco or motor oil."

"Uh, I wouldn't. But don't the lanes get greasy?"

"Nah. But let me tell you, it's a regular process. Can take up to an hour. And it's done by machine. In patterns. Too much oil and the ball grips the lane. Too little and it can veer off. It's a science."

"I never knew."

"Anyway, if they don't mess up the oiling, everything should be honky dory."

"At least the women won't cry. Except maybe for—" And then I stopped myself.

"Gloria. You can say it. We're all saying it."

"I'm sure she'll get over it."

"She better. Getting oil on the bowling ball is one thing, having it soaking wet from sobbing is a whole new game."

CHAPTER 29

My next call was to Lyndy. "Can you spare an hour of research? I'll order us a pizza and I promise you'll be done before your plans with Lyman. I think Orlando blackmailed the Harrises and cold revenge is what got him killed. I need your help to go over the correspondence."

"Make it a large pizza with extra green olives."

"You're the best."

Twenty minutes later, Lyndy was at my door with a six-pack of O'Doul's.

"Pizza's much better with beer. Even if it's nonalcoholic."

"Uber Eats should be here any second with a large Sardella's pie."

For the next five minutes, I explained everything to Lyndy and handed her Blake's file. "See what you find and I'll take Doris."

We had barely started when the pizza arrived. The large pie for Lyndy and me and a personal pepperoni one for Marshall.

"Don't worry," she said. "I can eat and read at the same time."

"Ditto. If we find anything that stands out, speak up."

"Okay."

The sound of chewing and swallowing was the only noise until Lyndy said, "I think I found the counterpart to that email Orlando sent to Harris. Here—see for yourself."

I reached across the kitchen table, careful not to brush against the remaining pieces of pizza, and took the paper. Sure enough, it read, "It would be a shame to spend your youthful years behind bars." Then, Orlando mentioned the forty percent.

"Funny," Lyndy said, "that Orlando would keep copies of emails he sent, knowing they would incriminate him."

I shrugged. "I guess he thought overwise. Not many people keep paper files these days. Which reminds me, I've got an entire flash drive to check out."

"What about Augusta and the men?"

"Oh, Augusta will want to dig her teeth into it for sure. Nate and Marshall are probably going to be too tied up even though I originally thought otherwise. This is proving to be quite formidable."

"And Doris?"

"Her file's not that thick and I'm itching to see what it says. Starting right now."

Lyndy laughed. "Face it, girl, you're going to be pulling an all-nighter on this one!"

As I bit into the last piece of pizza, I looked at my notations on the dates. It appeared as if Doris began working for Orlando once he relocated from Idaho to Arizona. There didn't seem to be an Idaho connection but it was too hard to tell.

"I wonder if there's a way to find out if Doris is from Idaho."

"There's a sneaky way." Lyndy winked. "Sun City West has an Idaho Club. See if you can get the roster. Then again, she may hail from Idaho but decided not to be in the club. Okay, here's a more diabolical way. Phone her pretending to be the membership chairperson for the club and invite her to stop by the next meeting. You can find out when that is from their rec center newspaper. I'm sure your mother has a copy."

"What if she's already in the club?"

"Tell her you're terribly sorry but somehow her name got on the list. Tell her you're new to the position."

"You ought to be working for our office."

"Nah. I like having regular hours that don't require homework."

"I'll get the info from my mom and the phone number from her directory. Sun City West is one of the few places that still sends out a printed telephone directory to residents each year. My mother uses it to prop open the door to the garage."

"They make special magnets for that."

"This came free." I chuckled.

Lyndy and I were able to complete our review of Harris, Blake and Doris and construct a hypothesis that seemed credible. We figured Orlando blackmailed Harris and Blake for his forty percent and somehow their partnership dissolved. Then, when Orlando started his new business in Arizona, he hired Doris to do the legwork of finding potential suckers. Of course, the final piece, Sherrille, was missing and I was way too tired to look at any more emails.

"Got to get going," Lyndy said. "Those theater tickets I mentioned are for tonight. At least we won't be eating again until much later. By then, my appetite should return."

"Thanks a zillion. I owe you."

"Tell me what you find out about Sherrille. Text me. Exhausted or not. I know you won't sleep until you do. And frankly, neither will I. This is getting to be way too much fun."

"Tell that to the book club ladies. They're all under the impression it's a serial killer. If nothing else, we can disprove that."

"In what world?" Lyndy grabbed her bag and walked to the door. "Don't forget. Text me."

"Have fun!"

I phoned Marshall once Lyndy left and told him I had gotten him a pizza for dinner. He texted back: *Did you find the lost treasure of the*

Incas?

My reply was short: *Even better.*

At a little before six, I heard the garage door open and was elated Marshall was home. I put his pizza in the air fryer and grabbed him a Coke from the fridge.

"Tell me about your day," I said when he stepped inside. "And I'll share the rewards of successful sleuthing."

"Can't beat that!"

The second Marshall sat at the table, I told him about my foray into Orlando's house, followed by the paper chase Lyndy and I engaged in. I thought he'd burst out laughing when I mentioned my mother's and Cecilia's comments about Orlando's pantry and dresser drawers.

"I'm surprised they didn't mention his medicine cabinets. That's one of the first places the forensic teams check out."

"Oh, trust me. They looked. Nothing exciting. Only antacids and they were over-the-counter. And yes, my mother and Cecilia commented on his choice of brands as well."

"Yeesh."

"I really need to find out if Doris is from Idaho. It may answer the nagging question I have. Was she acquainted with Orlando, hence, the Wainwrights, prior to relocating in Arizona, or did they meet here?"

"We can always call Rolo."

"He's got enough on his plate with Gloria's mess. Plus whatever other business he's up to. Nah, I'll have my mother poke around. Worst-case scenario would be Cindy Dolton at the dog park and I seriously hope it doesn't come to that."

"Just so you know, Bowman and Ranston are building a case against Mary Alice. It's impossible to disprove that forensic evidence."

"I know. But I'm convinced someone set her up."

"Us, too. We'll work behind the scenes to uncover what we can."

• • •

The next morning, we were up early and ready to head to the Wildflower for breakfast when my mother called.

"I'm glad I caught you at home, Phee. This is awful. Absolutely awful. Gloria's online friend was supposed to arrive this afternoon on a corporate jet so he could get to know her and spend Valentine's Day with her."

"Don't tell me. The plane broke down."

"No, one of his relatives was in a terrible accident in Venezuela. Also works on an oil rig."

Naturally.

I held my breath and waited for her to continue.

"The poor man apologized profusely to Gloria and said he'd make it up to her."

"Ten to one he's going to ask her for money. Tell her *no, no, no!*"

In a flash, a thought came to me. "Listen, we need to get going. Buy Gloria a box of tissues and call it a day. Talk to you later."

I told Marshall about the call and grabbed the burner phone to reach Rolo.

"Already on it. Like I said the last time, 'Doesn't your office ever communicate with each other?' Your boss called about five minutes ago. Spoke to one of the daughters. If he asks Gloria to send money, we can set a trap. I'll keep you posted. Heck, someone needs to!"

As I ended the call with Rolo, Marshall's phone rang and it was Nate. Sure enough, Sue-Lynn called him and he got to Rolo ASAP.

"Do you think Rolo will have any luck finding a real address for that scammer?"

Marshall shrugged. "If anyone can, it would be him, but I wouldn't gamble on it."

"At least Gloria can join the crew at Sardella's for Valentine's Day."

"Listen, we've both been so busy we haven't even talked about our plans for Valentine's Day. It's a workday and we'll be exhausted. What if we order pizza and celebrate it another way." He took his wallet out and handed me a card from the Corte Bella Spa.

"You got us a couple's massage? Oh my gosh! That's wonderful!"

I immediately threw my arms around him and kissed him. "Keep this top secret so my aunt doesn't show up."

"She was the one who suggested it. And got us a great deal! We can schedule it whenever you want."

"The sooner the better, because I have a sinking feeling that things are going to get out of hand as that red pin day approaches."

"Hate to say it, but I've had the same feeling, too."

With the lizards and itching powder as appetizers, I couldn't help but wonder what nefarious main course was in store for us. As far as I was concerned, those were not harmless pranks. They were warnings. Too bad we didn't know who made them.

CHAPTER 30

"I had a double shift yesterday," Lydia's email read. "Couldn't even stop for a meal. My sister told me she contacted your office. Can you believe it? That scammer is yanking my mother around and she's none the wiser. I'll call you later. Thanks."

It was Monday morning and I was already fortified with my usual cups of coffee. I forwarded the email to Augusta and sent a quick reply to Lydia— "Tell her not to send him any money!" Then, I walked to the outer office to see if Augusta had any ideas about thwarting Gloria from coming to the rescue of the con artist.

"I'd bug Nate and Marshall," I said, "but Nate's already working on it with Rolo."

"Too bad her daughters can't freeze her credit line but that would turn into one of those family dramas that lasts for decades."

"Hmm, maybe I could convince my mother to have Gloria ask for a physical address to send the money, and not an account. Then again, they'd probably reply with a bogus address."

"Got a better idea! When the crook asks for her money, have her say yes but not send anything. Then, when he contacts her again, she should tell him she already sent the money as requested but something went wrong with the account he gave. Then insist on an actual physical address, not a post office box. He'll be desperate and go for it. Then get Rolo on it."

"Oh my gosh—you're a genius, Augusta! An absolute genius!"

"Nah, I've just heard enough of these scams from my canasta group."

I returned to my office and phoned my mother to have her call Gloria.

"You read my mind, Phee. I was about to call you. Cecilia got a phone call from the attorney for Orlando's will and you'll never believe this in a zillion years—he willed her his car! His Lexus! Now all she needs to do is round up the required documents like the death certificate and a copy of the affidavit of inheritance and she can kiss her fifteen-year-old bronze Buick goodbye."

"She must be ecstatic!"

"No, the opposite. Said she didn't like the idea of driving around in something new and flashy. And that Lexus sedan is Matador Red Mica. That's what the attorney told her. Said it really stands out."

"Tell her she can give me the car and she can have mine. All I need to do is vacuum up the chocolate chip cookie crumbs from Starbucks and—oh my gosh—the car!"

"Yes, you said that. What about the car? It's in the garage. We never went into the garage the other day. We never even thought to see if a car was in there. Go figure."

"I'll have to call you back. Oh, and tell Gloria that when her Romeo asks for money, which he will, have her say yes but not send any. Then when he asks again, tell him she already sent it. I'll explain later."

"You're getting worse than your aunt Ina. Always rushing off half-finished talking."

"Uh, sorry. I'll be back. Call Gloria!"

As soon as I got off the phone, I called Marshall. "Hey, quick question. Do you know if the deputies or the forensic crew checked Orlando's car? It's in his garage."

"It was noted as being there according to the notes we got, but no, the forensics team did not dust for prints. There was no external evidence that indicated a crime had been committed there."

"Can you tell Bowman and Ranston to have them check it out? They'll have to contact Cecilia. She just inherited it."

"Holy cow!"

"I know. And she doesn't want to drive it. Too ostentatious for her taste. Anyway, I have a hunch it's where the murder took place. I'll tell you more later. Trust me."

"I always do, hon."

An odd scenario brewed in my mind and I knew I wouldn't rest until that crew from the lab scrutinized the car. I'd seen enough horror movies and thrillers to know that someone could have gotten into the backseat with a long thread of yarn and then strangled Orlando from behind. They'd have to be pretty muscular but a number of our suspects were. Then, the logistics of moving the body . . .

It would have to take two people. They could have easily shoved Orlando out of the driver's seat and into the back passenger seat. Then, they could have used his car to drive to Surprise, and then return it, empty, to his garage as if nothing happened.

I was positive I was on to something. With one exception—which two people? And what did they do with their own car? With plenty of work waiting for me, I pushed those thoughts aside and returned to my spreadsheets. An hour or so later, Augusta knocked on my door and announced, "July Fourteenth might have been when they stormed the Bastille, but it wasn't when Sherrille and Harris tied the knot."

"Huh?" I spun my head around and motioned for her to come in.

"You wouldn't believe how much digging I had to do. I was a regular mole. Got a break when I decided to use a site that checks public records. Small fee. Had them bill it to us. Anyway, Sherrille Bonita Wilson married Harris Wendell Wainwright on December fourteenth. Not July. I doubt the engraver got it wrong."

"Wow. Jonesy claimed he was never married, and Blake is single, but that doesn't mean he wasn't married prior. I'll ask Lyndy. She was scoping him out."

"One step ahead of you. I checked him out. Never married. Never widowed. Never divorced. He's a bachelor with a capital *B*."

"This is baffling for sure. If we knew what circle of friends Sherrille was with, it might help. Oh heck. I suppose I'm due for another chitchat with Cindy Dolton, like it or not."

"Think of it as a public service."

"More like a public nuisance with Streetman but I don't have too many other options. Between Gloria's so-called romance and those murders, I'm being stretched all over!"

"Well, limber up. Spring is around the corner and that brings in all the kooks and nutcases. Got to get these cases solved pronto."

"You would have made a great drill sergeant, Augusta."

"So I've been told."

It wasn't until the end of the day as we were about to close, when I phoned my mom. The guys were due in the office any minute and I needed to hurry.

"It's about time, Phee. I told Gloria what you said. Her friend sent her a lovely Valentine's Day bouquet and said that when things improved, he'd make the trip."

"Did he ask for money?"

"Not directly."

"What do you mean, not directly?"

"This is the strange thing: Gloria got a Facebook message from someone who claimed to be this man's friend. All of the details and information matched up so Gloria had no reason to believe the guy wasn't genuine."

Oh no.

"Then what?"

"He told her the man would never, *ever*, ask for money and would have his head if he knew his friend had reached out to Gloria, but—"

"Oh, I can fill in the 'but.' He asked if Gloria could send *him* some money to help the poor relative because their accounts cannot be accessed due to the fire."

"Yes, something like that."

"Don't tell me Gloria's going to do it."

"She's seriously thinking about it."

"Mom, call her right now and tell her *not* to send money but to ask for the specifics. Then, when the man contacts her again, have her tell him she *did* send the money. I'll explain later. Just do it. Please!"

"That doesn't make sense, but fine."

"Good. I'll phone you back in a while."

I immediately texted Lydia and told her about my conversation with my mother. Then I grabbed the burner phone and got Rolo on the line.

"Get me the address and any info you can," he said. "I'll take it from there."

"Will do. Thanks, Rolo!"

"Always a pleasure. This time, let your boss know what's going on."

I didn't have to wait long to honor Rolo's request. I heard Nate's voice as soon as I got off the phone and walked into the outer office. He and Marshall looked tired but not as ragged as I'd seen them lately.

"Got an update on Gloria," I announced. Then I went on to tell them the idea Augusta had, and the fact that Rolo was on board with it.

"You can thank us later, gentlemen." Augusta shuffled some papers on her desk and organized them into piles.

"Sounds like you've had quite the day." Marshall smiled and gave me a wink. "Ours was fruitful as well." Then he looked at Nate before continuing. "The deputies picked up on that U-Haul comment that some guy named Bentley made on your mother's radio show."

"Yeah, the mystery and fish show disaster program," I mumbled.

"Turns out, there was a stolen U-Haul at the same time, which gave them a reason to check things out with Sherrille."

"And?" I waited for Marshall to respond but I was chomping at the bit.

"They knew hers was legit, but it was a good cover for getting info."

"And? And?"

The men looked at each other like kids who had just cleaned out a cookie jar.

"She said with Harris gone, she decided to replace her bedroom set and had given the old one to a friend."

"What friend? Did she say?"

"Someone named Dot. She said, 'I gave it to my friend Dot, who also lives in Sun City West.' We couldn't really prod more out of her about the friend without raising suspicions, but good old Doris, the former Nomos waitress, goes by Dot."

"Do you think both of them had a shared motive for murder?"

"That's what we'll find out, if we ever come up for air. Meanwhile, we're looking into Jonesy and Mini-Moose for the deputies."

Augusta leaned an elbow across her desk and announced, "Won't that fit in nicely with your long overdue escapade to the dog park? I'm sure Cindy Dolton is expecting you by now." Then she laughed and went back to her paper piles.

"Let me guess," Nate said. "You're going to look into Sherrille's circle of friends via Cindy." He raised his head and nodded to Augusta. "Thanks. You saved me from asking her."

"What about me? I'm the one who has to deal with that neurotic little nuisance." I looked at my husband but all he did was laugh as well.

"Tell you what," Nate said. "Lunch is on me for the rest of the week. And that includes you, too, Augusta."

"Terrific!" Augusta nearly leapt from her seat. "Let's begin with Taco Tuesday tomorrow! The giant chimichanga at the Mexican place has my name on it!"

I rolled my eyes. "And the dog park has mine."

CHAPTER 31

"Look, Streetman," my mother called out when she let me inside the next morning. It was six and I had to have my head examined. "Your sister came to take you to the doggie park!"

"Not his sister!"

My mother ignored my comment and continued. This time to me. "Give me a minute. I want him to wear his special Valentine's Day vest. It's adorable. Shirley made it. He'll be the star of the dog park!"

He doesn't need a vest for that.

"Wait until you get there," she said. "Lots of the dogs will be in Valentine's Day outfits."

"As long as it's a vest and nothing complicated. He hates those fancy things."

A few seconds later, the little chiweenie was attired in a lovely red vest with white hearts emblazoned on it.

"I have to admit, it's cute. Shirley is amazingly talented."

"She made one for Essie, too. In pink! If you hold on, I'll show it to you."

"No time. Got to run. I'm hoping Cindy will know who Sherrille pals around with. The date on that ring didn't match her wedding date with Harris. Even though she told us it was his wedding ring. So, whose is it? Jonesy isn't married. Neither was Orlando. Blake neither. That's why I need to talk with Cindy."

"Good." The smug smile on my mother's face was hard to miss.

"By the way, thanks for getting the word out to Gloria yesterday. Fill me in later. Got to get going."

With that, I scooped the little dog into my arms and hustled to the car so he wouldn't be distracted. Minutes later, I walked him into the dog park and couldn't believe my eyes. It was a sea of red and pink outfits on mostly little white dogs, including Cindy's.

"You've got the right school uniform on," I said to Streetman as I unleashed him and let him run freely in the park. "Don't roll in anything," I shouted, but he was already halfway down the park and probably wouldn't have understood. Still, I felt compelled to warn him.

"Phee," Cindy called out from her usual spot by the fence, "I'm glad you're here! Come on over!"

"Hi! I was hoping you'd be here."

"If I'm not, someone better get to my place and see if I still have a pulse." She chuckled. "I take it you're wondering what I know about those murders. People have been chitchatting like crazy."

I nodded. "I need facts since we've got more theories than you can imagine. Do you know anything about Sherrille Wainwright and who her close contacts are?"

"Close as in romantic trysts or close as in girlfriends?"

"Both."

"For starters, I have it on good authority she's been quite cozy with Jonesy from Lizard Acres."

"What about Orlando? Was she ever involved with him?"

"Romantically? Not that I've heard. And believe me, I hear plenty."

"Before Jonesy, was she sneaking out on Harris with anyone else?"

"Not that anyone has ever mentioned."

"What about women friends? Card groups? That sort of thing."

"She's a friend of Doris Tucker's, who used to wait tables at Nomos. In fact, a while back when Doris worked there, she told me she planned on quitting because Sherrille got her another, more lucrative, job that didn't involve standing on her feet all day."

"Did she say where? With whom?"

"Only that it involved acquiring renters for senior residences, or something like that. I really didn't pay that much attention at the time. I was probably hungry and more interested in putting in my order."

"I know what that's like."

We turned our heads at the same time to see what our dogs were up to. Bundles was sniffing the ground but Streetman was more interested in sniffing the ruffled outfit that a small Maltese dog wore.

"Oh no," I said. "In a matter of seconds, he'll pull that thing off her and rip it into shreds. I forgot how he is with certain fabrics."

Not wasting a second, I ran toward him and thankfully averted the catastrophe of the day. Then, while Streetman resumed his sniffing and wandering, I returned to where Cindy stood.

"When he's done with his business," I told her, "I'm going to hightail it out of here before he gets into mischief."

"Better hope he hurries. Agnes Raul just drove in with her three French bulldogs. Look! They're all dressed like Cupid!"

I froze. I remembered the last time Streetman met up with Maurice, Pierre, and Jacqu. It was a frenzy of jumping, bumping, and rolling in icky grass. He loved those guys to the exclusion of anything else going on.

"Um, I think I'll leash him and walk him around the perimeter. Just in case."

"Smart move. Listen, I'll see what I can dig up on Sherrille and if I hear anything, I'll phone your office, okay?"

"Thanks, Cindy. I appreciate it."

With that, I charged over to the dog before he noticed his buddies, and with a quick scoop got him in my arms and on his leash. Then a short walk down the sidewalk and we headed back to my mother's house. The first words out of her mouth, after kissing the dog as if he'd been on a rescue mission, were, "What did you find out?"

I told her about the Sherrille-Doris connection and her immediate thought was similar to mine. Maybe they did know each other from back in Idaho. Lyndy suggested I find out and now was as good a time as any.

"Mom, do you have the Sun City West directory?"

"Behind the utility door to the garage. Why?"

"I need the number for the Idaho Club. I want to see if Doris is from there. Maybe she knew the Wainwrights and Orlando prior to moving here."

"Let me know what you find out."

"Fine. Give me a sec and I'll be on my way. Got lots of work to do."

For once, my mother didn't insist I kiss the pets and I was able to make a clean getaway and get to the office before it opened, complete with a hot Venti vanilla cappuccino in hand.

"I need to make a call, Augusta," I said as I walked in. "Back in a flash to give you the rundown."

"I'll give you yours fast. Bowman and Ranston got the MCSO forensic guys to get prints from Orlando's car this morning. Said once Cecilia stopped gasping for air over the phone, they got her permission and she followed them to Orlando's house. Had to be the crack of dawn."

"Good heavens. Did they mention if they found anything?"

"Nope. Only thing Bowman said was that he thought all retirees were up at five. Guess Cecilia was the exception."

"I'm sure I'll hear about it from my mother. At least they took me seriously."

Augusta snickered. "Nah. They took your husband seriously."

For some reason, the deputies needed follow-up interviews with a few of the bowlers, which meant Nate and Marshall had to add it to their already busy schedule. Meanwhile, I focused on my work and hoped it would go uninterrupted.

At a little past two, I was convinced I had gotten my wish, but unfortunately, I didn't. Apparently, the cyber-scammers knew exactly what to do in order to get Gloria to acquiesce and send them money.

"Gloria's online friend is in desperate need of funds," my mother wailed over the office phone line. "His relative will die if he doesn't get lifesaving surgery. It's not like here, Phee. It's Venezuela, for crying out loud!"

"It might as well be Mars! It's all a scam. We've been through all this.

Please don't tell me Gloria sent him money."

"No, she did what you told her. She let the man know that she wired the money but it didn't go through. He asked her to wire it again, this time to a different account."

"And she *still* wasn't suspicious?"

"Another bouquet arrived this morning. This time calla lilies. Those are Gloria's favorites."

"Tell her to stick with the plan. I'm phoning Rolo and Lydia."

I don't remember ever tapping numbers so fast on a cell phone. Thankfully Rolo picked up on the first ring.

"Give me your worst," he said. "I was expecting a call from your office."

I told him the cock-and-bull story that Gloria got from a would-be friend who pleaded for money. He wasn't surprised and in fact said it was usually for a kidney transplant.

"So now what do we do?" My voice was louder than normal and a whole lot whinier.

"If Gloria does what you said, we'll get an address. I'll call Lydia."

"You sure? I mean, I can do that for you."

"That's okay. Consider it billable hours."

Billable, edible . . . whatever

I thanked him and retreated back to spreadsheet Nirvana. With three hours of work left, I wanted to get home and enjoy a quiet Valentine's Day dinner with Marshall. We decided to grill steak and serve it with lots of fixings, topped off with a Lady Godiva cheesecake he bought from the Cheesecake Factory.

Thoughts of my soon-to-be blissful night ran through my mind until a quarter to five, when my mother phoned from Sardella's.

"Please don't tell me something awful happened," I said.

"No, nothing awful, unless you want to watch Herb consume his second pepperoni pie."

"Then what?"

"Sherrille is here with Jonesy. They're at the other end of the restaurant near the patio and when Shirley went to use the ladies' room, she heard them talking about Harris's car. Jonesy said that she should sell it before it's too late."

"That could mean anything. Did Shirley hear anything else?"

"Yes, but she missed the first part because someone bumped into her and said 'excuse me.'"

"Well, what *did* she hear?"

"She heard Sherrille say, 'That might mean we need to shut her up.'"

CHAPTER 32

"They're planning another murder, Phee. I'm positive. Both of them are the serial killers and they're only a few feet away from us."

"Whoa! Take it easy. Conversation snippets don't equal plots for murder. And don't get your table all worked up."

"I can't simply sit here like a bump on a log."

"Then order something else to eat. I'll call you in the morning. Unless there are bodies on the ground like the St. Valentine's Day massacre, we'll talk tomorrow."

I stretched my neck back and rolled it around at least twice. If nothing else, it helped with the tension. The fact that Sherrille was with Jonesy was no surprise. After all, they were chummier at her place when Myrna spied on them. However, the car comment stuck. What if whoever strangled Orlando in his car used the same MO to kill Harris? Too bad there was no way to check out Harris's car. Unlike Orlando, it belonged to his less-than-grieving widow.

Then there was Jonesy. On the surface he appeared to be concerned about New Media Entertainment, and in fact was seen having a verbal confrontation with Harris when I first saw them at the bowling complex. But it was Harris who threatened Jonesy, not the other way around. I remembered hearing him say that if Jonesy tried to stop him, it would be the last thing he did. Stop him from what? A business deal? Something to do with Sherrille? It could have been anything.

My head pounded and I stood and stretched. With the Red Pin Bowling Event only four days away, I worried that whoever sabotaged the bowling alley before would do it again. And then, the most diabolical thought sprung to mind—what if the saboteur did those things so that everyone would become complacent about them. Then, with another prank, they would be able to accomplish what they really had in mind—pulling off another murder while everyone was preoccupied with whatever melee was taking place at the bowling alley complex.

I tried to focus on my computer screen but decided instead to let Augusta know what I thought.

"You're conjuring up things that belong in a poorly written thriller." She pushed her chair back from her desk and walked to the Keurig. Her Starbucks blond roast with caramel looked inviting and I popped in a pod for myself as well. "Thanks for the compliment," I said.

"Those pranks serve one purpose only. And that's to make life miserable for the business owners and managers so that they'd either sell or leave. If everyone's really worried about that red pin event, they should hire extra security."

"Extra? They don't even have security. Sure, the posse swings around but it's not as if there's a dedicated security officer on duty. Or even one of the sheriff's deputies."

"There will be if a threat is made."

"Bite your tongue."

"Four days, huh? Sounds like you and Mr. Gregory might want to camp out there so that the place will have eyes and ears."

"And I'll have nausea and indigestion."

"Better than a third body."

"You're getting as bad as my mother. She's convinced Sherrille and Jonesy are serial killers."

"Huh?"

I then told her what my mother overheard at Sardella's.

"Selling the car is one thing, but shutting someone up may be more of a real deal than a figurative one." Augusta rubbed her chin and returned to her desk. "First thing to determine is this—who is the *she* that needs to be silenced?"

"If I knew that, I'd probably be able to piece all of this together."

"Do what you always do. Make a list and whittle it down."

"It won't be much of a list. According to Cindy, Sherrille only had one close contact, Doris Tucker."

"There you go! Possible victim three."

"Martha may also be on Sherrille's blacklist. She had issues with Orlando and the Wainwrights going back to their Pocatello, Idaho, days. When I overheard those women at Nomos, Martha mentioned that they were scoundrels, and that included Sherrille as well."

"You see. That wasn't so difficult. Now you're up to possible victim four. Keep it going and you might hit the top ten."

"That's not funny."

"At least it gives you a starting point. Not that I'm telling you what to do while the men chase around, but a deep archeological dig might pull up a few unexpected skeletons. But I wouldn't wait too much longer."

"Why do you say that?"

"Because inevitably, some other problem surfaces and next thing you know, everyone will be gasping for air."

"You're quite the optimist today, Augusta."

She winked. "I always try to bring a little joy into people's lives."

"Stick with the donuts."

When I returned to my desk, I pulled out the number I had written for the Idaho Club and placed the call. The expression "wing it" immediately sprung to mind as soon as I heard a lady's voice say, "Hello, this is Joannie from the Idaho Club. If you're calling about tickets for our potato fest this Friday, we only have a few left."

"Actually, I wondered if you could tell me if Doris Tucker is one of your members."

"You want to be seated at her table?"

"I, um, er . . ." And then, like a burp out of nowhere I said, "Yes. Please seat me at her table."

"Only one ticket?"

If I'd like to save my marriage . . .

"Yes, just one."

"And who shall I put this under?"

"Sophie Gregory."

"Fine. You can pay at the door. Cash or check. Twenty dollars. And it will be spectacular. The Oregon Club always boasts about their crabs, but they're not homegrown like our potatoes. Ours are home-raised. Can't say that about a crab."

"Um, I guess not. Can you tell me where the event will take place?"

"In the Summit Room at Palm Ridge Recreation Center. Six o'clock on the nose. And between you and me, you may want to arrive early. Some of our members start showing up at five in order to be first in line for the jumbo potatoes. Of course, *all* of our stuffed potatoes are delicious but those jumbos go fast."

"Thank you. I look forward to it."

Like a root canal. Miserable, but needed.

I picked up where I'd left off with the spreadsheets. Nate and Marshall returned a short while later because both of them had clients, who, according to Marshall, "gifted us with easier cases."

I finally caught up with Marshall in the late afternoon and asked him how the progress was going on those murders.

"Those second interviews paid off. Funny how people suddenly remember things they never thought to mention earlier."

"Like what?"

"Like the fact that before Mini-Moose took over as the manager for the billiard room, he was an accountant."

I shrugged. "That's not all that earth-shattering."

"It is when he turned out to be Harris's accountant."

"Holy moly! Do you think Harris strong-armed him into fudging things and the situation escalated to the point where it became physical?"

"I don't know what to think anymore, but I arranged to meet with him tomorrow morning at Dunkin' in Surprise. Less gossipers, good coffee. Should be an interesting chat."

"Um, speaking of interesting chats, I intend to have one at the Idaho Club's potato fest Friday night. And don't worry, you can pass on this one."

Marshall started to say something but before the words left his mouth, I explained about Doris and how it was a great opportunity for me to pry around.

"You're really getting into this, aren't you?"

I crinkled my nose and smiled. "Like an itch that needs to be scratched."

"Promise me one thing," he said. "When we get home and enjoy our quiet Valentine's Day dinner, let's not talk about Sun City West, the murders, or Gloria's cyber-romancer."

"You know that will never happen."

"True, but I thought I'd give it a try."

As it turned out, we had a lovely Valentine's Day dinner at home and set a date for our couple's massage. Regrettably, the following morning was anything but lovely. Lydia phoned me at seven to tell me that her mother received an alert from her bank that someone tried to open a line of credit but they thwarted it. Worse, however, was when she got another message from the friend of *her* online friend, only this time there were "sinister overtones," according to Lydia.

"Can you tell me exactly what the message was?" I asked. Marshall had already left for Dunkin' so I couldn't run anything by him.

"Hang on. I'll read it to you. My mother thinks this friend is trying to scam money out of *her* friend. Can you believe it? Hold on."

I washed my coffee cup while I waited for Lydia, all the while wondering what to do next with this latest development.

"Here goes, Phee. 'A woman with your means can easily wire the money. Try it again. Western Union should not have any trouble. Oil rigs do not have physical addresses. Please wire the money today. It would be a shame for someone to die needlessly.'"

A lump formed in my throat and for a second, I was still. "I see what you mean. The message can be construed to mean the fake relative's death, or a threat on your mother's life."

"I know. That's why I called you. You'd think my mother would be furious, and she is, but not at her romancer. Now what do I do?"

"First of all, workers on oil rigs get their mail from the company. It goes to that address. They then deliver the mail and any packages. Be there when your mom responds. Have her tell them to provide her with the company's address. I'll let Rolo know as well."

"You don't think she's in any real physical danger, do you? I know I asked this before, but I'm really worried."

"I don't believe so. It seems to be a cyber-threat. But still, it's chilling."

When the call ended, I raced into the shower and braced myself for a long day.

CHAPTER 33

"Talk about fast work," Augusta said the second I walked into the office. "Bowman called. He must have lit a firecracker under those forensic techs because he got a full report on the contents of Orlando's car. I texted it to Mr. Williams and Mr. Gregory because they're both out of the office."

"What did they find?"

"Not looking good for Mary Alice. They found tiny shreds of that robin's egg blue yarn on the driver's seat. Had to be real tiny so as to defy the eye."

"Okay." I took a breath. "All that means is that it substantiates the fact that the yarn was the murder weapon. It's not as if it had Mary Alice's name on it."

"Uh, actually it did."

"What I mean is, the fact that someone could have stolen it from her or cut it when she wasn't watching."

"There's more, Phee. They found two small charm dice with the letter *M* on one of them, and *A* on the other. Wedged inside the driver's seat. Some of the women in my canasta group have them on those homemade charm bracelets. If any of them forget their names, they can always look at their wrists."

I snickered. "An *M* and an *A*?"

"Yep. As in Mary Alice."

"Or Martha. That has an *M* and some *A*s. She's another player as far as I'm concerned."

"Not as far as Bowman and Ranston are."

"Now what?"

"Bowman didn't say. Betcha dollars to donuts Mary Alice is looking at an extended vacation in the Fourth Avenue Jail."

"Oh no. It's bad enough she went through that once. Then lack of evidence and it was dropped. Ugh. Not this time, I suppose. I imagine she'll call her bowling team and Gloria will call my mother."

As if by mystical communication, the office phone rang and sure enough my mother was at the other end of the line.

"You're in the wrong business," Augusta whispered as she handed me the phone. "You need to hang a shingle for a psychic."

"I'll pick it up in my office. Thanks."

I tossed my bag on the desk and picked up the phone. "Good morning. What catastrophe is on today's agenda?"

It wasn't as if I could tell her that I already knew, without violating the privacy of our office calls. Especially the ones from MCSO.

"Herb called. Kenny called him after Gloria called Kenny. Poor Mary Alice has been hauled into the posse office again. Seems they found incriminating evidence of her involvement in Orlando's murder. Not the yarn. This time it was something else."

She went on to tell me about the dice charms with the *M* and *A* on them, and sure enough, it did belong to Mary Alice. So much for wishful thinking.

"According to Mary Alice, who told Gloria, who told—"

"I know. I know. I know who she called. Keep going."

"Mary Alice wore her charm bracelet to bowling one night and it fell apart. It's only a string holding those little plastic charms together. Anyway, she found all the letters except the *M* and the *A*. She meant to buy replacements at Michael's but never got around to it. That's what she told the deputies but they didn't believe her."

"Did she call her lawyer?"

"Yes. Now do you understand why it's so important to nab the real killers?"

"That's what everyone is trying to do!" It was impossible to hide the exasperation in my voice.

"Not everyone. Those deputies are finished as far as they're concerned."

"Well, we're not." *Because the last thing Williams Investigations needs is to be hammered, badgered, and beaten by your unending phone calls.*

"Good. Keep me posted. What should I have Gloria tell Mary Alice?"

"I don't know. Try 'Keep a stiff upper lip,' or maybe 'It ain't over till it's over'?"

"You're not helping."

"Oh, I'm helping. In fact, I'm going to be at the Idaho Club's potato fest this Friday to dredge up information on Doris. How's that for helping?"

"It's a start. Too bad it's the Idaho Club and not the Oregon Club. The Oregon Club has Dungeness crabs for its food fest."

I rubbed my temple. "If you hear anything more from Mary Alice, let me know. I've got to get back to work." *Or at least get started.*

"Fine. But it's a two-way street. Besides, whatever you find out, I'll find out, too. Only my sources are quicker."

"And not always accurate. Don't spread any rumors about Mary Alice. Talk to you later."

I put the receiver back on the phone and booted up my computer. At a little past ten, Nate returned to the office. Marshall was still out on cases and also needed to confer with the deputies. The minute I heard Nate's voice, I raced to catch him before any of his morning appointments. As we spoke, Augusta listened in even though she feigned going over paperwork.

"I suppose you know about Mary Alice," I said.

"I do."

"And?"

He looked around the office, and even though it was only Augusta and me, he kept his voice low. "Even Bowman knows when he's been played and he's not likely to have that happen again."

"Huh? What do you mean?"

"He knows planted evidence when he sees it. Way too convenient."

"So Mary Alice will get off again?"

"Not exactly. Although that's what they'd like to have the public believe."

"I don't get it."

"Mary Alice will remain in custody but under house arrest. That way, the real perpetrators will believe they're off the hook and chances of them slipping up are bound to happen."

"I take it we're talking about Sherrille, Blake, Jonesy, Martha, and Doris."

"Possibly Mini-Moose. That's a substantial number of suspects but not unwieldy. That's why those interviews with all the bowlers on the other teams were so important. *That*, and the legwork to substantiate what they told us. Not to mention background checks on them to be certain."

"No wonder you and Marshall were running around in circles."

"Haven't stopped yet." Then he looked at Augusta and winked. "You can stop fiddling with the same pile of papers. I'll keep you both in the loop."

With that, he walked to his office and closed the door behind him.

"Should have known better," Augusta said. "He's not a detective for nothing."

"Just so you know, I'm going to be cozying it up to Doris at the Idaho Club's potato fest this Friday night."

"Too bad it's not the Oregon Club. Heard they have great crabs. Fresh ones flown in."

"My gosh! Who doesn't know about their crabs? No, it's the Idaho Club and they don't have to fly in their potatoes. Sherrille, Harris, Orlando, Blake and Doris are all from the same city, whichever one it was. I'm hoping to find out more at the dinner. Oh—and I managed to get a seat at Doris's table."

"And here I thought the men were the only detectives."

"They still are! This gal is making a fast track back to her bookkeeping and accounting."

"Not that fast. Look who's headed to our door!"

I looked out the window and was relieved it wasn't any of the book club ladies, or the men for that matter. And, thankfully, it wasn't my aunt or uncle. Instead, Lydia walked toward the door looking as if she hadn't slept all night. Her hair was mussed, and she usually pressed her scrubs, but not today.

"I'm so sorry to barge in on you like this, Phee," she said when she stepped inside the office, "but I'm an absolute wreck over this. That so-called friend of my mother's cyber-scammer contacted her this morning over Facebook. He gave her an address. It's a post office box in Phoenix! Now what do we do? I have a horrific feeling whoever is behind this is watching us."

"Come inside my office. We're calling Rolo."

I motioned for Lydia to sit while I unearthed my burner phone from the top desk drawer. Seconds later, I had Rolo on the line and on speakerphone.

"That's right," I said. "It's a post office box on South 35th Avenue, right here in Phoenix."

"Well, what do you know! Seems our cyber-players really *are* at our fingertips. They must be desperate for money to slip like that. Is Nate there?"

"No, he's on another case."

"Okay, when he gets in, have him call me. I'll have to jump ship since the deputies will need to be involved; but not before I figure out who these guys have Gloria mixed up with."

"Is she in jeopardy?"

"Not yet. They want the money. And fast, apparently. Once they get it, it will be another story. Then again, they may just keep stringing her along for more moolah."

"What should I tell her?"

"Hold tight."

"Got it. Talk to you later."

I gave Lydia a thumbs-up. "With any luck, our guys will be able to nab whoever is scamming your mother. Most likely they'll set up surveillance with MCSO at the post office once your mom lets them know when to expect the money. The postal clerk can notify MCSO first."

"I just want this mess over with. Even if it means my mother will be sobbing and shooting herself in the foot at the same time."

"Rolo and our guys think those crooks have Gloria confused with someone else. Can you think of anyone with substantial means whose name is the same? Or similar?"

"No. We went through this before. And not only with my mother but with me, my sister, and my brother. Nothing. Besides, my mother was targeted on Facebook under her name and profile."

Suddenly I realized I hadn't thoroughly looked at Gloria's page. Only a haphazard glance. "Give me a second." I went into the search engine and pulled it up. Then I gasped. I'd never looked at Gloria's middle name, but there it was—Leung.

"Lydia! Your mom has the same middle name as Leung Wong, the millionairess who married Barry Wong, the Hollywood producer."

"Oh my gosh! My father's name was Barry. But he was an optician. And if my mother is a millionairess, she's certainly hiding it well."

I laughed. "Don't you see? That has to be the connection. Those scammers don't always do deep dives into their victims. They use algorithms and things like that. No wonder they confused her with the other, wealthier, Wong."

"I'd like to be the other wealthier Wong."

Wouldn't we all?

"I think we know why she was targeted. Now all that has to happen is the sting, or trap, or whatever Nate's going to call it once he and Rolo talk."

"Thanks so much. I'm going to call my sister right away. Meanwhile, I've got a shift coming up so I've got to take off. And thanks again. Wow, the millionaire Wongs. Who would have thought?"

Lydia all but bounced out of my office. I heard her say, "Glorious day!" to Augusta before closing the outer office door behind her.

"What was that all about?" Augusta walked over to my desk with her arms in the air. When I finished telling her about my conversation with Lydia and my phone call to Rolo, she put her hand to her cheek and sighed. "Looks like Mr. Williams and Mr. Gregory better get themselves some decent snack food if they plan on a post office stakeout. Better keep your fingers crossed Bowman and Ranston are in good moods."

"I'll need more than keeping my fingers crossed. I may need to light a candle."

CHAPTER 34

"It's going to take a little more setup time than you think," Nate said to me when I caught up with him later in the afternoon. "Got your message and got Rolo on the line. Then Bowman after that. He said cyber-scams were not his deal since they have a separate department to handle those things. However, once I convinced him that it would involve surveillance and a bona fide physical arrest if we caught the perpetrator, he got ahold of the cyber-unit and worked out a plan. I swear that guy lives for the excitement."

"Please tell me it's a viable plan."

Nate nodded. "It is. First of all, Gloria would have to mail a bank check. In this case, the cyber-unit will create the check to look like the real deal. It's a safety measure so a real check wouldn't be processed via a cell phone app."

"How fast can they do that?"

"Fast. Since the post office box is in central Phoenix, it should only take two days at most for it to arrive from Sun City West. That means it will need to be sent tomorrow. The cyber-unit will take care of that. All Gloria needs to do is let the scammer know that it's on the way and that they can expect it on Saturday."

"Then what?"

"Then your husband and I get to watch behind the scenes at the post office, posing as employees. As long as they don't ask us to sort mail. MCSO will get all of that arranged. Bowman or Ranston, or maybe even both, will be there as well, but out of sight. Can't risk spooking whoever opens the mailbox."

"Oh my gosh! This could actually work and Gloria will be home free."

"That's the plan. Keep your fingers crossed."

"If it doesn't work, Gloria will be a mess that night for the red pin event. It starts at seven and it's a really big deal. From what Lydia and Sue-Lynn said, their mother is terrified of the new player in the mix but still thinks *her* guy is legit."

"Oh brother."

"Hey, any chance they'll let Mary Alice out of the house to bowl? According to Kenny, the team really needs her."

Nate shook his head. "Not if Bowman has his way. They have to convince everyone she's responsible for those murders along with unnamed suspects if they expect to nab the real killers. Marshall's been conferring with Ranston on this. I'm sure he'll tell you more when the two of you catch up."

"We've both been spinning in circles. Did he mention I'm going to the Idaho Club's potato fest to eke out information from Doris?"

"Uh-huh. Got to admit, you're quite the trooper, kiddo. Too bad it's not the Oregon Club. Heard they had huge crabs. Sure beats potatoes."

I pressed my palm on my forehead and pounded it. "Next time find us a murder with Oregon connections."

• • •

Before I knew it, it was Friday afternoon and only a few hours until my unofficial investigating at the potato fest would begin. Well, snooping around to be precise. Still, it all boiled down to the same thing—use my best listening skills and conversational techniques to draw out information that would otherwise remain hidden. Or pray someone opens up like a bursting dam and saves me the trouble.

"Are you all set for your 'snoop and pry' tonight?" Augusta asked when it neared five.

"As set as I'll ever be. All I need to do is go home, take a break, change my clothes and head over to Sun City West. Marshall's going to work late when he gets back here. He'll grab a burger and most likely fries."

"Yep, can't avoid those potatoes." She gave me wink. "If something juicy happens, text me."

"I doubt it'll be that earth-shattering. Funny though, Lyndy said the same thing."

• • •

Summit Room A was tastefully decorated with bright teal tablecloths and bouquets of white carnations. The buffet table, skirted in teal, held eight-quart chafing servers, silverware, and actual plates. A smaller buffet table, off to the right, boasted an assortment of desserts. If nothing else, I'd enjoy a good meal, even if it wasn't seafood.

A number of people were already seated at the tables and a few of them were milling about. I gazed around for Doris but didn't spot her.

"Hi, I'm Sophie Gregory," I said to the two women who were at the reception table as I entered. I took out a twenty-dollar bill and handed it to the redheaded one with round black glasses.

"Yes, I see you on the list. You're at table four. Drinks are off to the left. Water, soda, and coffee."

"Thanks." I grabbed a bottled water and as I started for my table, I felt someone's hand on my arm.

"This better be Phee or I'm in big trouble. My eyesight's not what it used to be."

I turned and sure enough, it was Bud from the Lane Chasers, Gloria's team.

"Hi! I totally forgot you're from Idaho. And I had no idea you'd be in this club."

"Oh, I'm not in the club. Too much yammering, yakking and blabbering. I just go to their food events since they're open to the public. What table are you at?"

"Four."

"Good! You can lead me there."

When we seated ourselves at the eight-person table, located close to the buffet, two couples were already there. They introduced themselves as John and Mary Higgins from Boise and Eileen and Stan Brenner from Rexburg. Then they promptly turned and continued the conversation they had started among themselves.

"Doris Tucker is going to be at this table," I whispered to Bud. "That's why I'm here. I'm trying to piece together more information about those deaths."

"Dot. Most people called her Dot. You think she had something to do with it? Is that what the deputies think? Dot was a darn good waitress when she worked at Nomos. Always fast on her feet. Too bad she left. Heard she found a better-paying job. Hmm, now that I think of it, she was friends with Harris's wife."

"Sherrille?

"Uh-huh. Harris met her at one of those senior home shows."

"How do you know all of this? Did Dot tell you?"

"No. The bowlers that I had lunch with did. Gee, that was ages ago. I can't even remember who they were. Maybe Fred, but I'm not sure."

"It doesn't matter. Shh! Here she comes now."

Doris arrived solo, which was a good thing. That way she wouldn't be busy chatting with a friend at the table. Her large girth, coupled with untamed curls, made her look like a female version of Samson.

Bud and I greeted her, along with the two couples across from us. I introduced myself again and told her I was the bookkeeper/accountant at Williams Investigations.

"Usually I'm not at these events," she said as she sat next to me, "but their cheese and bacon stuffed potatoes are amazing. And their jalapeño and Mexican cotija cheese is out of this world."

"Do you know what else they're serving?" Bud asked. "Don't want to stuff up on potatoes if filet mignon is on the way."

Doris laughed. "That's a good one. Usually they serve salads, breads, and those little hot dog appetizers." Then she squinted her eyes at me. "Williams Investigations. They're certainly making a name for themselves."

"I know. They're contracted with MCSO."

A few seconds later, the eighth person arrived at our table and Doris gave her a hug. "Madge," she said, "I haven't seen you since that day when those investigators spoke with us. It was right after your neighbor, Orlando, was found dead."

The thin gray-haired woman looked at us and said, "Awful, simply awful. The widows' club is growing on every street in Sun City West."

I sat, wide-eyed, not sure of how to respond when Bud stepped in. "What streets are they? I'll make a note."

If I thought Herb lacked discretion at times, Bud had him beat by a mile. To move things along, I quickly introduced Madge to the others at the table. Seconds later, a hefty woman with reddish streaks in her blond hair approached the podium to the left of the buffet table and welcomed everyone. With a long woolen tunic and tight leggings, she appeared to be in her late fifties or maybe early sixties.

"She better not speak for an hour," Bud whispered. Then, Doris whispered back, "It's Eugenia Stockton. She'll be quick when food's a few feet away from her."

"Good evening, everyone," Eugenia said. "I'm Eugenia Stockton, the president of our illustrious Idaho Club, and it's my pleasure to welcome you to our annual potato fest. This year we've added a few surprises to the menu, like chorizo and avocado potatoes, smoked Gouda and ham, and our Italian specialty, green olives with meatballs and pepperoni."

The audience applauded as if someone won an Olympic gold medal. When the noise died down, Eugenia continued. "For those of you who are new to the club, and those of you who are considering joining us, we have a number of ongoing activities and get-togethers. Please pick up a flyer at the dessert buffet, but wait until after the main meal. We'll be calling out table numbers so please remember your manners. Also, once everyone is served, please feel free to go back for seconds. We have plenty of our fabulous russet potatoes. No need to pile up your plates like last year and drop them on the floor. This is a baked potato event, not mashed. Now, without further ado, I am calling table number eight to the buffet."

"We better not be last," Stan said. "I always manage to get the table that's last."

Then Eileen asked, "Did they drop that many plates last year? We weren't here."

Bud immediately responded, "Plates, silverware, cups, you name it. It was the first time they served the pulled-pork potatoes and people piled them up."

Stan faced Bud. "While we're on the subject of things piling up, what's with those murders? We moved here to get away from that sort of stuff. Two murders in a short period of time, right here in a senior community, is very unnerving and upsetting. Makes me look over my shoulder all the time."

"I wouldn't worry," Madge said. "They were premeditated and personal, not some lunatic in our midst."

"Premeditated? How would you know that?" I literally jumped with my question.

"I'm an avid listener of the cozy mystery radio show and I've put my own clues together."

Wonderful. My mother and her friends can make trouble even when they don't know it.

I was afraid to ask but I had little choice if I was to get anywhere. "Um, can you be more specific?"

"Indeed, I can." Madge nodded once and smiled. "Sherrille Wainwright was at Orlando's door more times than I care to tell. And when he opened the door, not that I was deliberately looking, he hustled her inside and looked in both directions. What does that tell you?"

He was in a hurry?

None of us said a word and Madge continued with her explanation. "I don't want anyone to get the idea I was spying, but after all, I *was* directly across the street and some things were quite obvious. One day I heard them have a big row, and shortly after that, Orlando was dead on the ground in Surprise. Not random. Planned. And I'll wager Sherrille was on that planning board."

"Did you share your thoughts with the investigators who spoke with the neighbors?"

"They were just like the deputies. They only want facts."

Just then, another table was called to the buffet. This time, table one.

Stan shifted in his seat and looked around. "I hope they don't run out of the avocado ones."

Then Bud twisted his chair to face Madge. "Okay, that explains Orlando, but what about Harris? What makes you so sure his death was deliberate?"

"Because I happened to overhear the murderer confess."

CHAPTER 35

And just as all eyes at our table were on Madge, we heard, "Table four, it's your turn for the buffet." Suddenly, everyone stood, shoved their chairs into the table and raced off to the buffet. I sat, dumbfounded. I was about to learn from Madge who this "confessor" was, but unfortunately, Madge was no longer at the table. She stood, second in line at the buffet, chatting away with Stan and Eileen.

I stood and walked toward the line, now even longer since table three had been called. By the time all of us returned to our seats, the conversation had shifted to decent eateries in the West Valley.

Undaunted, I didn't wait for a conversational segue. I blurted out my question for Madge just as she scooped a giant spoonful of her Mexican cotija cheese potato and opened her mouth.

"Madge," I said, "I'm anxious to hear who you overheard. When? Where?"

She swallowed the contents on her spoon and sipped her water. "That's the thing. I heard the confession, but I didn't get a good look at the killer."

"I don't understand."

"Me, either," Bud said. "Weren't you wearing those glasses you have on?"

Madge sighed. "I was at one of those Thursday night movies at the Stardust Theater, *The Color Purple*, to be exact, and during one of the scenes, I overheard a woman say, 'Keep your end of the bargain and keep your mouth shut.' Then the other woman said, 'I thought you wanted that blue yarn to patch up one of your sweaters and were too cheap to buy the entire skein. Why don't you just sign a written confession?'"

"And you couldn't see who was talking?" I was incredulous.

"No, it was dark and they were somewhere behind me."

"Madge," I said, "whoever it was didn't use the word 'murder,' just confession. It could have referred to stealing yarn."

She shook her head. "It wasn't. Later on in the movie, I heard her again. This time she said something like 'not spending the rest of my days behind bars.' They don't put you behind bars for petty theft."

"What about when the movie got out?" Bud asked. "Could you take a good guess who it was?"

Madge shook her head. "It was a madhouse and most of the audience was women. They complained about sciatic pain and elbowed their way out of there."

I wanted to elbow my way out of the potato fest, but I came for a specific reason and I wasn't about to give up so early in the evening.

The next ten or fifteen minutes were spent in relative silence as everyone at my table dove into their stuffed potatoes and side dishes. When table six was called, Mary put down her fork and announced, "I suppose I should say something about what my house cleaner told me, but that would be telling tales."

"Nah," Bud replied. "Think of it as doing a service for the community."

Yep, like picking up litter.

Mary sighed. "I agree with Madge. Those murders weren't random. My cleaning lady also cleans the Wainwrights' house and she told me she overheard Sherrille and Harris having a giant fight a few weeks ago. The cleaning woman found a gold wedding band under a nightstand and brought it to Sherrille's attention. Instead of thanking her, Sherrille went ballistic and screamed for Harris to 'get in the blasted bedroom now!' The poor cleaning woman was beside herself and thought she'd lose her job. What's that saying? Oh yes, No good deed goes unpunished."

"Did she hear anything else?" I asked.

Mary's face flushed as she spoke. "I hate being a gossip."

Get used to it. Everyone is. Come on, come on!

"We don't know who your cleaning lady is," I said. "It doesn't matter."

Terrific. I think I just broke one of the Ten Commandments.

"Sherrille kept asking Harris what he was hiding. She screamed over and over again, 'Do you have another wife? Are you a bigamist?' My cleaning lady wasn't eavesdropping. She was in the next bedroom and they were loud."

"Did he answer? What did he tell her?" Doris spoke with her mouth full and it all garbled together. Still, we understood what she asked.

"Harris said he's not a bigamist and that the ring was his wedding ring from another marriage. One that dissolved before he met Sherrille. He happened to find that ring while rearranging some of his things."

"And she believed him?" Bud snorted.

"No. Not in the least. Then she demanded to know who the first wife was and why he never told her."

"And?" Doris swallowed her last bite of the potato and wiped the sides of her lips with a napkin.

"That was it," Mary said. "My cleaning lady told me she went into another room and didn't hear anything else."

I looked at everyone's faces before I spoke. "Mary, did your cleaning lady get the sense that Sherrille would have been angry enough to . . . well, do something she'd regret?"

"You mean murder her husband?"

"Well, uh, yeah. That."

"I don't know. All she said was the last time she heard anyone argue like that was when she watched *Who's Afraid of Virginia Woolf* on Turner Classics."

"Couples argue all the time," Eileen said. "I wouldn't read too much into it. But that conversation in the Stardust Theater was certainly unsettling."

"Hey, look at the good side." Bud smiled. "It means we can't possibly have a serial killer around here, only unhinged, jealous, crazy women. And tomorrow night, some of them will be bowling."

Then the table talk morphed into tomorrow night's red pin event before it reverted back to decent restaurants that didn't cost an arm or a leg.

I decided to forfeit the desserts and explained that I had work the next day. I told Bud I'd see him at the bowling event and stood to leave. Then, while everyone headed to the dessert buffet, I discreetly asked Doris if she wouldn't mind chatting with me for a few minutes.

"Doris," I asked as we walked down the corridor, "you and Sherrille are friends, right?"

She nodded and I continued. "Do you think she'd be angry enough to turn a verbal argument into a physical one? Apparently, she argued with Orlando and had a major row with her late husband."

Doris shrugged. "I would hope not, and I've only seen her go after people verbally. But she's really a nice lady and she actually found me a better job than working at Nomos and coming home reeking of French fries."

"Was that the job with Orlando?"

"You know about that?"

"Like I said earlier, I work for an investigative agency. Lots of things cross my desk but I keep them to myself."

"Good. I'm sure that's common knowledge by now. Those deputies and investigators asked a lot of questions of a lot of people. I wouldn't be surprised if I was on the suspect list."

"Everyone is. What about Sherrille and Orlando? Any love interest?" *That sort of thing can cause all sorts of words to be flung everywhere.*

"Madge thought so. Even went as far as telling one of the investigators, but no. Her relationship with Orlando was all business as far as I know. They had some issues back in Idaho and the Wainwrights severed business ties with Orlando, but that's as much as I know."

"Thanks, I appreciate it. Um, I know this really is none of my business, but do you think you'll return to Nomos? From what I hear, lots of customers miss you."

"Believe it or not, Martha called to ask me the same thing. Funny though, she called the day before Orlando was found dead. Talk about coincidence."

Or murder.

CHAPTER 36

Marshall was up before dawn, dressed and ready to meet Nate at the office before their post office stakeout on South 35th Avenue in Phoenix began. I was still in bed and struggling to open my eyes.

"Had my first cup of coffee and will fortify myself at the office before we head downtown," he said. "Keep your fingers crossed we catch this cyber-scammer."

"Who's joining you guys? Bowman or Ranston?"

"Ranston, as far as we know, but Bowman hates to miss the fun so it wouldn't surprise me if he showed up as well. By the way, you walked out of that potato fest with lots of clues."

"And a stomach that feels as if an elephant landed in there! Most likely I'll pop into the office to get caught up. Besides, Augusta always likes the company."

"And the chitchat." He leaned over, gave me a kiss. "She'll want to know what you found out last night, too. Frankly, it kept me awake thinking. We'll talk later. I'll keep you posted."

"Be careful," I said. "You never know what to expect."

He squeezed my shoulder. "That's what makes it interesting."

• • •

Augusta all but jumped out of her chair when I walked into the office carrying a box of baked goodies from Boyer's Café in Sun City.

"Wow! Boyer's! Glad you decided to work this morning."

I opened the box of fruit-filled croissants, shortbreads, and brownies and smiled. "Got lots of work to catch up on and thought I'd do a better job with a decent sugar intake."

"Works for me. And thanks! Mr. Williams left a message that he and your husband will be on that stakeout, but of course you already know that."

"Uh-huh. Hoping we hear something this morning."

"I think we will." Augusta took a coffee-caramel brownie and broke off a piece, which she promptly tasted. "Mmm, this is heaven with chocolate chips inside, too!" Then she continued. "That scammer is hot for his or their money. It won't be long until they check out the post office box."

"That's what Bowman and Ranston are counting on. They'll bring him or her in for questioning and go from there. He can't be arrested for opening a post office box with his own key, but once the contents are

160

discovered, those deputies will piece everything together."

"Let's keep our fingers crossed."

The next two hours went fast as I breezed through invoices and double-checked the spreadsheets I'd been working on. At a little past eleven, Marshall texted me: *Good news, bad news. Both deputies here. We nailed the guy who opened the PO box. Young kid. Late teens or early twenties maybe. Said he responded to a courier ad to pick up the mail. Said he had no idea about cyber-scamming. Headed to MCSO main office on Jackson Street. Will keep you posted. Let Augusta know. Though she's probably reading this over your shoulder.*

I texted back: *Shall do. Keep me posted!* I threw in hug and heart emojis before closing the app.

"What do you think will happen now?" I asked Augusta. I refilled my coffee and took a sip before grabbing a shortbread cookie.

"Hopefully Bowman will scare the daylights out of the kid and he'll tell them where he's supposed to deliver the contents. Better keep your fingers crossed it's nearby."

Lamentably, it wasn't. Marshall texted an hour and a half later: *Turns out the kid is a college student at ASU and needed some extra cash. Saw the ad on Craigslist and responded. He's supposed to mail the contents of the PO box by priority mail to another box, this time to Avondale. Will stay in touch.*

I texted back a smile emoji because I didn't know what to say. Augusta, however, had it all figured out.

"I think I saw this on an old 1930s movie. They keep moving the mail around and around. Bet Avondale isn't the final stop. You'll see. This merry-go-round could take a few days."

"And lots of county resources, not to mention time."

"Then again, our guys know the right questions to ask. Maybe the kid isn't as innocent as he seems."

"Let's hope."

Sure enough, Augusta was right. Not about information the kid had, but about who purchased those post office boxes. It turned out that their downtown office attacked the situation like a pit bull after a juicy steak. Five PO boxes were purchased by the same party and they were spread out all over the Greater Phoenix area. Good thing they moved fast or Marshall and Nate would have been chasing their own tails for days on end. Not to mention Bowman and Ranston.

"I can't believe it," I said. "They've got a name and an address. This nightmare for Gloria is finally going to come to an end."

So much for wishful thinking. The deputies didn't waste a minute but the results weren't as expected. They located the man who purchased the

PO boxes, but like the kid who did the first pickup, he, too, was hired through a Craigslist ad.

"Got to give those scammers credit," Marshall said when he called me around noon. "But they forgot one thing—Rolo Barnes! He was able to track the payment method and origin for us. And in record time. Something about needing to accommodate his new diet with the proper kitchenware. Heaven help our budget!"

"Now what?"

"Now the gumshoeing paper chase, that's what. Nate and I will need to meet with the bank involved and track down their client."

"What about Bowman and Ranston?"

"They gave us their blessing. You know Bowman. Loves the action, hates the work that comes first."

I laughed. "Um, speaking of action, you haven't forgotten about that Red Pin Bowling Event tonight, have you?"

"Wish I could, but no, I didn't forget. What time does it start?"

"At seven. I figure we can eat first and let our food settle before we get there. According to my mother, Gloria and Kenny's team expect to see us rooting for them. Lydia and Sue-Lynn will be there as well so you'll be able to chat with them about the investigation."

"Don't bother asking your mother to leave Streetman at home. Best we can hope for is that the little darling arrives in his doggie stroller."

"I cringe at the thought. At least Thor will be home. He's way too big to sneak in there."

"Thank goodness for small favors. Nate and I will grab lunch downtown and I should be home by two thirtyish."

"Good. I'm hankering to share those tidbits from last night with you. I really think we can narrow down Orlando's and Harris's killers."

"Yeah, and with our luck, they'll be bowling tonight!"

I should have told Marshall to bite his tongue, but it wouldn't have done any good. The catastrophe that was about to explode at the bowling alley would have been unstoppable. Just like the perpetrators of those murders.

CHAPTER 37

I scrambled up some ham and eggs for a quick dinner before we headed out to the bowling alley. Once in the car, all we could talk about was what I learned from Doris and Madge last night.

"Think they'll be showing up to the red pin event tonight?" Marshall asked.

"Doris mentioned she was going because she knows everyone on those teams. She said it was going to be a close competition between the Lane Chasers and the Desert Scorpions. She also mentioned other teams but I can't remember their names."

"Let's keep an eye on her. She certainly had the opportunity to help herself to Mary Alice's yarn, but Madge would have recognized her voice at the theater. It's like one step forward, two steps back."

"I imagine most of the Lizard Acres and billiards crowd will show up as well. It's quite a big deal according to my mother. In fact, she read me the article in the *Independent* that said, and I quote, 'It's an exciting and intense time when the red pin falls in the head position for players in each lane.'"

"Hon, it's an intense time when the Valentine's Day chocolates go on sale for half price."

"What a tangled web of suspects for both murders, starting with Orlando's. Martha and her late husband lost a fortune moving into one of those life-care communities he represented. Harris and Blake could have held a grudge against him as well, dating back to events in Idaho. Sherrille is the anomaly. She obviously got Doris a job working for him so that would mean, unlike her husband and son, she didn't carry a grudge. Aargh! This is confusing as heck."

"I know. And it gets even more so. The only crystal-clear evidence was Mary Alice's yarn and she didn't have a motive. Or opportunity. Then there's the late Harris and the alive-and-well son, Blake. Most likely they fumed over that forty percent demand that Orlando made. There's motive for you."

"And that's only Orlando's murder. What about Harris? We know Sherrille was, and still is, having an affair with Jonesy, yet she went bonkers when she found Harris's old wedding ring. And, it was no secret he took lots of business trips. Maybe he *did* or *does* have another family. Oh my gosh! I'm worse than my mother."

Marshall laughed. "As long as you don't announce it over the radio at the top of your lungs to drown out Paul."

J. C. Eaton

By the time we finished dissecting suspects and moaning about how long those murder investigations dragged out, we had arrived at the bowling alley. Sure enough, the parking lot was packed and we had to walk from a spot behind the pickleball courts.

It was dark at that hour but the combination of solar and electric lights provided enough illumination, so I didn't have to worry about tripping over anything.

As we approached the lower entrance facing the auto restoration building, we heard a familiar voice. "Phee! Marshall! Isn't this exciting? If Gloria can hold herself together, her team might stand a chance at winning. They let Mary Alice out on bail. Or maybe it wasn't bail. I'm not sure."

I spun my head around and it was Myrna and Louise, with Myrna's voice booming.

Then another voice that sounded like a landmine exploding. "I'm here for the excitement. I figured things come in threes and we already had the lizards and the itching powder!"

It was Paul and I wanted to choke him right there and then. "We don't need any more excitement," I said. "The tournament will be enough."

"If Gloria doesn't have a breakdown." It was Louise. "I think she's worried sick that her online boyfriend or whatever you call him is being scammed or worse."

No, she is.

"The sheriff's office is looking into it. Gloria has nothing to worry about." I gave Marshall an elbow poke and he added, "Phee's right. Not a thing to worry about."

Then, as we opened the door to the complex, I spied my mother with Streetman and Essie's double stroller. "No, not a thing to worry about. *Two* of them!"

Behind my mother stood my aunt Ina in a flowing red skirt, a red blouse, and a black pashmina. Bright red ribbons were woven into her braids and from a distance she resembled an abstract version of Little Red Riding Hood.

As my mother motioned us over to her, I heard my aunt say, "Harriet, must you bring the dog and cat with you everywhere you go? I don't bring Louis and I'm married to him."

Then, my mother's response, "The dog has separation issues."

Marshall leaned over my shoulder and whispered, "The entire place will have issues by the time the night is done. Check it out—Bowman and Ranston are in Lizard Acres. I just caught sight of them."

"What? Why on earth would they be here?"

At that moment, Myrna, Louise and Paul thundered their way past us and into the alley itself. It was a regular crowd scene in the entryway as

164

people made their way into the bar or the alley. With Nomos closed, the complex felt tighter and cramped. Just then, Lyndy and Lyman approached us.

"Marshall, Phee, I need a word with both of you." Lyman tugged on his sweatshirt until it covered the belt on his jeans. "I wanted to give you a heads-up. I called the sheriff's office to alert them that something may be in the wind tonight."

Oh my gosh. First Paul, now Lyman.

"They got the message," Marshall said. "Bowman and Ranston are both here. What's going on?"

"Nothing definitive but a lot of scuttlebutt from the players on my team. They've been hearing rumors all week that whoever has been messing with the bowling alley has something planned for tonight."

I looked around, and other than a louder than usual crowd, everything seemed perfectly normal. That should have been my first clue not to let my guard down. As Marshall and Lyman spoke, Lyndy and I stepped off to the side and had our own conversation.

"I tried calling you but it went to voicemail." Lyndy threw her palms in the air.

"Oh good grief! I forgot that I muted the phone. Oh well, it wouldn't have mattered. I didn't think you'd be here."

"I didn't either but maybe we'll be able to pick up more murder clues. Looks like the entire community showed up. Never knew bowling was such a big deal."

"Apparently it is here. Along with bagels, bocce, and mystery books. Of course, those are just my mother's friends. And speaking of which, I see a bunch of them chatting behind that rope in the bowling alley."

"Your mother's male friends are here, too. Look! Isn't that Herb with something in his mouth?"

"A pretzel. A giant pretzel. They started to serve those at Lizard Acres. Bill, Kevin and Wayne are there, too."

"Any word on Gloria's situation?"

"It would take me all night. Let's just say *ongoing* for now. I'll fill you in tomorrow."

"All set?" Lyman asked Lyndy.

"Might as well find a spot to park ourselves. Catch you guys later!"

As the two of them walked toward the counter in the bowling alley, Marshall approached and squeezed my shoulder. "You go on in. I'll head to Lizard Acres to chat with Bowman and Ranston."

I glanced at the bar and it resembled a subway during rush hour. Still, I was able to spot Sherrille as well as Doris. They stood a few feet away from each other but that was soon to change. I wondered why I hadn't heard anything about a service or memorial for Harris, but then again, if Sherrille was complicit in his demise, I doubted she'd be in a hurry to memorialize him. As for Blake? It was anyone's guess. He could have been greedy enough as well, even though nothing pointed in his direction.

Next thing I knew, Lydia and Sue-Lynn made their way toward us.

Is there anyone who isn't here tonight? The Girl Scouts should be selling cookies.

"Have either of you seen my mother?" a frantic Sue-Lynn asked. "We checked with the team and Erik said he saw her a while ago but hasn't seen her since."

I looked at Marshall and then at the sisters. "She has to be around here. The tournament starts in less than twenty minutes. Did you check the ladies' room?"

"Uh-huh." Lydia stretched her neck and looked around as she spoke. "We didn't see her car in the parking lot either, but there were tons of cars on both sides of the complex so maybe we missed it."

Marshall looked around as well. "Could be she got a ride with one of her friends. We'll look around. Don't panic. I'm sure she's fine."

Sue-Lynn grabbed Lydia by the wrist. "Let's check the ladies' room again, okay?"

"I'll ask around. We'll look for you inside."

As the sisters took off for the restrooms, I moved closer to Marshall and kept my voice low. "You don't suppose she's off crying somewhere over that guy, do you?"

"Wouldn't surprise me. But where would she go around here? There are people everywhere."

"The dog park is across the parking lot and no one is there at this time. I'll drive over and you can keep an eye out here."

"Be careful."

Five minutes later, having surrendered our decent parking space, I drove to the dog park and sure enough, there was Gloria sobbing her eyes out on one of the benches beneath the canopy. I walked over and sat next to her, hoping no one left a bag of unpleasantries on the bench. It wouldn't be the first time.

The dim solar lighting made it difficult to see Gloria's face, but her sobs were audible.

"Phee! How did you know I was here?" she asked.

"Lucky guess. Everyone is worried about you. The tournament starts in less than fifteen minutes."

"The announcer will blab first. I still have time. Oh, Phee, this is awful. I'm positive my friend is being taken advantage of by a ruthless scammer. The deputies think *he's* behind the demands for money but that's not like him."

Just then, we heard voices carry in the still night air. They came from behind Meeker Mountain, a mound of rocks that was somehow sacred to Sun City West. I put my finger to my lips and we stopped talking and listened.

"Are you sure we don't have a choice?" It was a woman's voice and one that I'd heard before.

"Unless you fancy spending the rest of your life making license plates."

"Fancy." I know I've heard someone use that word in conversation. But who?

"Do you recognize those voices?" Gloria asked.

"Sort of. Shh! Keep listening."

"She knows too much," the first voice continued, "and we can't risk it. Tonight's got to be the night. Big crowd scene. I brought a lock pick. Getting her car open won't pose a problem. I know what she drives."

Then the voices faded out and we couldn't understand what else was said.

"They must have rounded the back part of Meeker Mountain," Gloria said. "Goodness! I think they're about to murder someone!"

CHAPTER 38

"I've got to let Marshall know about what we heard. Gloria, can you pull yourself together for the game? Everyone is counting on you. Come on, I'll drive you back. I'll let you off in front and then find a parking spot. All right?"

Gloria wiped her eyes with a wet, wadded-up tissue. "I suppose. I don't want to let my team down."

"Um, your daughters are here, too. I saw them when we walked in. That's why I drove here. When they didn't see you, they got concerned."

"Oh dear. We'd better get back. I'm ready. I hope what we think we overheard wasn't about murder."

"Me, too." *But I doubt it.*

Seconds later, I dropped Gloria off and found a better parking space. Then I rushed inside to find Marshall but ran into Bowman instead.

"There's something going on behind Meeker Mountain," I blurted out. "And you need to see who's there."

"Not another naked couple like we had a few months ago? Why do those jazzed-up seniors pick Meeker Mountain? I need to be right here in the bowling complex. I'll phone it in for the posse to check out."

"No, not a naked couple. Ew! I was in the dog park talking with Gloria and we heard two women talking about killing someone."

"They actually used the words *kill* or *murder*?"

"Alluded to it, but it was pretty obvious. You need to find out who they were. They mentioned recent events."

"I'll phone the posse. They can take names. *If* those women are still there. Most likely they're back here with this sea of humanity in the bowling alley."

And then, Bowman took off before I could finish my thought.

"Wait!" I shouted. "Hold on! Wait!" I rushed after him, colliding with at least three people. Bowman spun around and crossed his arms. "Now what? I was about to text the posse station."

"Good. They need to send a few cars to circulate around the parking lots in front and out back. With posse presence, it may deter whoever those killers are."

"*Alleged* killers, or *imaginary* killers. You may be overreacting."

"I'm not hard of hearing. It was pretty clear."

"The posse is making its rounds throughout the community. I can't bring all those cars here because of something you overheard."

"I think all the action in the community is right here. Right now. At least bring in a half dozen or so."

"We're not ordering donuts, Ms. Kimball. Gregory. Aargh. I am making the call. Are you satisfied?"

"Yes. Thank you."

While Bowman took his cell phone from his pocket, I charged off to see if I could locate Marshall. Instead, I ran into my mother and the circus that accompanied her.

"Phee!" she called out while pushing the dog and cat stroller toward me. "I heard Gloria is AWOL."

"Not anymore. I just dropped her off."

"Where was she?"

"At the dog park."

"With Thor? I don't think they'll allow a dog that size in here. And why was she in the dog park when she's supposed to be in that tournament?"

"Long story." I stood on my tiptoes and looked around. "Over to the left! Gloria's here."

"Come on, Harriet." Myrna and Lucinda, who stood by her side, gave her a nudge.

"Lordy, what a crowd," Shirley said. "Cecilia and Louise saved us seats by those front tables near the lanes. We'd better hurry."

"Did they save any for us?" Herb shouted. Behind him were Bill and Wayne. I imagined Kevin was in earshot as well.

"I don't know," Shirley responded.

And with that, the entire entourage wove its way to the lanes like *The Blob* from the 1950s horror movie, only they didn't devour everyone in sight, they merely trampled on them.

If I thought the place was crowded when Marshall and I first arrived, I seriously wondered if it exceeded occupancy code now. At least Lyman had the foresight to phone the deputies. Maybe his "gossip radar" wasn't far off, especially after the Meeker Mountain conversation Gloria and I heard.

"Hey, hon, I've been looking all over for you."

I turned and Marshall was by my side. "You're not going to believe this," I said, "but I think I might have overheard Orlando and Harris's killers. Let's move over to that alcove by the billiard room and I'll explain."

When I finished, he took out his phone and grimaced. "I'm texting Nate. He may want to join the fun. Maybe it's only a feeling I have, but given what you heard, and the fact that this crowd seems antsier than usual, his presence may be needed."

I nodded. "Good idea."

We walked to the tables by the lanes and sure enough, my mother's crew had commandeered three of them, adjacent to where Gloria and

Kenny's Lane Chasers were seated. With mouthfuls of snacks and enough soft drinks to last well into next week, everyone seemed contented. The stroller was at the edge of the table so that meant we needed to keep a wide berth, lest we knocked it over.

"Sit over here," my mother directed. "Next to your aunt Ina. She went to get some chips."

I took a seat but Marshall decided to wander about, just in case. Across from our tables were Lydia and Sue-Lynn. They waved and I waved back. For the time being, all was well with the world.

For the life of me, I tried to recall the voices from Meeker Mountain and associate them with the suspects we had. Unfortunately, I couldn't. Shirley, who was seated to my right, tapped me on the hand. "Oh, dear. I'm afraid Gloria's heart isn't in the game."

"You're not the only one. Look! Kenny's trying to give her a pep talk. He's jumping up and down in front of her and raising his hands in the air."

"Oh my gosh! That's not a pep talk. It looks like something is biting him." I got up from my seat and, bowling protocol or not, I ran over to him without wearing proper bowling shoes.

"What's going on?" I couldn't see anything on him, but obviously, there was.

"Something's biting me. Darn it. I'm taking my shirt off!"

In a flash, Kenny tossed his Lane Chaser shirt on the ground and Gloria shook it out. And while there was nothing on his body, a small lizard crawled out of his orange bowling shirt.

"It must have been a leftover from that debacle not too long ago," she said and handed him the shirt. "Looks like we're about to start. The announcer arrived."

I couldn't help but wonder how many more *debacles* would be in store for the evening but my thoughts were interrupted by the announcer.

"Good evening, everyone, and welcome to our long-awaited Red Pin Bowling Event. As you know, we have eight teams competing this evening and here goes the first game:

"The Desert Scorpions versus the Lane Chasers
"The Pin Spinners versus the Happy Rollers
"The Desert Bloomers versus the Alley-Oops
"The Ballbarians versus the Bowling Stones

"As you know, the winners of the first game are matched with another winning team until the final elimination game. Now, gear up, everyone! The first game is about to begin."

Marshall slid into his seat and told me Nate would arrive shortly. "Said he hoped for an excuse to get out of the house since Mr. Fluffypants was driving him crazy and wouldn't stop talking."

"Great." I chuckled. "He can trade an obnoxious parrot for the book club ladies tonight."

"Or Paul. Isn't that him over there, passing some photos around?"

"His recent catches. I was privy to see them earlier this week."

"Just so you know, I checked the parking lot. At least three posse cars are circling around. Hope that deters anyone from whatever they have planned."

"It might not deter them. Only relocate them. In a few minutes I'll mosey through the billiard hall as well as the outer perimeter. Seems the deputies have the bar covered."

"Guess I'll be glued to the action here."

A second later, the game began and the first bowlers approached their lanes. Erik started off the action for the Lane Chasers and had the first strike of the evening. For a minute, I thought the team was off to a good start, but I should have known better.

My aunt Ina arrived with a bag of potato chips and a bucket of popcorn. As she walked past Streetman's stroller to sit next to us, her long black pashmina caught on the arm and it teetered and teetered while she tried to get it to stand upright. That resulted in popcorn getting spewed all over and my mother barking orders like a four-star general.

"Ina, straighten out the stroller! Make sure my Streetman and my Essie are all right. Put your popcorn and chips down! I'm coming over." She pushed her chair back and bumped into everyone in the vicinity as she approached the aisle that separated the tables.

I jumped up to offer assistance but it was too late. The stroller cascaded to the ground and the meshing caught on the lip edge of the table and ripped. In a nanosecond, Streetman was at large.

"Harriet!" Myrna shrieked. "Your dog is loose!"

My aunt returned the stroller to its upright position and thankfully the cat was safe and sound in her part of the contraption. Too bad the same couldn't be said for the dog. He gobbled up all the kernels he could find and then eyeballed the bowling balls that were in motion.

"He's after that bowling ball, Harriet, do something!" This time it was Louise who shouted. And it wasn't any old bowling ball. It was Fred's brand-new three-dimensional ball with Betty Boop in the middle.

"Streetman!" my mother shouted. "You get back here right now!"

Too bad my mother forgot that her dog had selective hearing and a total disregard for obeying commands. I looked on in horror as that sneaky little chiweenie raced after the bowling ball, only to find himself slipping and sliding on the freshly oiled lane. Still, it didn't prevent him from following the ball and knocking down all the pins.

"Looks like your dog made a strike," Herb said. "Sign him up. The

Lane Chasers could use him."

At that point, the announcer stopped the competition and asked everyone to remain seated. "We have this under control," he said.

We do? In what alternate universe?

And then, the worst violation of bowling etiquette and procedure ever. In her wedge heels, my mother charged down the lane calling for her dog. In a matter of seconds, she slipped and skidded a few feet, landing on top of the lane's gutter.

Kenny and Fred rushed to help her up but they, too, struggled to maintain their balance.

"Can you hear me, Harriet?" Myrna yelled. "Whatever you do, don't bring your dog to our bocce tournament! We have enough problems."

I rolled my eyes and watched as the men removed my mother from the bowling lane and tried to coax the dog into leaving the pin-return area.

"He doesn't listen," I said. "He only responds to bribes. Hold on, I'm going into Lizard Acres to see if they have any cheese."

Amid the grumbles from the crowd, not to mention the bowlers, I rushed out of there to find some little tidbit to entice Streetman. What I didn't expect was to find Blake and Sherrille engaged in what appeared to be another of their heated arguments. This time in front of the now-closed Nomos Bistro.

Rats! I may miss a full-blown confession thanks to that unruly chiweenie!

CHAPTER 39

The only words I could catch as I charged into Lizard Acres were Blake's. "At least save face and do it." Do what? Harris's funeral? Continue to promote New Media Entertainment? Break up with Jonesy? Confess to murder? What?

They didn't notice me walk past them and I didn't acknowledge them either. Instead, I wrangled with the crowd at Lizard Acres to get to the bar, and hopefully get a piece of cheese from their kitchen. I glanced around for Bowman and Ranston but the crowd was thick and they could have been anywhere. Same with Marshall and Nate, who were probably there by now.

I nudged a couple as I leaned my elbow against the bar and called out for Jonesy, who was at the other end. "This is an emergency," I said.

He looked up. "Beer or wine?"

"Cheese. For a dog."

"I don't think I heard you right." He sauntered toward me and I explained what was going on in the bowling alley.

"Holy cannoli! If that doesn't top it all. Hang on. I'll see what I can find in the kitchen."

As I watched him go into the kitchen, I caught sight of Martha chatting with another woman. No doubt, the red pin event brought out everyone.

Seconds later, Jonesy returned with two slices of Swiss cheese. "Good luck! No charge!"

I thanked him and scurried out of the bar and back to the bowling alley. By now, Streetman's ruckus had escalated. The little stinker turned the bowling lane into his personal ice-skating rink and slid back and forth, having the time of his life. To make matters worse, Erik, Fred, and Kenny all tried to catch him while leaning over into the lane.

With the tournament on hold, the Pin Spinners, Happy Rollers, Desert Bloomers, Alley-Oops, Ballbarians, and Bowling Stones joined the Lane Chasers and the Desert Scorpions for a bird's-eye view of the fiasco.

"I hope you're happy," I muttered to my mother as I handed her a slice of Swiss cheese. "You've got to get him out of there."

As I glanced back at the Lane Chasers, I saw Gloria take out her cell phone and dab her eyes.

"I've almost got him," my mother called out as Streetman snatched the cheese from her. But just as her arms reached out to grab him, he bolted out of the lane, jumped into another one, and skidded all around. That's when he sniffed the air and made a mad dash toward Doris, who was seated a few tables over with an open bag of Cheetos. Her oversize pocketbook rested against the bottom of her chair.

This nightmare is never going to end.

With a remaining slice of cheese in my hand, I rushed to get to Doris's table before the dog did. No such luck. Streetman knocked over the contents of Doris's bag, letting loose a wallet, tissues, cough drops, glasses, papers, pens, lipstick, plastic utensils, wipes, business cards, and heaven knows what else on the floor.

"Sorry," I said as I tried not to step on the contents of her bag. "Got to get this dog." I frantically waved the cheese in front of me but knew I couldn't entice him and catch him at the same time.

"Will someone grab this dog?" I shouted. "I've got his attention."

"Does he bite?" a man asked.

Bites, snaps, growls, bares his teeth . . . you name it.

"Only if he's stressed."

Then, a miracle happened. Lydia and Sue-Lynn rushed over and together they snatched up Streetman and removed him from Doris's table. My mother immediately grabbed her little prince, thanked the sisters, and returned him to his stroller while a thundering round of applause took over the bowling alley. Then she handed me a small laser mouse.

"This is Essie's. You've seen it before. I have two of them. Hold on to it in case she escapes."

"She better not! That's all I can say!" I got down on my knees and picked up the contents of Doris's bag, all the while apologizing to her. *And he isn't even my dog!*

"Don't worry about the tissues and napkins," Doris said. "Just toss them. Got a message on my phone. I need to go to a quiet place and return the call. Thank goodness the phone was on the table."

I handed her the larger items and rounded up the ones for the trash. With the exception of a few business cards that I stashed in my pocket to give her when she returned, I had everything cleaned up in a matter of seconds.

Flushed and out of breath, I returned to my seat just as the announcer resumed the tournament.

"And that's why your dog should stay home," I whispered to my mother.

"It wasn't his fault. Your aunt knocked his stroller over."

"A stroller that doesn't belong in a bowling alley with a neurotic dog and cat in it!"

"Shh!" Bud waved his arms. "I can barely see. I need to hear what's going on."

As if nothing had happened, the tournament resumed as Erik walked Bud to the line and positioned him for his roll. I held my breath and was amazed the ball actually knocked down seven pins, including a red one.

"We're on a roll!" Fred shouted.

With his second roll, Bud knocked down another pin. I was astonished.

Next up was Gloria. She approached the lane like a high schooler headed for detention.

"You can do it, Mom!" Sue-Lynn called out.

At that moment, Marshall tapped me on the shoulder and whispered, "Nothing happening on this side of the parking lot. Let's talk."

I got up and followed him to the outside entrance, thankful I'd worn a heavy sweater since the February night air was chilly.

"What's going on? Have you seen Nate?"

"He's on the other side of the building, scoping out that end of the parking lot. What was that commotion in the bowling alley earlier? Don't tell me. A machine malfunction?"

"Worse. A Streetman malfunction. He got loose and slid his silly self all over the oiled lanes."

"How'd you get him back?'

"Got an hour?"

"Never mind. Tell me when we get home. Ranston thought he overheard something about trouble in the billiard room so he went over. Bowman's keeping an eye out in the bar and I'll watch the parking lot. You might as well go back and enjoy the tournament."

"*Enjoy* isn't actually the word I'd use, but yeah, I should go back. After I dump some tissues and napkins into the trash, compliments of Streetman's find. Thanks for keeping me posted."

"Anytime." He gave me a kiss on the cheek and stepped outside. I looked around for a trash bin but there were none in sight so I walked into the ladies' room and dumped the contents of my pocket onto the sink counter so I could separate tissues and napkins from business cards.

And as I did, I knew, without any shadow of doubt, who one of the killers was.

CHAPTER 40

I stared at the name in front of me and looked around to make sure I was the only one in the ladies' room. Then, I phoned Augusta.

She spoke before I could take a breath. "Are they sending in a militia at the bowling alley? Your name came up on caller ID."

"No, but they might. Augusta, you need to stop everything and look up something. I'm sorry if I'm interrupting one of your canasta games."

"Only thing you're interrupting is the *Yellowstone* marathon. I could look at Kevin Costner all day and night."

"Put Kevin Costner on hold. I found Doris Tucker's Arizona driver's license and it reads 'Doris Olsen Tucker.' The *O* in the middle would make her initials DOT. That's what everyone calls her—Dot. But why would the name Tucker appear after Olsen?"

"Maybe when her husband died, she went back to her maiden name. Lots of women do that."

"I think she was married to the man who ratted out the Wainwrights. Can you find out if Doris Tucker was married to a Clyde Olsen, who was a contractor? Check Pocatello, Idaho. In fact, check everything you can on Clyde Olsen. If he was alive today, he'd be in his late fifties or sixties."

"Got it. Clyde Olsen. The whistleblower that Mr. Williams mentioned. The one who suffered a deadly accident, right?"

"Uh-huh. Only I don't think it was an accident."

"You think the Wainwrights made it appear like an accident and now Doris wants stone-cold revenge?"

"And how! And worse yet, I think the whodunits are going to knock off the who-knows-it tonight."

"Speak English. Maybe I should just show up with reinforcements. The boys are hankering for some action."

"Tell Mr. Smith and Mr. Wesson to stay home. I need you to find out about Clyde."

"On it! I'll text as soon as I find something."

"Thanks, Augusta."

"My pleasure. And don't you become a target. Got it?"

"You sound like Nate and Marshall."

"Good!"

When I ended the call, I returned to the bowling alley. The tournament was in full gear as if none of the malarkey had ever happened. Bowlers approached the lanes and took their turns, including Gloria, who had finally stopped sniveling and sobbing.

Cassie amazed everyone with two strikes that enabled the Lane Chasers to win the first round. Now they were up against the Ballbarians with a ten-minute break in between. It was down to four teams with the Desert Bloomers and the Pin Spinners facing off.

"I need to stretch," I said to my mother. "Be back in a bit."

"Do you want to take the dog?"

"No! He can stretch when you get home."

I stepped out of the bowling alley and into the billiard room. Whatever rumor Bowman heard, nothing appeared out of the ordinary. Mini-Moose was laughing and chatting with the crowd and in the rear of the room, I spotted Lyndy and Lyman having their own good time. I was thankful she'd met a decent man who had a terrific sense of humor and treated her well.

Next, I meandered to Lizard Acres and the same could be said for the atmosphere in there. It was as if the chaos that took over the beginning of the tournament dissipated as the evening wore on. I began to think that maybe I'd been wrong about what Gloria and I overheard, but seconds later, Augusta texted me and goose bumps covered my arms.

Doris Tucker married a Clyde Olsen in Chubbuck, Idaho. That's north of Pocatello. Call me.

This time, I stepped outside and made sure I buttoned my sweater to the top, rivaling Cecilia with those black cardigans of hers. I walked a few yards past the entrance and backed up against the wall. Then I phoned Augusta.

"That was fast," I said.

"It is when you've got Rolo on speed-dial and an extra burner phone in the house. He helped with the first part of your request."

"I only made one part."

"Well, I added another and you're going to want to hear it."

I took a breath. "Tell me."

"Doris Adelaide Tucker was married to Clyde Olsen, a contractor in Pocatello who had the misfortune to work on a high-rise project for the Wainwrights. He blew the whistle on them for shoddy materials that they were using on a job site. Said they misrepresented their initial proposal to the city council and put the workers in jeopardy."

"Uh-oh. I believe I know the rest. Bud explained some of it. He's from that area."

"Did he explain that Clyde fell from a scaffold and as a result could no longer work? He passed away not too long after, leaving Doris in financial difficulties. Seems like a heck of a good motive for murder, wouldn't you say?"

"And then some. I wonder how Sherrille fits in to all of this. She was the one who got Doris her job with Orlando when he relocated to Arizona and ran that senior care community business."

"A payoff."

"Huh?"

"Honey, from what I know, Sherrille's no dummy. Last thing she needed was for Doris to badmouth her husband and son's New Media Entertainment business. What better way than to entice Doris to keep her mouth shut? But along with that shut mouth came her plan for revenge."

"Oh my gosh. You might be right."

"Hey, it's not only nepotism that puts people in jobs that everyone else wants. Sometimes it's downright *quid pro quo*. And in this case, the *quid* would be Sherrille getting Doris a better job and the *pro quo* would mean Doris zips her mouth shut."

"Augusta, planning revenge is one thing, carrying it out is another. I think Doris is one of our killers. And I know she's not working alone."

"Like I said, *be careful* and let the deputies and our guys handle it. I'll keep my phone near me if you need me tonight. And remember, the boys are always at the ready."

Just what we need. Augusta Hatch with her fingers on the trigger.

I walked back inside to see Bowman running from the billiard room into Lizard Acres. And he wasn't the only one. A crowd started to form and the words I overheard on Meeker Mountain looped back into my head— *Tonight's got to be the night. She knows too much.*

I saw Marshall straight ahead and rushed to catch up. In a frantic move, involving more sidestepping and elbowing than I imagined possible, I was finally able to grab him by the arm.

"What happened? Don't tell me those women Gloria and I overheard pulled off another murder in Lizard Acres. They mentioned the parking lot and a car."

"No, Nate texted me. There was a small lizard encased in one of the ice cubes in someone's drink. The woman went berserk and naturally, the crowd reacted. I'm leaving the deputies to deal with this mess. You might as well go back and watch the rest of the tournament. I'll keep an eye on the parking lot from this entrance and Nate will do the same out front."

"Look at this." I handed him Doris's driver's license and studied the expression on his face.

"Olsen. The contractor. Darn good motive. Wish we had more to go on."

"She had motive and means. As a waitress, she could have easily snipped that yarn from Mary Alice. Plus, she could have been one of those voices I heard."

"I know. The posse cars will keep circling the parking lot until the tournament is over. Best we can do at this point."

"I know. I better go see how the Lane Chasers are doing."

By the time I walked back to the bowling alley, the Lane Chasers had beaten the Ballbarians and were about to take on the Pin Spinners for the final game. I ambled back to my seat at the table and ran into Herb, who had an armload of small potato chip bags, pretzel bags, and Dorito bags.

His voice all but shook the walls. "Hey there, cutie! Had to use my last change on the vending machine. They've got Lizard Acres closed temporarily. Something to do with someone's drink. It better not have been poisoned."

"Poisoned? Someone's drink was poisoned?" It was Paul, who was a few feet away showing more photos of fish to some poor woman.

"What?" a man from the crowd shouted. "Someone got poisoned in Lizard Acres?"

"Murdered? We had another murder tonight? Right under our noses?" This time it was Madge, who, like Herb, had an armload of vending machine snacks.

Within seconds, people scrambled to spread the rumor like hair lice in a kindergarten, and I knew if it reached my mother's table, the book club ladies would waste little time circulating and embellishing it.

With no time to waste, I all but tackled the poor announcer, who had just introduced the final competitors.

"You've got to make another announcement," I said. "No one was murdered in Lizard Acres."

Unfortunately, the announcer had earbuds in and didn't hear my full sentence, resulting in him repeating what he thought he heard. Only he did it with the microphone on.

"What's this you said about a murder in Lizard Acres?"

And that was all it took to put the final game on hold as the crowd hurried to the door.

I reached for the mic and in my loudest voice, I shouted, "Wait! Stop! No one was murdered. And Lizard Acres is closed for now."

"Why are they closed if no one was killed?" someone yelled.

"Food issues in the kitchen. Everyone, please return to your seats."

It took a few minutes for the bowling alley to return to normalcy but that couldn't be said for Lizard Acres. As I looked out at the lobby, I saw that it was still closed and that some posse volunteers stood in the entryway. I hoped they weren't called away from their cars because that would mean a wide-open opportunity should it turn out there was a real threat from those women on Meeker Mountain.

Resigned that there was little I could do at that point, I moved toward my mother's table. And in doing so, I caught a glimpse of Doris and Martha in what appeared to be a rather serious conversation. I maneuvered closer to them and even though the noise level was far from low, I was able to hear them.

"Text her and tell her to meet us at her car. Do it but give me a lead to get there first. She'll be parked in front of the social hall but way down by the road. Heaven forbid anyone park near that Mercedes of hers and put a scratch on it."

Oh my gosh. The second player is Martha.

I shot off a text to Marshall but there was no response. Same with Nate. I figured both of them must have gotten tied up with that Lizard Acres fiasco. I wasn't sure who the third party was, or who owned the Mercedes, but I had a good hunch. And if I was right, Sherrille Wainwright would be the next victim.

I turned away from Doris and Martha but kept them in my side vision. Then I followed them out of the bowling alley and prayed they wouldn't turn around to see me. Thanks to the situation at Lizard Acres, there were no posse cars on this side of the building and the lower part of the parking lot appeared darker than usual. A light pole out, maybe?

It didn't matter. If Sherrille Wainwright was going to be victim number three, I'd have to stop her before she got to her car. I positioned myself behind a mesquite tree and waited for Sherrille. Martha took off and thundered downhill to the lower part of the lot. I spotted her figure by a white Mercedes but she vanished in an instant. Apparently, the woman knew how to pick a car lock.

So this is how it's done—skootch down behind the driver's seat and when the engine starts, surprise the person with a quick toss of yarn over their head, a tight pull, and good night for good!

I imagined Doris would wait until she spotted Sherrille by the car and then make her move. That meant I'd have to prevent Sherrille from ever getting there. Looking around, she was nowhere in sight. And neither was anyone else.

I bit my lip, took a breath, and pulled my sweater tighter. Then, of all things, a dark SUV pulled up near Sherrille's car and dropped her off. Rats! She had gotten a ride from someone, maybe even Blake, but whoever it was took off within seconds.

Knowing that if I were to yell at her and race down there, Doris would distract her and Martha would exit the car, leaving me to look like a fool. I had no choice. Like it or not, I had to catch them in the act, or at least catch then initiating it.

By now, I watched as Doris made her way to the car. I skirted off to the side and ducked behind the parked vehicles at the top and midsection of the lot until I reached the one Chrysler van that was adjacent to the Mercedes.

It was a miracle I snuck behind the van without being seen. Now, all I had to do was wait until Sherrille got inside her car and Martha made her straight-out-of-the-movies move. Unfortunately, a slight tremor in my hands appeared out of nowhere and I clenched them as tight as I could. I should have thought about Sherrille but instead, my only thought was that this is the scene in all those movies where someone sneaks up from behind.

I turned my head and was relieved that Martha and Sherrille were in the car with Doris leaning over the window and talking. Her voice carried in the quiet night air and what I heard astonished me.

"It's about time you got here. I take it you got my text."

"Yeah. Now all we have to do is find *her*. We were right about one thing, Doris. Tonight's the night. Everyone is going nuts inside that place. No one's even here and those posse cars are parked out front. They needed the volunteers in Lizard Acres. And by the way, why are you sitting in the backseat, Martha?"

Oh no! She's going to make her move!

"Because your front seat has pet hair."

"Oh brother. Good thing for us Mary Alice is never without yarn. Got lots of leftovers. Okay, I say we send you, Sherrille, back inside to find her. Tell her you need to speak privately with her and ask her to walk with you away from the building. I doubt she'll suspect anything."

"Then what?"

"Then we do what we've done."

They're going to kill Mary Alice! With her own yarn, no less!

I didn't stop to think about the why. I reached into my bag to get my cell phone but a motorcycle sped down RH Johnson with so much noise that it took me by surprise and I dropped my bag on the ground.

"Someone's here!" Martha shouted. "Behind the van!"

That was the second I knew my plan was about to fail.

CHAPTER 41

As I bent down to retrieve my bag, Sherrille and Doris approached me, with Martha only a few steps behind.

"I imagine you overheard us," Doris said.

"I did."

"That's too bad," she replied.

"Everyone will be exiting soon. You won't get away with murdering Mary Alice."

"Mary Alice?" I thought Martha would burst out laughing. "Why on earth would we want to kill her? And what? Lose our favorite fall guy, or in this case, fall girl."

"I don't understand." With the bag hanging by my side, I tried to discreetly unzip it and turn on my cell phone but Sherrille caught sight of my plan.

She took a small taser from her pocket and directed it at me. "Drop your bag on the ground."

I did as she said. Next, she kicked my bag off to the side and it slid under the van.

This is SO not good.

"You saved us the bother, Phee," Sherrille said. "It was you we hoped to snare, not Mary Alice. Don't take us for fools. We know what you and your mother have been up to. Not to mention those friends of hers who can't keep their mouths shut."

"So you plan on killing me right here in the parking lot?"

"Don't be ridiculous. We're all going to take a nice little ride. Isn't that right, ladies?" Sherrille looked at Doris and Martha, who both chuckled. Then she aimed the taser at me and motioned for me to get into her car. "Please. Take the passenger seat. Be my guest."

She opened the door and I put my left foot inside, but instead of getting into the seat, I remembered something in my right pocket. Slowly, so as not to cause suspicion, I reached into the pocket and retrieved Essie's laser toy.

Then, with a speed I didn't know I had, I flashed it in front of Sherrille's eyes so as to blind her momentarily. "Give me the taser if you don't want this to be permanent," I said.

"Don't do it, Sherrille," Doris yelled. She stood behind Sherrille and I moved the laser toy again. This time shaking it so that the red beam bounced in front of Doris's face. It caught her off guard and she stumbled into Sherrille, who dropped the taser. This time, it was me who got out of the car and kicked it out of reach and under the Mercedes.

"Don't just stand there," Martha shouted. "Grab her."

"I'm warning you," I said. "This laser has two speeds and I used the mild one. The pulsating one came with a warning for use. Make one move and you'll never cook another meal at your bistro."

Then, with the laser pointing at Sherrille, I said, "Hand me your car keys. And don't throw them."

She extended her arm and put the keys into the palm of my hand. In that instant, I pushed the siren button on the key fob and kept it on full blast. Then, I looked at Doris and Martha. "Your keys, too."

I wasn't sure if the signal would work, but it was worth the try. "No quick moves or this goes on pulsating."

Martha handed me her keys, followed by Doris. I immediately pushed the siren alarms and prayed the signal would reach. Sure enough, I heard two distinct noises from the top of the parking lot.

Come on, someone. Go outside to see what the ruckus is.

"Stay where you are," I shouted. This time in a voice like a canon.

"You can take the fall," Martha said. She shoved Doris toward me and turned to run. I was terrified they'd know I bluffed about the pulsating signal. But in an instant, a bowling ball came out of nowhere on a straight line in Martha's direction, picking up speed thanks to the parking lot's incline. I watched, wide-eyed and mouth open, as it slammed into Martha's ankle. She let out a yowl and fell to the ground. What followed next were a series of expletives as Sherrille and Doris looked on.

"I heard everything!" Cassie shouted. "I walked to my van to get another bowling ball since the oil pattern on the lane hates my other ball. At first, I thought all of you were just chatting and went about my business, but then, well, I heard what I heard."

Martha got on all fours and tried to stand but the blow from the bowling ball resulted in her wobbling for a few seconds before she limped back to Sherrille's Mercedes.

Just then, a car turned into the drive off of 138th Avenue, but instead of going into the supermarket, the driver approached us and got out of his car. His stocky build and three-piece suit were unmistakable.

"Uncle Louis!" I shouted. "What are you doing here?"

"I should ask you the same thing. What happened? Someone's battery died?"

"No. You're looking at three murderesses who tried to add me to their list. Call 911. Call Marshall. Call Aunt Ina."

"I'll start with 911."

It was only a minute or so but it seemed like a hundred. Next thing I knew, Bowman and Ranston drove to the bottom of the parking lot with their red and blue flashers on and that annoying siren of theirs.

"This isn't what it looks like," Sherrille announced as Bowman pulled up next to Cassie's van, slamming his car door behind him.

"No, it's worse!" Cassie said. "And I heard it all. Arrest those women for murder. Full-blown, first-degree murder!"

"Who are you?" Bowman neared Cassie while perusing the situation in the parking lot.

"Cassie Wyatt. I'm one of the Lane Chasers and I came out here to get a different bowling ball. My team is in the final leg of the tournament. I can't stand here. They need me. And by the way, you guys have guns. Don't be afraid to use them."

Before Bowman could say a word, Cassie raced to her van and drove it to the front entrance, ignoring the *No Parking* sign. I looked as she took off and prayed she didn't run over my bag.

"Take notes!" Bowman shouted to Ranston.

My uncle Louis and I stared at them without saying a word. I needed a few seconds to get my thoughts in order, but Sherrille didn't. She put her hands in the air and then clasped them together as if it was a stage performance. "Whatever those women tell you, I was not part of their murder scheme."

"Cut the crap, Sherrille. You were as much a part of this as Doris," Martha said.

"What?" Doris pointed a finger at Martha. "You were the brainchild if I'm not mistaken."

"I don't care who was the mastermind. I'm booking all of you for suspicion of murder." Bowman took out an iPad and proceeded to fumble with it. "Darn technology. I liked pencil and pad better." Then he handed the iPad to Ranston. "You fill this out."

Ranston put his pad in his jacket pocket and whispered to Bowman, "Which homicide?"

"Oh, never mind. We'll sort it out at the posse station."

In all of the chaos, the sirens on Martha's and Doris's cars kept blasting. That sent a crowd of folks into the parking lot and down toward us when they caught sight of the red and blue flashers. To add to the situation, the crowd included Paul, Herb, and Wayne. At least my mother and the ladies were still in the bowling alley, as far as I knew.

Bowman must have called the posse because a few seconds later, two posse cars appeared.

"I want one woman in each car," Bowman said to the posse volunteers. "Mrs. Wainwright can be the first to get in." He pointed to the posse car and Sherrille dutifully got inside. Then, Martha in the next posse car, and finally, Doris, who stood in front of Bowman and Ranston's car waiting for a directive.

"I really should get back to the bowling alley," I said. "And I need to grab my bag. It was under Cassie's van."

"Not so fast. We need your statement as well. Meet us at the posse office."

"Just give me five minutes to touch base with my mother, and my husband."

"Touch base now, because your husband is headed this way."

Sure enough, Marshall strode toward us, only a few feet ahead of the crowd.

"Cassie came screaming into the bowling alley lobby," he said. "We were in the billiard room and heard her." Then he gave me a hug. "Are you all right?"

"I'm fine. Thanks to Essie's toy. I'll explain later. If it wasn't for Cassie and then Uncle Louis showing up, that might not have been the case."

Louis nodded at Marshall. "Just got done with a birthday gig and thought I'd pop over and surprise Ina. She's always saying I never get to do things with her because I'm always playing the sax. Now I know why. Always the unexpected around here."

"Phee!" Lyndy's voice halted whatever else my uncle was about to say. "Lyman and I heard what just happened. Cassie announced it when she barreled through the door. Oh my gosh! All three of those women killed Orlando and Harris?"

"What? Who killed Orlando and my father?" It was Blake. He elbowed his way to us and looked around. "Where's my mother? Someone said she was out here."

"In the posse car on the left," Ranston said. "You might want to save her some time and call your lawyer."

"What? Are you implying my mother is a murderess?"

"We don't imply. We gather evidence and make arrests. I suggest you drive to the posse station and have a brief chitchat with her."

Blake charged to the posse car and shouted at Sherrille through the window, "What did you do?"

Meanwhile, a frantic Jonesy appeared in time to hear Blake yelling at his mother and then to anyone who would listen. "They think she killed Orlando and my dad."

While Blake and Jonesy continued to shout at Sherrille through the car window, I approached Bowman. "You know this is going to be a long, long night. May I please return to the bowling alley to see the end of the tournament?"

He opened his mouth to speak, but I beat him to it. "And keep my mother and her dog from going to the posse office?"

"She's got the dog with her?"

I nodded.

"Fine. Make sure that little snapper-yapper goes home. We'll expect you later for a statement."

"With pleasure."

The posse cars with Sherrille and Martha pulled out of the lot and turned onto RH Johnson Boulevard en route to the posse office. Then, once Doris got into the backseat of Bowman and Ranston's vehicle, they opened the doors and got in.

"Hold on." Nate rushed over from a few yards away. He then walked to the driver's side of the car and spoke with Bowman. "One more person needs to be booked. But not for felony murder. More like vandalism and endangerment. That *is* the correct term for wanton or reckless behavior, isn't it?"

"Who? What?"

Nate tilted his head in Blake's direction. "The young Mr. Wainwright is the party responsible for the lizard outbreak as well as the itching powder incident."

"You can't prove anything," Blake said. "Not a darn thing."

"Oh, I can't prove it but Mini-Moose sure can."

By now, the small circle of curiosity seekers had grown to encompass most of the lower parking lot. They budged, elbowed and nudged their way to get a closer look at Blake, who stood adjacent to Nate, all the while complaining about the red and blue flashers that the deputies refused to turn off.

"You see," Nate said, "Mini-Moose was positive someone was stealing all the napkins and straws from the bowling alley as well as Lizard Acres and the billiard room. So, a few months ago, he bought six nanny cams from Amazon and set them up in those rooms without telling anyone. Said he didn't want to make the patrons nervous. Then Orlando wound up dead and Mini-Moose forgot all about those napkins and straws. That is, until tonight."

"Is that so, Mr. Wainwright?" Bowman asked. "You sabotaged the bowling complex?"

"I'm not saying anything to anyone without my attorney present."

"Then your attorney may want to watch the footage from those nanny cams. Mini-Moose made a copy for our office and Mr. Williams will be dropping them off once the complex clears out."

Again, Blake reiterated what he said before. "I won't speak without my lawyer."

Bowman shrugged. "No skin off my back. I collect my salary whether you talk to me or your lawyer." Then he turned to Ranston. "Read him his rights. Looks like the evidence will hold up in his case."

Then, back to Blake. "You'll have to share the backseat with Mrs. Tucker. And not a word out of either of you."

Nate moved closer to us and explained that he planned on sticking around at the bowling complex since Bowman and Ranston wouldn't be there. "I'll drop off the videos and then head home. Boy, what a night."

The three sheriff's vehicles left the parking lot, leaving the spectators to take whatever morsels of information they might have overheard and spin them into their own versions of who killed whom.

"I didn't hear everything," Herb called out to Marshall and me. "Who did what?"

Marshall spoke loud enough so that anyone in the vicinity would hear. "You'll have to catch the early morning news. Meanwhile, I suggest everyone return for the tournament. It should be ending pretty quick."

"I'm surprised my mother and the ladies didn't rush down here," I said.

"That's because it was super loud in the alley with everyone cheering on their teams. Come on, we might as well enjoy the final minutes. Last I heard, it was pretty close between the Lane Chasers and the Pin Spinners."

When we approached my mother's table, it was Gloria's turn. I stood and held my breath she wouldn't get a gutter ball. Apparently, I wasn't the only one. The room quieted down as if everyone shared the same thought.

We watched as the ball moved gracefully down the lane until it hit a dry spot from the oiling. Then, it veered off and a chorus of exasperated sighs filled the room. Then, all of sudden, it hit another spot, wobbled and moved slowly down the center toward a bright red pin smack dab in the front.

I was afraid if the ball moved any slower it would stop before reaching the pins. Gloria must have had the same idea because she motioned with her hands for the ball to keep moving. Then, to our astonishment, it knocked down a few pins and those pins knocked down others and before we knew it, Gloria had a strike.

The cheers from her team and friends drowned out any conversation.

"Do you think they know about the arrests?" I asked Marshall.

He shook his head. "I doubt it. Cassie probably didn't say anything because she didn't want to spook the team. Don't worry, when the tournament is over, she'll make up for it."

My mother, who was fixated on Gloria, heard Marshall's voice and turned to us. "Where have you been? The game will be over in a matter of minutes and it is neck and neck. Mary Alice is next. Looks like Cassie just whispered something to her. Must be she's wishing her luck."

Or telling her who stole her robin's egg blue yarn.

I prayed I was wrong. Sadly, I wasn't. Instead of Mary Alice approaching the lane with a bowling ball, she announced, "I'm going to the posse office. Now! Bud is next on the lineup."

"You can't go, Mary Alice," Kenny shouted. "You're our last chance."

"Thanks a lot," Bud said.

Mary Alice put her bowling ball in its bag and took off. Her parting words were "I'll make sure they pay for this!"

CHAPTER 42

"Uh-oh," I said to Marshall as Mary Alice stormed out of the bowling alley. "I hope she meant *pay* in a figurative sense."

"Hate to do this, but I think I'm going to be needed at the posse office. Want to join me or get a ride later with your mother?"

"Are you kidding?" I elbowed my mom and whispered, "Tell me who wins. We're following Mary Alice."

"Why is she going to the posse office? Do you know?"

"Um, I can take a guess. I'll call you in a few minutes, and whatever you do, don't go over there."

"Why would I go over there? Oh look, Kenny and Fred are helping Bud with his approach."

I rolled my eyes. Given the score, which was in full view on an overhead screen, it would take a full-blown miracle for Bud to ensure the Lane Chasers emerged victorious.

"We'd better hurry," Marshall said. "No telling what she'll do."

I waved goodbye to my aunt and uncle as well as the book club ladies and the men. A few minutes later, we pulled up to the posse office and went inside. No sign of Mary Alice but that didn't mean anything. She might have gone home first to . . . to what? Get a gun? I tried to dismiss that thought and instead focused on the room.

It had had a slight makeover since the last time I was in there. Newer chairs and office arrangement. A few posse volunteers were in the outer room, where Doris sat on one side and Martha on the other.

I peered into Bowman's office and spied Sherrille seated with her arms crossed. It was a similar setup in Ranston's office, only this time it was Blake and he wasn't seated. Instead, he paced up and down, looking at his watch every few seconds.

"Must be he's expecting his lawyer," I said to Marshall.

Then, like a microburst out of nowhere, Mary Alice thundered inside and shouted, "I want those two women arrested for theft. Outright theft! Does anyone hear me?"

Who couldn't?

Bowman and Ranston both left their offices and raced toward her. Mary Alice still continued her outburst. "Do you have any idea how expensive robin's egg blue yarn is? It's a rare and coveted color!"

Undaunted, Bowman walked to one of the desks, picked up a form, and handed it to Mary Alice. "You'll need to fill out this complaint. Include a receipt for the purchase should your complaint result in an arrest."

"You already arrested them, didn't you?"

I've heard Bowman groan before, but this time, it was much louder. "Not for stealing blue yarn!"

"And implicating me for murder. I want a new arrest. A brand-new arrest!" Mary Alice was adamant.

"Fine!" Bowman handed her another form and told her to complete that one as well. Then he noticed me and pointed to the conference room. "Good. We'll need a statement. Make yourself comfortable. I want to hear this firsthand, too, once you've completed and signed your statement. Those forms are on the credenza along with pens."

"No problem."

"Help yourself to the coffee but there are no guarantees that it's fresh."

"I'm fine."

I went into the conference room, closed the door behind me and watched as he and Marshall spoke. When I completed my statement and opened the door, I overheard Bowman tell Marshall that an off-duty deputy swung over to the bowling alley to bring Cassie in for her statement.

Seconds later, a middle-age man in khakis, long-sleeved shirt and tie walked in. He carried a briefcase and asked to speak with Blake and Sherrille Wainwright. Yep, they wasted no time rousing their lawyer from whatever he was doing on a Saturday night.

Looking around, every corner had its own mini-circus going on. Still, everything was under control. Then, Bowman and Marshall walked to the conference room and joined me. For the next ten or fifteen minutes I explained what had happened and provided my explanation of the motives behind the murders.

"You're not going to release them, are you?" I looked directly at the craggy deputy.

"Heck no! Once we have Ms. Wyatt's statement, and we can verify it parallels yours, Mrs. Wainwright, Mrs. Tucker, and Mrs. McMillan will be taken to the Fourth Avenue Jail, where they'll wait for an arraignment. They'll make a plea and bail will be up to the judge. Of course, it's Saturday night so don't expect anything until Monday."

"What about Blake?"

"We'll hold him here for seventy-two hours and go from there. His crimes lean in the direction of misdemeanors but some types of vandalism are considered felonies. He'll be arraigned as well."

I'm not sure if it was sympathy on Bowman's part, but he looked at Marshall and me and said, "You might as well go home. We've got enough deputies and posse volunteers here to make sure no one makes a break for it."

"I doubt Martha will. Cassie's bowling ball struck her ankle pretty hard."

"Hmm, I'd better call an EMT or next thing you know, she'll sue us." Then he got up and walked to his own office.

"Might as well leave while the moment's right," Marshall said. "We'll get the whole story in the morning."

"And you'll probably have to show up here."

"Could be worse. Could be one of the book club brunches."

"Oh no! That reminds me. I'd better call my mother."

"Do it from the car."

No sooner did Marshall start the engine when I placed a call. Only it wasn't to my mother. It was to Augusta, who peppered me with questions.

"You don't say? Too bad that bowling ball didn't wipe out both of her ankles. Thanks for letting me know. I'll expect Monday to be busier than usual."

"Does that mean you'll bring donuts?"

"Nope. Strudel, fruit turnovers and apple fritters. Trying to eat healthy."

I laughed. "Good deal."

Next, I phoned my mother, whose voice was a foghorn. "I had to find out everything from Cassie after you and your husband took off to follow Mary Alice. Cassie said you were nearly murdered! Had I known, you could have taken Streetman with you for protection."

Like a cap gun in a war zone.

"Are you all right?" my mother went on. "I tried your phone but your voicemail was full."

"I'm fine. Marshall's fine, but Doris, Martha and Sherrille will be spending the night downtown. And please—don't say anything to anyone until tomorrow. Okay?"

"Not a problem. We'll all be celebrating at Bagels 'n More at eleven tomorrow. Good thing Shirley thought ahead and reserved us three long tables."

"Celebrating?"

"The Lane Chasers won! Bud actually made a strike! I don't know who was more surprised, him or the team."

"That's wonderful. Enjoy yourselves."

"You mean, *ourselves.* You have to be there, too, Phee. You're the only one who knows what really happened. If you don't tell us, we'll have to piece it together from Mary Alice and Cassie. Oh, and Paul."

"Paul? He arrived on scene later."

"He might have arrived later, but that busy mouth of his didn't. He'll be yakking to everyone tonight."

I shuddered. "Fine. Eleven. Bagels 'n More. Marshall may not be there. Most likely he'll be with the deputies."

"They can come too."

"Doubtful. Exceedingly doubtful. See you in the morning."

Marshall looked over at me and burst out laughing. "I can picture it now. Paul will spin a fish tale like nobody's business and the book club ladies will come up with their own scenarios for what took place. For once, I'm keeping my fingers crossed Bowman and Ranston call a meeting so I'll be tied up."

CHAPTER 43

I was right about Nate and Marshall having to show up at the posse office the next day. Only it had more to do with Gloria's cyber-scam romancer than the arrests made for murder. According to Bowman, the women turned on each other like hyenas after food. Still, their official pleas wouldn't be made before a judge until Monday.

As for Blake, his lawyer got him released on a desk appearance ticket since he didn't pose a real threat to the community; and, truth be told, his sabotaging of the bowling complex was more of a fraternity prank than a serious felony, although some of the residents may have felt otherwise.

Bagels 'n More was packed when Marshall and I got there. In spite of checking his text messages every few seconds in the hope he'd be called away, poor Marshall had no excuse to bow out of brunch.

It was a Sunday morning and eleven was usually the time church members arrived after services. However, news had traveled fast about the arrests and it seemed as if everyone in Sun City West wanted to hear the latest.

With the exception of Cecilia and Lucinda, who went to a later service at St. Stephens, all of the book club ladies were there, including my aunt. The pinochle men and the Lane Chasers were there as well, with a couple of additions—Paul and Mini-Moose. I imagined Jonesy kept a wide berth given the circumstances.

I invited people as well—Lyndy and Lyman. It was high time they got introduced to the reason pharmaceutical companies make antacids. As I said my hellos, they approached the tables and I introduced them.

Marshall and I sat at the end of a table with Gloria next to me and my mother directly across. Thankfully, Herb and Paul were at the third table down so I didn't have to worry about looking at photos of fishing spots or fighting for the cream cheese spreads on the table. And, to ensure we'd get out of the place before dark, two waitresses took the orders instead of the usual one.

With few exceptions, most of the folks could recite the menu by heart, but still, it was a process just to listen to the orders. Watching our waitress gave new meaning to the expression nerves of steel.

"Do you have small-curd light cottage cheese?"

"It says gluten-free but is it GMO?"

"Are the tomatoes locally sourced? I don't like hothouse tomatoes."

Once the orders were in, the topic immediately jumped to last night's arrests and all eyes were on Marshall and me.

"The news anchors on KPHO said arrests were made in the murders of Orlando Fleish and Harris Wainwright but they didn't elaborate. They said to stay tuned for further developments in those cases," Myrna said.

"Channel 10 had the names—Martha McMillan, Doris Tucker, and Sherrille Wainwright." Louise leaned over to look at Myrna.

"Name, rank, and serial number. That's all we'll get." Kenny took a gulp of his coffee and turned toward me. "You were in the thick of it, Phee. Tell us what happened. Cassie said you were nearly murdered in the parking lot."

"It was harrowing, that's for sure. I'll piece together what I know, since it won't come as a surprise and I'm pretty sure it will be all over social media by the time we get out of here."

Just then, Cecilia and Lucinda walked in and rushed to our table. Cecilia couldn't wait to speak. "It was all over church that Martha and Doris conspired to kill Orlando and Harris like those men did in *Strangers on a Train*."

"What train? Where? I can't hear everything back here at the far table." Bill stood and repeated his question.

A chorus of "It's an Alfred Hitchcock movie" followed, and that's when I prayed our orders would arrive soon. I looked at the two women and bit my lip. "What else did you hear?"

This time Lucinda jumped in. "Sherrille was having an affair and had to get Harris out of the way. Three different women told me that this morning. And get this, Sherrille was convinced he was a bigamist."

"Um, why don't you two sit down and flag a waitress for your orders? I'll tell everyone what will soon be common knowledge."

"Go on, Phee," my aunt Ina said. "Once the food gets here, no one will care."

If nothing else, my eyes got plenty of exercise rolling around in my head. "Fine. Here goes. Martha never forgave Orlando for suckering her and her late husband into deeding their house to a senior care community that promised to have them live in luxury for the rest of their lives at no additional costs other than the agreed-upon amount. However, the fine print held something else and the rates went up and up until the couple could no longer afford to live there. When they tried to salvage some money, they were unable to do so, and the husband died from stress-related causes. She lost everything."

"That's horrible," Shirley said. "Perfectly horrible."

I nodded. "Revenge. One of the best motives."

Wayne sat further up in his seat and spoke loudly. "What about Doris? I always liked her service in the bistro."

"A bit more complicated. Her husband, Clyde, worked for Harris in

Idaho and was a whistleblower who revealed Harris's shoddy deals and false promises. Doris always believed Harris was responsible for the so-called accident that claimed the life of her husband. Again, revenge."

My mother looked directly across the table and narrowed her eyes. "I don't get why Sherrille was involved. People have affairs all the time but they don't go around killing each other. Just suing them for money."

"It's strange, Mom. That's for sure. Especially since Sherrille was the one who got Doris the job working for Orlando. One would have thought Doris would want nothing to do with Sherrille, but—lo and behold—Doris was greedy for the money and Sherrille had to find a way to prevent Doris from blabbing all over about the Wainwrights. Especially since they were about to start a new project in Sun City West."

"But what about her murdering her husband?" Bill asked. "Did she or not?"

"She's being charged with it, along with the others." I took a sip of my coffee and went on. "Sherrille had lots of issues with her husband. She wanted Blake to take over the business so they could retire, but Harris refused. Then, she found what she thought was evidence he was married to someone else at the same time, but it turned out it was a prior marriage." Then I looked at Marshall and whispered, "Augusta checked it out for me. You and Nate really should give her a raise."

"Okay, okay, we got it. Hurry up and tell us what happened before the food gets here." By now, Herb had finished off the complimentary mini-bagels and spreads and was waiting for his breakfast.

I told them how the three women teamed up to pull off both murders by cleverly having Doris steal some of Mary Alice's yarn so the evidence would point to her. They used Orlando's own vehicle as the staging ground and dumped him off in Surprise. When it came time for Harris, they did the same thing but instead, got his body into the pin-return room at the bowling alley because Martha had a key to the complex."

"How'd they move the dead weight?" Lyndy asked. She looked at Lyman and he shrugged.

Then Paul spoke. "Have you ever looked at those two? They're like linebackers."

"Um, not to say anything disparaging"—*because I've already said more than I should*—"but Paul's right. Both women are incredibly strong. I've seen Martha hoist fifty-pound ice cube bags as if they were five pounds. Add adrenaline to the mix, and you've got—"

"Chopped liver! My order is here!" Myrna shoved her mini-bagels aside and made room for her breakfast plate.

From that moment on, the only talk was about food and how the Lane Chasers were going to celebrate their victory.

"Curley's bar!"

"No way! The Homey Hut!"

"Not on your life. Tailgator's."

"Paul is banned from there."

And finally, "Sardella's!"

I finally began to relax, but it was short-lived. I looked over at Gloria, who had her head buried in her cell phone, and saw her crying.

Oh no. He's dumping her. The cyber-ratfink scammer is dumping her. Must be he or they are on the run.

I started to say something but she beat me to it. "Can anyone here loan me thirty grand?"

CHAPTER 44

"What?" Herb asked. "Insider trading? A tip on a horse race? A slot machine that's paying off?"

And like that, no one paid any attention to Gloria. I leaned over and spoke in a low voice. "Whatever it is, we'll deal with it. We can chat later."

She grabbed a napkin, dabbed her eyes and proceeded to spear some home-fried potatoes with her fork. For now, all was well.

• • •

By the following morning, news of the arrests was all over the media— TV, radio, internet, and gossip chain. The only thing missing were the details describing how the women pulled off two murders without anyone batting an eyelash. But that changed at midday with an announcement from channel 10 saying they would feature a special on what was now dubbed the "Bowling Alley Murders," even though Orlando met his demise in his own garage. Go figure.

"You need to pat yourself on the back for getting that one right," Augusta said when I told her what the deputies told us. Martha and Doris drove to Orlando's house on the day of the murder and parked down the block. While Doris knocked on the door, Martha waited unseen on the side of the house and used a universal remote to get into the garage. She skootched down on the car floor behind the driver's seat and waited it out. The plan was for Doris to tell Orlando her car battery died a few houses down and ask him to drive her to the dealership, where it was going to be towed.

When they got into the car, Martha wasted no time doing the deed. She then drove her car to Orlando's and, since it was a two-car garage, they were able to maneuver the vehicles so that Orlando's body could be placed in Martha's car. Then, off to Surprise and a clump of thick bushes.

"Harris's demise came easier because Sherrille was in on it. Same scenario, more or less." I looked at Augusta and shrugged.

"Yeah, why mess with a good plan? Although I can't figure out why they stuffed him in the pin return?"

"In order to cast suspicion on one of the bowlers. And set up Mary Alice. The deputies would insist Mary Alice had an accomplice and they would try to make the evidence line up. Plus, it's real easy to stuff them in a pin return. Once the mechanism starts to move, there's lots of open space for a body. All they needed to do was manually turn it off and give the corpse a good shove."

"Makes sense to me. Good thing you stepped up."

"I didn't exactly step up. I stepped *in*! Taser and all! If that hadn't happened, those murders would still be unsolved."

"Nah, I had more faith in you, and our guys. Speaking of which, they're still at the posse office tying up some loose ends with Bowman and Ranston."

"Yeah, Marshall said as much. Any word on Gloria's situation from Rolo? She was a mess yesterday at breakfast."

"Something's brewing. I'm not sure what. Got a fax from him a few minutes ago before you came out here for coffee. Here, read it yourself." Augusta walked to her desk and handed me the paper. All it said was "Casa Grande," followed by a description of an Emeril Lagasse air-fryer-convection-oven-toaster-broiler-grill combination that all but did the dishes.

"Whoa. I think this means he was able to locate the cyber-scammer and that bum is in Casa Grande. Do Nate and Marshall know?"

"Yep. I photo'd it and texted it to them."

"And?"

"Still waiting."

Just then, my cell phone pinged and it was a text from Marshall: *Headed to Casa Grande. Heads-up from Rolo. Got the cavalry joining us as well as MCSO over there. Back later.*

"Yahoo, Augusta! They may catch that guy or guys yet." Then I paused. "Poor Gloria. This will devastate her."

"Romance is overrated. Tell her to spend her money on a decent tenderloin charbroiled to perfection."

"I'm not sure that's going to make her feel better, although now that you mention it, I want a hamburger for lunch."

I spent the remainder of the day one step away from nail-biting. I waited to hear from Nate and Marshall while Augusta fielded calls from Lydia, Sue-Lynn, and Shirley, who told her Gloria was too distraught to dial the number correctly.

"No matter the outcome, it'll be bad news for Gloria," I said when I reappeared in the front office later that day for more coffee. "Her romance will fizzle like one of those sparklers on the Fourth of July."

"Yeah, but her bank account will remain unscathed."

I retreated back to my office and looked at the time—four ten. Then back again for another word with Augusta. "You would have thought we'd hear something by now."

"They're working with Bowman and Ranston, plus a cyber-response team in Casa Grande."

Then, everything at once. The phone rang, a text appeared on my cell and the burner phone on the edge of Augusta's desk rang as well.

"Get the burner!" I shouted. "It's got to be Rolo!"

Augusta grabbed it and gave me a thumbs-up. The call ended in a nanosecond and she chuckled. "Better get that Emeril Lagasse thing he wanted."

• • •

It was after six when Nate and Marshall returned to the office. Augusta and I stuck around because we wanted to hear all the salient details and because we ordered jumbo pizzas when Nate phoned us that "it was a successful bust!"

To say that the guys were exuberant would have been an understatement. They were both pumped up and beaming, even though it had been an exhausting day.

Nate's voice shook the walls. "Rolo was right all along. A regular cyber-café. And we nailed them. The county cyber-unit will most likely get the credit, but we'll rake in our consultant fees in addition to extraneous costs."

"Rolo?" I asked.

He nodded. "And then some. We phoned Lydia and Sue-Lynn. Both ladies were over the moon that the 'romance nightmare' had come to an end. They're with Gloria now."

"Can Gloria press charges?" I widened my eyes and waited for a response.

"I'm afraid not, hon," Marshall said. "She didn't lose any money, although I suppose she could make a case for harassment. That would be up to her."

"When she stops crying."

"Well, let's stop yakking and open the door! Pizza delivery is here!" Augusta motioned to the delivery man to put the pizzas on the credenza. Then, pointing to the break room she said, "Napkins, plates, and drinks are all set up. Let's eat!"

I phoned my mother when Marshall and I got home and told her what had ensued. If I thought Gloria would be crushed, my mother wasn't far behind.

"I don't know how I could have been mistaken about that man. He seemed so real. So genuine."

"That's part of the scam, Mom. These guys are pros. According to the deputies, they're part of a greater network that operates in LA as well as Lagos. That's why the connection bounced around so much."

"Who's going to break it to Gloria?"

"Her daughters already did. Best thing you can do is be a good shoulder for her to cry on."

"I'll plan some nice playdates for Streetman and Thor."

Oh yeah. That should brighten anyone's day.

"Uh, sure. Good idea."

"I wonder who's going to run Nomos Bistro now that Martha will be serving time instead of food."

"Someone will step in. It's a good business."

"So is our current bowling alley complex. Please tell me Blake will be behind bars, too. That way, New Media Entertainment will leave us seniors alone."

"From what I hear, that won't be a problem. No one will back his business given the adolescent behavior he exhibited."

"Let's keep our fingers crossed."

"I always do. And by the way, good choice buying Essie those laser toys. It saved my life."

"Actually, your quick thinking did that. You get it from my side of the family. Your great-tante Rosie was always a quick thinker. One time she—"

"Mom, I'm exhausted. Let's talk about Tante Rosie another time, okay?"

"Fine. We'll do it when everyone celebrates at Sardella's. Or, we can have the girls meet at the Homey Hut this week."

"Sardella's will be fine. Absolutely fine. And please tell me there aren't any more of these events cropping up soon."

"Only the giant puzzle at the library. It's going to start early this year. Besides, what could possibly happen with that?"

And there it was—the next invitation to disaster.

EPILOGUE

In the week that followed, Tim Justin outdid himself with two exposés on channel 10. The double homicides and a cyber-scam whose players had been outmaneuvering cyber-units across the United States for over five years. The Associated Press picked it up and next thing everyone knew, Sun City West was besieged with reporters from CNN, FOX, MSNBC, BCC, and Headline News.

"This is horrible," my mother told me when the first show aired.

"All the reporters?"

"No. The fact that none of us can get into a beauty parlor. Those reporters are interviewing people and we want to look good for the cameras."

The rec center board held a business meeting and decided to nix the New Media Entertainment project and instead focus on "aesthetic projects to enhance the community," whatever *that* meant. As far as the book club ladies went, it meant an extra pie night at the Homey Hut.

Cecilia decided to put Orlando's house up for sale and donate money to her church as well as save enough for any emergencies that would befall her or her friends. Lucinda said Cecilia really wanted to cover the cost of all the holy water she'd been sneaking out for years.

According to Herb, Jonesy was taking things in stride and told the guys he never planned to get involved with a woman again. Herb immediately set up a wager with the pinochle crew to see how long that would last.

Lyndy told me that Lyman was still in shock, having witnessed his first book club–pinochle crew brunch at Bagels 'n More. I told her he'd get used to it if they came more often. She wasn't too sure.

By mid-March, things had returned to a certain normalcy in Sun City West. And then, out of nowhere, Gloria received a dozen roses but couldn't find the card. A frantic Lydia phoned me but within minutes, she phoned back.

"It's okay, Phee. My mom found the card. Thor removed it and chewed the edges but she could still read it. It was from Fred on her bowling team and he asked her to join him for lunch and a movie."

"Will she?"

"When she stops smelling the roses."

Yep, all was well in Sun City West. For now!

ACKNOWLEDGMENTS

Without the help, expertise, and support from our Sun City West community, none of this would be possible. We owe so many thanks to so many of you!

First and foremost, to Jeffrey Tracey and DJ Williams, for the super tour of Johnson Lanes and for showing us the best places to hide a body. Bowling will never be the same! Corine Bleckwenn, Jim Montgomery, and Steve Writz, so many thanks for your bowling expertise!

To our incredible Beta Reader Editors, Regina Kotokowski in Sun City West, Arizona, and Susan Schwartz in Coorparoo, Australia, for scrutinizing our manuscript and eyeballing every nuance. We can't thank you enough!

Larry Finkelstein and Gale Leach, you keep our computer and website running! We are dinosaurs without you! So glad we have friends in the twenty-first century!

Of course, none of this would have been possible without Dawn Dowdle, our agent at Blue Ridge Literary, who passed away last year. Your voice rings in our heads and we were so blessed to learn so much from you. You are missed every day.

Dar Albert from Wicked Smart Designs, our covers are like magnets for readers! Wow—you amaze us!

To our editor, Bill Harris, and the phenomenal staff at Beyond the Page Publishing, we are genuinely appreciative of all you do.

Finally, we thank you, our readers, for hanging out with our quirky characters!

About the Author

Ann I. Goldfarb

New York native Ann I. Goldfarb spent most of her life in education, first as a classroom teacher and later as a middle school principal and professional staff developer. Writing as J. C. Eaton, along with her husband, James Clapp, she has authored the Sophie Kimball Mysteries, the Wine Trail Mysteries, the Charcuterie Shop Mysteries, and the Marcie Rayner Mysteries. In addition, Ann has nine published YA time travel mysteries under her own name. Visit the websites at: www.jceatonmysteries.com and www.timetravelmysteries.com

James E. Clapp

When James E. Clapp retired as the tasting room manager for a large upstate New York winery, he never imagined he'd be coauthoring cozy mysteries with his wife, Ann I. Goldfarb. His first novel, *Booked 4 Murder*, was released in June 2017, followed by ten other books in the series and three other series. Nonfiction in the form of informational brochures and workshop materials treating the winery industry were his forte, along with an extensive background and experience in construction that started with his service in the U.S. Navy and included vocational school classroom teaching. Visit the website at www.jceatonmysteries.com.

Made in United States
North Haven, CT
07 July 2024